Title:	Murder Runs in the Family
Author:	Tamara Berry
Agent:	Courtney Miller-Callihan
	Handspun Literary
Publication date:	April 29, 2025
Category:	Mystery
Format:	Trade Paperback Original
ISBN:	978-1-4642-2117-0
Price:	$17.99 U.S.
Pages:	256 pages

This book represents the final manuscript being distributed for prepublication review. Typographical and layout errors are not intended to be present in the final book at release. **It is not intended for sale and should not be purchased from any site or vendor.** If this book did reach you through a vendor or through a purchase, please notify the publisher.

Please send all reviews or mentions of this book
to the Sourcebooks marketing department:
marketing@sourcebooks.com

For sales inquiries, please contact:
sales@sourcebooks.com

For librarian and educator resources,
visit: **sourcebooks.com/library**

Also by Tamara Berry

Murder Runs in the Family

TAMARA BERRY

Published by Poisoned Pen Press, an imprint of Sourcebooks

P.O. Box 4410, Naperville, Illinois 60567-4410
(630) 961-3900
sourcebooks.com

[Library of Congress Cataloging-in-Publication Data]

Printed and bound in [Country of Origin – confirm when printer is selected].
XX 10 9 8 7 6 5 4 3 2 1

1

"A detective without a crime to solve
is like a hat without a head."

—*DEATH COMES CALLING*, SEASON 1 EPISODE 9

AS AMBER WINSLOW STEPPED DOWN from the city bus, everything she owned in the tattered backpack slung over her shoulder, she had one thought and one thought only: *Man, I wish I was old.*

She'd seen retirement communities before, of course. Usually in the pages of a sleek brochure or on billboards edged with graffiti, the faces of the residents wreathed in smiles as they lounged poolside, ate chef-prepared meals, and visited doctors who only had good news to share. As was the case with most advertisements, she'd assumed they were one big corporate lie. *No one* was that happy to visit a doctor, especially when their organ functions had been in decline for years.

But this place? Well...she was starting to rethink that whole your-thirties-are-the-best-decade-of-your-life thing. If being retired meant living year-round in a desert oasis that looked like a luxury Palm Springs getaway, she was ready to fast-forward about forty years.

"Excuse me?" She strode up to the gated entrance, where a security guard dressed in head-to-toe blue polyester stood sweating in the heat of a sweltering Arizona July. "Are you the person I should talk to if I want to flirt my way past these locked doors?"

The security guard, who bore the bowlegged stature of a cowboy of old, looked as if he were one or two short years away from taking residence inside the Seven Ponds Retirement Community himself. His slicked-back hair was threaded with more gray than black, his skin as deeply lined and cracked as if he'd lived a lifetime under the sun. He cupped one hand around his ear. "What's that, dear?"

She hooked a thumb at the barred entrance, her smile wide. The fence surrounding the community was eight feet tall, at most, with spikes so fat at the top they were practically stepping stones. She could scale the thing in ten seconds flat—and do it under cover of the decorative acacia trees lining the east side—but that wasn't the point.

She was no longer a woman who skulked and hid in the shadows, hunting her prey until it begged for mercy. She walked through front doors like normal people.

More's the pity.

"I'm trying to visit my grandmother, but I don't have an appointment and I'm not expected," she explained, still with that beaming smile. She tried tossing her hair for good measure, but the desert air had turned it into a limp, sweaty tangle hours ago. "I figured I could break in the hard way, or I could just bat my eyes at you and hope that works instead. Is it? Working, I mean?"

The man laughed, a short, raspy sound that felt as though it carried undertones of emphysema. "You don't need an appointment to visit family." He ducked into the booth and pulled out a clipboard. "Just write down your name and who you came to see, and I'll buzz you straight through."

She grabbed the pen and scribbled out both her own name and that of her grandmother, a woman who existed in her life as nothing more than a story she was told at bedtime.

"Judith Webb?" the security guard asked as he took the clipboard back. "Who's that?"

All at once, the fatigue of the cross-country journey hit Amber like a bag of dimes—and she meant that as literally as possible. It was a little-known fact that a roll of dimes weighed more than any other kind of packaged coin. One would think to go for the quarters or nickels for maximum impact, but dimes were tricky like that: small and unassuming, the last ones picked for any job requiring brute force.

But take a few of those suckers to the head, and you'd rethink that approach.

"This is Seven Ponds Retirement Community, right?" Amber asked, straining to read the sign. Maybe she'd have to scale the walls after all. Maybe breaking and entering was her only hope. She could see the facility's pool from here—cold and refreshing, surrounded with red-striped umbrellas that looked positively decadent. "And I'm still in Draycott, Arizona?"

The man clicked his tongue. "That you are."

"But she doesn't live here? Are you sure? I thought…" Her voice trailed off, her lower lip between her teeth as she rummaged around in her backpack until her hand closed on a crumpled printer page. Finding her grandmother's whereabouts hadn't been easy, but Amber wasn't only adept at scaling walls and braining bad guys with dimes—she could also find the proverbial needle in a haystack, provided the needle was a person and the haystack was an existence somewhere on the planet. The grainy newspaper photo of a smiling older woman in a wide-brimmed gardening hat picking tomatoes wasn't much to go on, but there were several clues in the background.

That was the real trick to finding people—not looking at *them*, but at their surroundings. Cacti and red rocks as far as the eye could see? Those were easy. Anyone could point to Arizona or New Mexico from there. But the basket the woman was filling with garden produce bore a unique five-star pattern—one that Amber had painstakingly tracked down to an art style from the Yavapai tribe. The basket was probably a cheap tourist knockoff, but even cheap tourist knockoffs had to come from somewhere.

In this case, they came from Draycott, Arizona—a city with over a dozen retirement communities, yes, but only one that boasted that particular garden trellis. Based on a PR puff piece she'd found online, the purple cone flowers and hot lips sage had been planted at this facility a decade ago with the intent to draw butterflies to the area.

So, yeah. Tracking her grandmother to this location had been a stretch, but it had been a *well-researched* stretch.

"Wait. Is that your grandma?" The man chuckled and tapped the newspaper page with one forefinger. As before, his laugh was underscored with a dry, painful-sounding cough, but Amber found herself warming to it—and not just because his words were music to her ears. "If it's Jade McCallan you're after, why didn't you say so? She'll probably be at the bowling alley this time of day. Her team has been sweeping the league this year. I've got fifty bucks riding on her wicked hook."

"*Jade McCallan*," Amber repeated, testing the syllables out on her tongue. The name was familiar, but not for any reason that Amber could put her finger on—not that it was difficult to believe that her grandmother would have changed her name at some point in her checkered career. According to the stories she'd heard growing up, her grandmother had lived a life less ordinary in every sense of the phrase. "No wonder why she was so hard to track down."

The man seemed to understand her without need for explanation. "Jade doesn't make anything easy. Least of all her wicked—"

"Right. Her bowling hook is off the charts," Amber agreed. Now that she knew she'd tracked her quarry, she was impatient to get inside. "Does this mean you'll let me in?"

"Oh, I was always going to let you in," the guard said with a friendly wink. He pushed a giant red button labeled OPEN and stood back to watch as the wrought-iron gate groaned and scraped its way across the pavement. "Anyone willing to flirt with an old man like me to get what she wants isn't going to be stopped by an eight-foot fence."

Amber blinked, startled and a little nonplussed to find that he'd read her character so easily. She *was* willing to flirt to get her way—in fact, it was one of her greatest investigative skills—but most people were oblivious to the phenomenon while it was happening.

"Hang on a sec." She didn't step through the entrance. "How do you know I'm not going to cause trouble once I'm inside? Maybe I'm a hit woman. Maybe Jade is my next victim, and you just signed her death warrant."

This time, his laugh rattled the cough loose. "Honey, I've never met an apple so identical to the tree it fell from. You tell your grandmother that if she doesn't win today, she owes me my fifty bucks back. I'm not made of money."

Contrary to the security guard's expectations, Amber found her grandmother lounging poolside.

For the longest moment, all she could do was stand on the opposite end of the Olympic-sized pool with her heart in her throat. Judith Webb—or *Jade McCallan*, rather—aged seventy-six, originally from Washington, currently residing in Arizona, known to absolutely zero of her three grandchildren, was a sight to behold. And coming from Amber, that was saying something. She'd seen enough of the world, both good and bad, to believe that nothing could surprise her.

An elderly woman in a string bikini sipping cocktails at two o'clock in the afternoon surprised her. Especially when she looked up at Amber, lowered her oversized sunglasses, and cried out in delight.

"Oh my stars. I don't believe it." She was on her feet so fast that the cocktail sloshed over the edge of her glass. And then her arms were opened wide, her coral lips spread in a smile as she gestured for Amber to come to her. "It's you, isn't it? Amber Winslow? *My* Amber Winslow?"

Amber didn't know what compelled her to dash around the pool and fall into her arms, but she suspected it was the unabashed joy she saw in the older woman's expression. People were *never* that happy to see her, particularly when the people in question shared her blood. The last time she'd gone home for the holidays, her brothers had actually staged an intervention before she was allowed through the front door.

We just want to make sure you aren't planning on bringing your oversized PI boyfriend this year, Derek had said. *Last time, he pulled his gun on Mikey and almost shot him in cold blood.*

I still have nightmares about it, Mikey had agreed. *I'll be paying off the therapy bills for years.*

Which, obviously, had been an exaggeration. Bones hadn't "pulled his gun" so much as flashed his holster when he took off his jacket for dinner. Unfortunately, Bones not only went by a name designed to strike fear into the hearts of the people he was hired to investigate, but he was also six feet four inches of carefully honed ex–Navy SEAL musculature. He was deadly with almost any weapon, covered in as many scars as tattoos, and smiled in a way that made every heart in a ten-mile radius flutter.

If you asked her, it was the last one that had really bothered her brothers. Amber had seen the way both of their wives had to roll up their tongues when Bones had taken off his jacket.

Not that any of that mattered now. She and Bones had broken up, and she'd left all six feet four inches of his carefully honed ex–Navy SEAL musculature back in Seattle where it belonged.

For some reason, her grandmother's hug reminded her of him. Part of it was the way she wrapped her arms around Amber's neck and took command of the embrace, but it was more than that. Her grandmother hugged like she *meant* it—and that Amber, by extension, meant something too.

Tears sprang to her eyes before she could remember to blink them back.

"My sweet child, I never thought I'd live to see the day. Come and sit down. Do you want a drink? Two drinks? Camille! For the love of God, make yourself useful and get us a pitcher of something. Can't you see my granddaughter is parched?"

Amber felt herself being half led, half dragged to a poolside lounger with a tropical towel spread out over the top. The towel was damp, but she didn't mind as she was pushed into it and her legs were lifted into a reclining position. Her jean shorts rode indecently high up her thighs, but considering how close her grandmother's right nipple was to popping out of her bikini top, she figured it didn't matter.

As before, however, the quick and easy reading of her identity unsettled her.

"How are you so sure I'm your granddaughter?" she asked as she lifted a hand to shield her eyes against the sun's glare. "Did the security guard at the gate tell you I was coming?"

"Julio? Please. He wouldn't notice if an armed battalion was making its way inside." A pitcher appeared on a tray next to her grandmother, along with a woman in a glorious hand-beaded caftan that Amber was pretty sure had been shown at a Paris runway just last week. "Bless you, Camille. Now go away so the two of us can have a nice, long chat."

The nice, long chat was preceded by the biggest margarita Amber had ever seen. Her grandmother pressed it into her hand and stood towering over her until she took a sip, much like a child being forced to take her medicine before bed. Satisfied that it went all the way down, her grandmother then settled into the lounge next to her, careful to tuck all her wayward parts back into her swimsuit as she did.

These wayward parts weren't as numerous as Amber's earlier assessment had made them seem. Her grandmother was in remarkable shape for a woman her age—her skin tanned but not leathery, faint lines of her musculature visible whenever she moved. Even her waist-length hair was a marvel of preservation, the dark brown underlayer streaked with chunks of white as if Mother Nature had taken a fan paintbrush to her head. Since Amber's own hair was the same rich mahogany color—albeit one she wore in a messy bob—she hoped the effect was a genetic one.

"You're *much* prettier than you look on your socials," her grandmother said as though making a similar sweep of Amber's appearance. Since her eyes were hidden behind huge Gucci sunglasses, it was hard to tell. "I think it's because you always cock your head to the right when you pose for pictures. That sort of thing does nothing for your chin. What you want to do is thrust it out a little—smooth out that extra bit of skin above the throat. The women in our family have a tendency to double-chin at the least provocation. You'll want to watch out for that as you get older."

Amber clutched her margarita glass as though it was the only thing keeping her from spinning out—which, in many ways, it *was*. That cold glass and the sharp tang of lime were the only clues that she was actually in this moment: sweating and overwhelmed and facing a woman she'd been taught her whole life cared for no one but herself.

"My socials?" she echoed. "You mean like Instagram and stuff? You're online?"

If she wasn't already in a fair way to loving her grandmother, the ripple of laughter she let loose would have done the trick. Like the tinkling of bells at Christmastime or a wind chime in a balmy spring breeze, it unlocked a sensation Amber didn't know she'd been hiding away.

"Bless you, child, I'm on them all. Instagram, TikTok, Facebook, Nextdoor—I've got my bases covered."

"You're on *Nextdoor*?"

"Oh, yes. It's quite popular here at the retirement community. We're currently using it to track down the Admiral's missing tortoise—the last sighting of the poor dear was near the pickleball courts, but if you ask me, Lincoln mistook him for a rock and refuses to admit it. He's ninety-eight years old."

"Lincoln?"

"No, the tortoise. The Admiral inherited him from his great-aunt—oh, nigh on forty years ago now." She touched the side of her nose. "He's not really an admiral, you understand. We're not even sure he was a member of the military, but at our age, one doesn't like to pry. Every closet here has at least half a dozen skeletons. You should see how festive it gets at Halloween."

"Oh," Amber said—just that, just *oh*. She might have felt silly about her inanity, but her grandmother didn't give her time.

"Julio started a betting pool to see who'll live longer: the Admiral or the tortoise. I've got a thousand riding on the tortoise, but don't tell the Admiral I said so. The poor man thinks he's going to live forever."

Her chatter thus at an end, Amber's grandmother sat back, took a sip of her margarita, and sighed happily. In that moment, two thoughts occurred to Amber. The first was that she was *never* going to forgive her mother for keeping this treasure of a woman away from her for so long. Growing up, Grandma Judith had been a bogeyman of all the world's evils wrapped up in one: she was a vain woman, an irreverent woman, a woman who refused to settle in one place long enough to put down a semblance of a root. She treated responsibility like a four-letter word and, worst of all, had given her only daughter the most deplorable name known to mankind.

Of all the listed sins, Amber had a feeling her mom counted that one as the worst. Moonbeam Effervescence was a tough name for most people to pull off. For her type A, born-again mother who actually *enjoyed* her career as a bookkeeper at her church, it was tantamount to tattooing the sign of the devil on her forehead.

The second thought came riding hard on the heels of the first.

"Whoa, whoa, whoa." Amber sat up, heedless of her drink sloshing around. "How do you know about my socials? All my accounts are private, and I only let a select pool of people follow me."

Her grandmother waggled her fingers at Amber. "Give me your phone."

Amber hesitated. It wasn't that she didn't trust this bright, cheerful old lady she'd just met, but, well, she didn't trust this bright cheerful old lady she'd just met. She didn't trust *anyone* after a ten-minute acquaintanceship. Bones was the one responsible for that particular quirk. A private investigator was by necessity a suspicious sort of person—and one like him, who could saunter into a biker bar and command respect using nothing but the deep timbre of his voice, was worse than most. According to him, he'd never met anyone who didn't want to kill, dismember, or otherwise maim him.

At the moment, she included herself on that list. Their breakup hadn't exactly been amicable.

"I'm not going to log into your banking app or snoop through your dirty photos, so you needn't look at me like that. I only want to show you something."

Amber pressed her thumb on the screen and handed over the phone, though she was careful to keep an eye on her grandmother's movements. "What makes you think I have dirty photos?"

Her grandmother slid her sunglasses down her nose and stared at Amber over the top of them, her deep brown eyes twinkling. Those eyes were so much like her own that she almost gasped out loud with recognition. The man at the gate—Julio—had been right. It was like looking into an image of her future.

"You're a thirty-one-year-old woman with a fantastic body and no wedding ring in sight. You have nudes."

Amber snorted, but she couldn't deny the truth of this—and, since her nudes were carefully locked inside a photo security app, she let the rest of her guard slip down. Unless her grandmother was a secret hacker as well as an intoxicated chatterbox, there was no way she'd be falling down that particular rabbit hole.

"Here." Her grandmother clicked the screen a few times before handing the phone back. "That's me. Your privateinvestigatorprincess account started following me on Instagram about a year ago. Imagine my surprise when I followed you back only to find your sweet face plastered all over the screen."

Amber wasn't proud of how long she had to stare at her phone before her grandmother's meaning penetrated. On paper, Amber was the least successful member of her family—the only one without a college degree or regular source of gainful employment, the only one to eschew marriage for a string of bad boyfriends and even worse breakups—but she'd always secretly felt she had the sharpest wits. Not that the competition was particularly stiff when you considered how long it took her family to finish a game of Trivial Pursuit, but still.

Scrappy street smarts counted for something. Not much, obviously, but something.

"Is this a joke?" Amber asked once she finally finished assimilating what—or rather, who—she was looking at. *Jade McCallan*. Of course. *That* was why Amber had recognized the name. Jade McCallan was the producer of the *Death Comes Calling* true crime podcast—one of a hundred such productions that had cropped up over the past few years, and one with which she was intimately familiar.

Like so many things about her life, that familiarity wasn't her doing. For some strange reason, Bones had been obsessed with true crime podcasts. The last thing Amber wanted to do during their all-night stakeouts together was listen to tales of other people tracking bad guys, but Bones had insisted she not only listen but take notes. *You wanna be the best, babe, you gotta live and breathe this stuff,* he'd said as he snacked on an endless succession of protein bars and relieved himself into an empty Gatorade bottle—a thing that Amber had tried once and only once before deciding she'd prefer to sit in dehydrated discomfort. *Listen to how the* Death Comes Calling *people figured out this guy's location using nothing but pollen from one of those rare corpse plants.*

Since Bones had taught her literally everything she knew about investigation, she'd listened. And learned a thing or two. And also decided that nothing—and she meant nothing—would get her to set foot anywhere near one of those stinky plants during full bloom.

She'd also come to enjoy that particular podcast and the narrator behind it, a retired police detective with a low, gravelly voice that made her feel that the world was somehow safer because he was in it. Hence the follow on socials—and her delight when the account actually followed her back.

"How do you know Horace Horatio?" Amber asked, blinking first down at her phone and then back up at her grandmother. "He's a detective. An old man. And you—"

"Am positively *surrounded* by old men," Her grandmother spread her arms wide and gestured at the scene around them. Although the majority of the people lounging around the pool were female, Amber did spot several balding heads and fluttering Hawaiian shirts. "At first, I tried narrating the podcast myself, but no matter what I did to my voice, I always ended up sounding like a frail old grandmother. That's why we invented Horace. My friend Raffi plays the part, but the writing is mine. You like it?"

"I...uh. Yeah, actually. It's very entertaining." Amber felt sure the ground was likely to open up any second and swallow her whole, so she forced her focus where it mattered: on the facts. "But I don't understand. You run a true crime podcast? That I've been following on socials for over a year?"

Her grandmother nodded before taking a long, satisfied sip of her margarita. For all that the earth was moving and shaking under Amber's feet, her grandmother seemed remarkably in control of herself.

Or—no, wait. She was *enjoying* herself.

"And you never once thought to reach out to me to say something?"

That one stopped her grandmother flat. The smile fell from her bright coral lips, and she went so far as to set her glass down before turning to face Amber. "I wanted to, my darling. I really did. In fact, I almost—"

Amber narrowed her eyes as her grandmother cut herself off midsentence. "You almost what?"

Instead of answering, her grandmother countered with a question of her own. "Your username...privateinvestigatorprincess. That's not just a cheeky handle, is it? You track people down? Solve mysteries and all that jazz?"

A hot, tight sensation started to leak out from the center of Amber's chest. She got that same feeling every time she thought about the life she'd recently fled, but nothing—and she meant nothing—would induce her to go crawling back to it. "I used to. I, uh, recently broke up with the guy who introduced me to that world, so I'm not really part of it anymore."

"Because he owns the entirety of the PI community?"

Amber blinked. Between her general exhaustion, the rapid pace of her grandmother's conversation, and the margarita on an empty stomach, she was starting to feel dizzy. "I'm sorry. What?"

"This man—the one who introduced you to the glorious world of investigation. He's the be-all and end-all of every decision related to the profession?"

"Of course not," Amber said. Then, because more explanation was obviously necessary, "But I'm not licensed or anything. I just kinda went along with him on his jobs—at first, because it was the only way I could spend time with him, and then, well…"

Amber let her voice trail off. Even though her grandmother seemed unlikely to judge her too harshly, she was loath to share her deepest regret. The regret wasn't that she'd lost her handsome, well-built boyfriend of three years, or even that she'd been rendered homeless when she'd snuck away from him in the dead of the night. It had little to do with the lack of possessions in her backpack and even less to do with the fact that she had no one to turn to but a stranger living fourteen hundred miles away.

No, it was that when she'd left Bones back in Seattle, she'd also left all the heart-pounding, adrenaline-pumping rush of the chase with him. Three years of her life she'd given that man, and all she had to show for it was a penchant for intrigue and nowhere to put it.

Amber forced a smile, pushing down the swirling, drowning sensation that had been threatening to pull her under for weeks. "Let's just say I'm an enthusiastic amateur and leave it at that."

"Excellent," her grandmother said. "An enthusiastic amateur is exactly what I need."

Amber was almost afraid to ask. Nothing about this meeting was going the way she'd intended—instead of cajoling her way into her grandmother's good graces, begging for shelter from a kindly old woman who was the only family member who hadn't yet cast her to the wolves, she was day drinking and getting sunburned with a murder podcaster.

Still. She asked anyway.

"Need for what?"

"Fresh blood," her grandmother said with all the air of one conferring a high treat. "Our podcast ratings are at an all-time low, and a hot young thing like you is exactly what we need to pull them back up again."

2

"If a man dies in the forest and no one
is there to see it, do the police *really*
need to bring in all those guns?"

—*DEATH COMES CALLING*, SEASON 3 EPISODE 1

THAT NIGHT, AMBER SLEPT LIKE the dead.

Most nights, sleep came on Amber like a skittish animal, creeping close only to dart away at the last second. Anything out of the ordinary—a rustle of leaves, the whir of the refrigerator, even a top sheet that was too scratchy—had a way of keeping her awake for hours. Bones had always said that sleeping next to her was like bunking down with a seismograph that hadn't been properly calibrated.

Maybe it was how nice her grandmother's condo had smelled, like a field of lavender blooming in the sunlight, or perhaps it was the fact that she'd been sitting on a Greyhound bus for too many days, but the moment her head hit the pillow of the guest bed that she'd been graciously offered, she was out. And she was out *hard*.

She also awoke to the scent of fresh coffee and something baking in the kitchen. Since those two things had never been a part of her wake-up routine before, she had no trouble identifying where she was.

I'm home.

She jolted the rest of the way awake, amused as much as alarmed by the thought that her grandmother's hyper-air-conditioned condo could be anything approaching a home. For one thing, it wasn't large enough to house two people, especially when one of them had a personality the size of Jade McCallan's. For another, well…

Amber averted her eyes as she swung her legs out of the bed and padded toward the living room. She couldn't say for *sure* that oversized nude painting hanging above the guest bed was a highly stylized portrait of her grandmother, but that unique purplish-brown hair color was making an awfully convincing case.

"Good morning, darling," her grandmother called as Amber stepped into the combination kitchen and living room. Blinding streaks of Draycott sunlight streamed in through the filmy curtains, indicating that the morning was well advanced. "I wasn't sure what grandmothers are supposed to do in situations like this, so I invited Lincoln over to make you breakfast. He has eighteen grandkids, so he knows all about this sort of thing."

"Eighteen grandkids?" Amber echoed as she slid onto a stool and accepted the milky cup of coffee her grandmother held out to her. She sipped cautiously, but she needn't have worried—it was exactly the way she liked it, with one too many sugars and enough milk to cool it to a reasonable temperature. "That sounds…busy."

"Nah. The trick is to keep food in front of them all times." The elderly Black man rummaging around her grandmother's snack-sized kitchen turned to face her. He was too large for the space, tall and well-built with shoulders like a linebacker, but the effect was softened by his frilly apron and glasses so thick that Amber could barely see what color his eyes were behind them. But what she *could* see seemed kind, especially when he slid a plate of croissants in front of her. "You just watch. Your mouth will be so busy chewing that you won't be any trouble after this. I got my daughter's triplets through their terrible twos using nothing but pancakes and my famous sugar-free oatmeal cookies."

Since the first bite of croissant that Amber took was so light and buttery she actually moaned out loud, she could see how that might work. "Oh, wow. Did you really make these? From *scratch*?"

Lincoln chuckled in a way that shook his whole body—and, by extension, the whole kitchen. "See, Jade? I told you she'd be like putty in your hands. Get her to agree to your schemes now, while her mouth is full."

"Schemes?" Amber asked. Then, as the rest of the previous day's events came rushing back, she pushed her plate away. She should have known these were bribery croissants. Anything that delicious had to come with strings attached. "I already told you. While I appreciate the offer to be a part of your podcast, I can't. I'm not qualified to do any kind of crime solving. Despite what my socials say, I'm not really a PI. I'm not really *anything*."

"Don't be absurd. You're my granddaughter." The words were spoken with a hint of pride, but not enough to outweigh the sudden note of steel in her grandmother's voice—or her expression, which looked not so much like steel but titanium.

Amber blinked, but by the time she opened her eyes again, her grandmother was wearing her bright, sunny smile again.

Amber took a cautious sip of her coffee, unsure how much of what was happening was real and how much was a product of her imagination. Never, in her wildest dreams, had she imagined this kind of reception from her grandmother. She'd come to Draycott partially out of curiosity and partially out of desperation, so unmoored after her breakup that she'd felt *anything* would be better than crawling home to her parents' house—or, worse, the beige McMansions that belonged to her brothers. Nothing short of the direst necessity would get her to stay in one of those for longer than an hour a time. She'd once used a Chanel hand towel in Derek's guest bathroom, and the hell she'd paid for it would have covered half the student loan debt in the country. *Apparently* the towels for family were in kept in a drawer instead.

So to find herself not just welcomed with open arms, but being fed, offered part-time work, and tucked into bed in thousand-thread-count sheets was, well, *odd*.

Before she could dwell too much on it, a knock sounded at the door. Giving a delighted clap, her grandmother moved to answer it.

"That'll be Raffi," she called over her shoulder. "He's dying to meet you to discuss the details of how we can work you into the podcast. We'll have to cast you as Horace Horatio's sidekick if we want to really sell it. I hope you're a good actress. We need something more official than the ex-girlfriend of a Seattle PI. How do you feel about playing a down-on-her-luck deputy who was kicked out of the force for questioning the status quo?"

Fortunately, no response was required. As her grandmother disappeared into the hallway, Amber was left alone with Lincoln and—even better—a brief moment of silence.

"Is she always like this?" Amber wrapped her hands around her mug for warmth. Her loose-fitting tank and sleep shorts were no match for the icy blasts of air curling around her feet. "My mom warned me that she was like a tidal wave, and that the moment I entered her vicinity I'd find myself engulfed by her, but I assumed that was an exaggeration. The two of them don't get along. They never have."

"You don't say." Lincoln chuckled and started to stack the dirty dishes into the sink. From the easy way he moved around the kitchen, Amber assumed he'd been here for many an impromptu breakfast.

Which, considering the naked artwork in the guest room, totally tracked. *You go, Grandma.*

"Does that mean she's talked to you about my mom before?" Amber tried not to sound as eager as she felt. "And about…me?"

Instead of answering the question, Lincoln grabbed a dish towel and started wiping down the flour-streaked counter. "If you want my advice, young lady, you'll save yourself the trouble and agree to be on the podcast. Your grandmother has a way of getting what she wants in the end. Half the people at this retirement community are part of it in some form or another." He paused as if considering. "Well, six or seven of us, anyway. We're quite popular around these parts."

Amber sipped in thoughtful silence. It wasn't that she didn't *want* to help her grandmother out—really, it wasn't. Many a murder podcaster needed no more qualifications than an insatiable appetite for the macabre and the ability to make a nuisance of oneself among law enforcement officers, and it wasn't as if she had a whole lot else going on in her life right now.

But assuming she ignored the nagging memories at the back of her mind—the laughter that had shaken through Bones whenever she'd offered advice on how to build his business, the way he'd laughed even harder when she suggested he might sign the training paperwork so she could get a PI license of her own—there was still the small matter of Bones listening to that podcast with an almost religious fervor.

The last thing Amber wanted was for him to hear the sound of her voice and come running. Knowing him, he'd probably assume she did it on purpose—and that the trail of crumbs was all part of her plan to win him back.

Which, ugh.

There was also the small matter of her grandmother's delight at seeing her when she showed up out of the blue yesterday. Finding a soft place to land was nice, obviously, especially considering the current state of her bank account, but there'd been a suspicious lack of surprise when her grandmother had engulfed Amber in her arms.

In fact, now that she thought about it, it seemed odd that her grandmother had known about Amber's professional background and had, in fact, been following her socials for a year. *Not to mention she knew exactly how I take my coffee and that the fastest way to disarm me is with food and a friendly, soft-spoken stranger in the kitchen.*

Amber sat up straighter as the full implication of this sank in. She'd done enough stalking in her lifetime—the legit kind—to know when things started feeling a little too *Cape Fear* for her own good.

Her grandmother returned to the kitchen at that exact moment. Amber opened her mouth to make her excuses and hightail it out of there—she was needed in another state, there was a family emergency, a meteor was about to strike the earth and she only had twenty-four hours to live out her final earthly dreams—when she saw the stricken expression on the older woman's face.

Gone was the life and vibrancy. No more was the sparkling laughter on those bright coral lips.

Lincoln must have seen it too, because he rushed to her side. Misjudging the angle, he smacked his hip into the kitchen counter and let out a howl of pain. That was how Amber got to her grandmother first, and that was why Amber was the one who caught her as her knees gave way and she started to sink to the terra-cotta-tiled floor.

"That wasn't Raffi," her grandmother said, her voice wavering as if it had been struck by a tuning fork. "It was the police. The Admiral is dead. They found his body in the podcast studio earlier this morning."

3

"If the Grim Reaper ever takes a night off,
I have an idea or two I'd like to try."

—*DEATH COMES CALLING*, SEASON 5 EPISODE 2

ACCORDING TO THE BROCHURES, SEVEN Ponds Retirement Community was a luxury residential facility offering a "transitional retirement experience."

The luxury part was self-explanatory, evident in every aspect of the extensive grounds. In addition to the pool, complete with private cabanas and a full-service tiki bar, there was a bowling alley, six different restaurants open throughout the day, a tai chi garden, a pickleball court, a dog park, an arts and crafts facility, individual vegetable plots assigned on a first-come first-serve basis, and a bona fide movie theater.

The transitional retirement aspect was less visible. At first glance, the whole community appeared to be made up of rows of individual condominiums laid out in a grid-like pattern around the shared services. The condos weren't overly large, and they had no yards to speak of, but the residents zipped down the roadways in golf carts and had the general air of people enjoying a slice of communal living while maintaining their independence.

It was only once you got to the main facility near the back that the true purpose of this place started to creep in. As Amber ushered her grandmother out of Lincoln's golf cart and through a set of sliding glass doors, she realized she was standing in what amounted to a nursing home.

That it was a *nice* nursing home was obvious, what with the marble tiles and trickling fountains, but there was no mistaking the scent of antiseptic that hung heavily in the air. Or the quiet hush that surrounded the place like a storm about to break.

"Excuse me?" she called to the receptionist behind the desk. Like Julio the security guard, it was difficult to tell if the woman worked here or was one of the residents. She was a tiny slip of a thing, her features so birdlike that a gust of wind seemed likely to whisk her away, but she had on a bright red wig that imbued her with a sense of strength and purpose. Like Ronald McDonald at a board meeting.

"How can I help you, dear?" the woman asked, glancing up. The moment she caught sight of Jade being propped up by Amber on one side and Lincoln on the other, she immediately clicked into action. "I need one of the orderlies to get here with a wheelchair, stat," she barked into an intercom on her desk, which boasted another of those enormous red buttons like the one Amber had seen in the security booth yesterday. "Better bring the oxygen and the defibrillator just in case. Jade doesn't look too good."

"If you get anywhere near me with that defibrillator, Peggy Lee, I *will* have a heart attack to spite you," Amber's grandmother said as a man came squeaking around the corner. He was dressed from head to toe in white, his scrubs so crisp they looked as though they'd been cut from paper. Jade took one look at the wheelchair he pushed and grimaced, but that didn't stop her from sinking gratefully into it. "I'm fine. Just a little weak in the knees, that's all. My granddaughter insisted that I come in to get checked over."

Amber blinked, surprised to hear her grandmother telling the orderly a bald-faced lie. Yes, after seeing how shaken her grandmother was, Amber had insisted she sit down. She'd even offered her a stiff drink despite the early hour. But her grandmother had eschewed both, insisting instead that Lincoln drive them both to the clinic without a moment's delay.

"I expect you've heard the news by now," her grandmother said in a voice that wobbled across several different octaves. None of Amber's detection skills were necessary to decipher what that particular vibrato indicated. This was no medical visit—it was a *social* one, and her grandmother was about to cash in on her exciting new development big time.

"What news?" Peggy Lee's eyes grew wide behind the pair of colorful readers perched on the end of her nose. Like Amber, she seemed to understand the nature of this visit without explanation. "Has something happened? Did they finally find the Admiral's tortoise? I swear I saw his beady eyes poking out from under the yucca during my speed walk this morning, but he darted away before I could get a good look at him. It's a pity Hermann's tortoises are so small and look so much like desert rocks. At this rate, he'll just keep escaping us."

The orderly cleared his throat. "I told you already, Peggy Lee. That was a candy wrapper someone had tossed on the ground. You made me check three times."

Amber found her eyes sliding over to the man with sympathy. She may have been at Seven Ponds for less than twenty-four hours, but she was developing a sense for how things went down around these parts. The residents were well-to-do, intelligent, and—it seemed—bored to flinders. They also had unfettered access to more than one bar and high-speed internet. The combination was…interesting, to say the least.

"That poor tortoise." A look of genuine regret flashed across her grandmother's face. "We'll have to double our efforts to find him now. The Admiral would want him to be at the funeral."

The bombshell had all the impact her grandmother could have hoped for. Demands to hear the details, genuine tears on the part of Peggy Lee, and an uncomfortable series of low-throated grunts from Lincoln filled the air. If that wasn't bad enough, the glass doors slid open to reveal two uniformed officers looking less than pleased to have been scooped by a woman twice their age.

"Ms. McCallan, what's going on?" asked the older and sterner of the lot, his hat tipped so low over his eyes that he looked to be ninety percent mustache. "I thought we told you to keep things under wraps until we concluded our questioning."

"Did you?" Jade asked. She lifted a shaking hand to her head, looking even frailer than when she'd first stumbled in here. "Oh, dear. I didn't mean to cause trouble. It's the shock, you see. My heart isn't what it used to be."

Amber decided she'd heard enough. She wasn't sure what the police protocol was in a place like Seven Ponds, where death was the eventual way out for everyone, but she did know that her grandmother was behaving like a woman who cared less about the loss of her friend and more about making sure she was at the center of it. She also knew that any attempts to obstruct police activity was likely to reflect back on *her*.

Bones might not think that the three years Amber spent by his side, filling out the paperwork he didn't want to do and diving deep into research of a detailed and mind-numbing nature, counted as official training, but she did. She knew exactly how law enforcement worked—and more to the point, she knew how to handle them.

"Lincoln, will you please accompany my grandmother and the orderly to a quiet room somewhere?" Amber flashed a bland smile. "She needs rest and plenty of fluids. I'm sure you can rustle up a nurse somewhere around here."

"Not Nasty Nancy," her grandmother was quick to interject. She gave a ladylike shudder before continuing. "The last time she gave me an IV, she missed my vein six times. I swear she does it on purpose. Heroin dealers have better bedside manners."

Amber had to tamp down her sudden snort, but she was nothing if not professional. She nodded for Lincoln and the orderly to continue on their way. "Find a nurse who isn't Nancy, and I'll be with you shortly."

Her grandmother cast her a look that held a hint of suspicion and a healthy dose of approval. She also moaned in a way that made the police officers loath to follow her, which Amber expected was the real goal. Thus left to handle this situation on her own, Amber kept her smile airy, attached not so much to her brain as to her more obvious attributes.

"I'm so sorry about that, Detective..." she let her voice trail off, her eyelashes brushing softly against her cheek. Her attempts would have worked better if she'd had time to check a mirror before she'd dashed over here, but beggars couldn't be choosers. With any luck, yesterday's mascara would have become sexily smudged rather than the painted eyes of a raccoon.

"Just officer," the mustachioed man grunted. "Officer Peyton."

"Well then, Officer Peyton. I'm sorry if my grandmother let her tongue run away with her." From the sheepish way he rolled his shoulders, Amber guessed that either her makeup was safe or the man had a thing for raccoons.

"She didn't mean to interfere with your investigation, I swear. She just forgets things sometimes. You know how it is. Physically, she's doing better than ever, but mentally…"

"No need to apologize," Officer Peyton said. "My grandmother was the same way. Once they reach a certain age, it's a straight path down that hill."

An annoyed *tsk* sounded from the reception desk. Amber tucked an arm behind her and waved Peggy Lee to silence.

"Is that what happened to the man who died?" she asked as she lowered her voice to a reverent hush. "Old age? Natural causes?"

"Hmph. Well, now. I'm not at liberty to say." The mustache wavered again, so Amber did what she did best. She played innocent, she played pretty, and she played dumb: the trifecta of disarmament.

"I'm so sorry," she gushed. "It must be difficult, getting these kinds of calls and then being pestered by Nosey Parkers like me. I don't know how you do it, day in and day out. The things you must have seen as a dedicated officer of the law…"

Officer Peyton straightened up so much that the hat and the mustache finally separated into two distinct entities. He was younger than he'd first appeared, the drooping ends of his facial hair not gray so much as sandy brown. The other uniformed man at his back went through the same motions, though no amount of straightening could hide the stoop in his posture or the paunch that sat heavily over the top of his belt.

That was when she noticed that a *third* man was watching them from across the hall. He wasn't dressed in a police uniform but gray joggers and a loose-fitting T-shirt, his arms crossed over his chest as he leaned against the doorframe and watched her attempts at flirtation.

"You've got to be kidding me," he muttered.

One of the things Amber prided herself on most in this world was her ability to recall specific details about a person long after they'd exited the scene—she was basically a sketch artist's dream come true. She already knew that Peggy Lee had a flat brown mole the shape of Utah on her temple, that her grandmother's tan was streaky on her feet in a way that implied at least part of the color came out of a bottle, that Lincoln's thick glasses helped to obscure a slight laziness to his right eye. Officer Peyton's mustache hid the nicotine discoloration on his front teeth, and his fellow officer had painfully enlarged pores on his nose.

But this guy. This leaning guy. This guy who seemed to be on to her tricks....

He pushed off the doorway with grunt and ducked into the room behind him. As soon as he disappeared from view, she could no longer recall *any* details about him. He'd been tall but not too tall. Young but not too young. Hair…brownish? Skin…whitish? Eyes…had he even had any?

She shook herself. *Obviously*, the man had eyes. She must be losing her touch.

"I won't be upset if you're not at liberty to share anything about the Admiral's death," she said to the two remaining officers. "It's just that I've never seen my grandmother like this before. She must be really shaken up."

Officer Peyton reached a hand out and awkwardly patted her shoulder. "It's all right. Death is always difficult. And for it to have happened in your grandmother's podcast studio of all places, well, it's a good thing we got there when we did, is all I'm saying. I can't imagine a ticker like hers would've appreciated the sight."

"The sight?" both Amber and Peggy Lee spoke up at once. Since their combined voices were loud enough to echo off the walls, Amber lowered her voice. "What do you mean? Was he…hurt or something?"

"Well, now. I didn't say *that*. Until we get the autopsy report back, we can't disclose an official cause of death. But the scene was… That is, the amount of overturned furniture…" Officer Peyton trailed off and looked back at his coworker. From the wary glance that passed between them, it was clear Amber was going to have to extract this next bit of information by either force or guile.

And since force had always been Bones's thing, guile was all she had left.

"You're absolutely right, Officer," she said. No combination of words in the English language were likely to butter up a man as fast as those ones.

"I am? I mean, I *am*. Yes." He blinked. "About what, exactly?"

Amber leaned forward, a conspiratorial tilt to her head. Then she remembered what her grandmother had said about her double chin and smoothed her neck out instead. "About my grandmother's ticker. There's no way she could handle a job like yours. You must have the heart of a lion to do what you do, day in and day out, always seeing humanity at its worst."

"Something mighty fishy about this whole business," the second policeman said, his voice curt. When Officer Peyton didn't stop him, he smoothed his shirt over his belly and added, "Mighty fishy indeed. Facilities like this usually handle their own deaths, you understand. Straight to the funeral home, no need for us to come out. Only reason we were asked to take a look was because of the"—he dropped his voice to a barely audible whisper—"anonymous tip."

"Anonymous tip?" Amber echoed. "What do you mean?"

The officer shook his head, his expression grave. That flat, stony press of his lips imbued the rest of his unimpressive build with a sudden respectability. "Call came in during the wee hours of the morning. Loud noises, it said. Signs of a struggle. Something terrible going on."

The thought that her grandmother's friend had died of anything other than old age filled Amber with a sharp, sudden unease. Most of the cases she'd worked on with Bones had been typical private investigator fare—cheating spouses, missing persons, insurance fraud, and the occasional bit of industrial espionage.

Never anything that carried the weight of so much finality. Never *murder*.

"That's terrible," she said and meant it. "Has anyone told his family?"

"I'll call them in straightaway." The answer came from behind her. Like her, Peggy Lee seemed to have deflated at the news, her bright red hair suddenly a little too garish for her hunched posture and the way she cradled the phone in the crook of her neck. "Unless you'd rather I have them meet you at the station?

"Here is fine," Officer Peyton said. "I'm sure his family will appreciate hearing the news in a familiar setting."

"I wouldn't be so sure about that," Peggy Lee muttered, but so softly that Amber may have misunderstood.

With a thanks and a nod for the officers, Amber ducked down the hall in search of her wayward grandparent. She didn't know the woman very well yet, but one thing she felt for sure: once Jade knew that her friend had died under questionable circumstances, she was going to need a lot of support to get through the ordeal.

———————

"So I said to her, 'If you can't even *spell* vulva without breaking out into hives, how do you think your wedding night is going to go?'"

Amber halted at the threshold to the room where she'd been told she'd find her grandmother, one foot hovering above the ground. For the longest moment, she thought no one had noticed her, and that she'd be able to get away undetected, but luck wasn't on her side.

"Ah, Amber. You've come at the perfect time. I was just telling Lincoln some of my favorite stories about your mother."

"Nope. I'm not here." Amber threw up her hands and started backing away. "If the stories you have about mom involve any body parts that aren't, like, hands or feet, I'm out."

Her grandmother tsked and waved to usher her inside. "You can be anything you want in this world, child, but for the love of everything, please don't tell me you're a *prude*."

The amount of censure in her grandmother's speech could have moved mountains. All at once, some of the stories Amber's mom used to tell about Grandma Judith came rushing back.

One summer, she put me in sleepaway camp so she could join a nudist commune out in some mountain range no one had ever heard of. Only she didn't fill out the form properly, so I was put on the bus to the Boy Scouts. They couldn't get hold of her once I arrived, so I had to spend the whole summer sleeping on the exam table in the clinic. The nurse was the only other woman there.

Or *For senior prom, all I wanted was a black velvet dress with puffed sleeves and an iron-on lace collar. I begged and pleaded, but she refused to spend money on something she said was only fit for a funeral or an elderly matron on* Dallas. *I had to go in one of her discards—a low-cut red satin jumpsuit that was at least two sizes too small for me. The teachers were so scandalized they wouldn't even let me through the door.*

At the time, the stories had seemed like a gross exaggeration—her mother's way of justifying her refusal to let Grandma Judith anywhere near them—but Amber wasn't so sure anymore.

Especially once her grandmother waved her in and patted the seat next to her.

"Don't worry. I'm just teasing. I know you're nothing like Moonbeam Effervescence—or, I'm sorry, *Effie*. Would you like a vitamin IV bag? They're wonderfully refreshing. It's like doing cocaine but without the comedown afterward."

"Um."

"They're perfectly safe. I get at least one a week. They're what keeps me looking so young."

Lincoln chuckled and propelled Amber to the chair next to her grandmother. The room was small, but in addition to the lounge chair where Jade was hooked up to the IV, there were several cushioned seats where Amber assumed people had similar infusions of vitamin cocktail therapy. Which, now that she thought about it, was probably just another "luxury" detail in the transitional retirement process.

"The nurse says your grandmother will be back on her feet as soon as she's hydrated," Lincoln assured her. "We got lucky. Nasty Nancy is only on call today, so Marta put in the IV. She can glide a needle in like Luke Skywalker hitting the Death Star."

Amber barely had time to assimilate this before he winked. "That bit of knowledge comes from having eighteen grandkids too."

She had no choice but to fall into the seat he indicated, though she didn't feel at ease as she sat back and tried to figure out how best to broach the subject of the Admiral's death. Fortunately—or not—the choice was taken out of her hands by the arrival of Julio, once again clad in the too-heavy polyester of his security guard outfit.

"The day of reckoning has arrived," he said as he entered the room, his breath rattling and his steps labored. Sweat streaked down his forehead, but all he did was wipe the perspiration with the back of his hand before extracting a small notebook from his front pocket. "I've come to collect your balance, Lincoln. I've got you down for—"

"Two hundred," Lincoln interrupted. "I know. I'll have to write you a check when I get back to the condo. I don't have the cash on me right now."

"Reckoning?" Amber asked, glancing back and forth between them. "Balance? Surely you don't mean—"

"Isn't it ghastly?" her grandmother asked with a dainty shudder. "We're a macabre, greedy lot, but when you've seen as many friends die as we have, it's a necessity, not a choice. We wouldn't be able to get out of bed otherwise. What's my take? Last I checked, the odds were seven-to-one in my favor."

"Eight-to-one, actually," Julio said as he once again consulted his notebook.

Realization dawned on Amber with a start. "Grandma, you don't mean the money you're going to win because the Admiral died before his tortoise, do you?"

Her grandmother practically lit up. "Excellent. I knew you were paying closer attention than you let on when I was chattering by the pool yesterday. You're going to be a great addition to our podcast team."

"Grandma!" Amber cried again, this time with real distress. Her grandmother and her elderly friends might be accustomed to gambling on death, but it wasn't such a prevalent occurrence in her life that she was willing to treat it so cavalierly. Petty theft and larceny? No problem. Fistfights in the streets and bar fights that got a little out of hand? She'd seen her fair share.

But this was different. This was *forever*.

Lincoln reached over and patted her shoulder. "I know, dear, but what can we do? The Admiral lived a good, long life surrounded by friends who cared about him, which is more than a lot of folks can say."

Julio touched his forehead and made the motion of a cross over his chest. "In the name of the Father, the Son, and the Admiral's blessed tortoise, amen."

Amber could only shake her head. She used to think that Bones was the most cavalier person on this planet—his rough edges honed down to a razor's blade—but she was starting to rethink that stance. Bones could snap the neck of every person in this room with a flick of his wrist, but he'd at least feel a pang of guilt afterward. Possibly even two pangs.

She decided to sit on the news about the anonymous tip and the possibility that there was more to the Admiral's death than met the eye. Since the police officers hadn't seen fit to inform her grandmother about the gory details, there was plenty of time to cross that bridge once they got there.

"Wait." Her brow furrowed as a thought occurred to her. "Didn't you say that the Admiral's tortoise is on the loose?"

Her grandmother clucked her tongue. "For almost a month now. It's a wonder we can't find him. He's the only creature on earth who moves slower than we do."

"Then how do you know for sure that the Admiral died first?" Amber asked. "For all you know, the tortoise has been dead for weeks and you just haven't found the body yet. Technically, that means the Admiral out-lived him."

As soon as the words passed her lips, Amber regretted them. *Not*, as one would expect, because it was a callous thing to say when a man had been found dead inside a podcast studio less than six hours ago, but because of the way her grandmother cackled with delight.

"Ladies and gentlemen, may I present my granddaughter!" she cried with an energetic clap. The IV bag swung ominously on its stand, but Lincoln must have been used to her way of reacting to things, because he was quick to lay a hand on top of hers.

"Brilliant, Amber," her grandmother added. "Positively *brilliant*. Don't you dare write that check yet, Lincoln. Until we find the tortoise either dead or alive, it would be unethical for me to claim any of my winnings."

It seemed the height of irony to be discussing ethics at a time like this, but Amber knew when she was outnumbered. When backed into a corner, fighting would only end up making the situation worse. The most she could hope for was to slink away when everyone else was occupied.

Unfortunately, this particular corner was a tight one—and she was beginning to realize that these weren't people who gave anything up easily.

"You're absolutely right." Julio stuffed the notebook back in his pocket. "I don't know what I was thinking."

"You just lost a close friend," Jade said with a magnanimous air. "One can't expect you to have everything figured out. But it's all right. Amber is on the case."

"I'm sorry. I'm what, now?"

A beep from the IV indicated that the line had run dry. Taking it as a cue to end the conversation as well as her vitamin infusion, her grandmother yanked the needle out of her hand and tossed it aside. It dangled from the end of the line, a lone drop of blood bubbling at the tip.

"Well, you're a PI, aren't you?" her grandmother asked as Lincoln helped her to her feet. "Or close enough to count?"

Amber blinked, unable to tear her gaze from that drop of blood. "Yes?"

"Then I'd like to hire you as payment for you continuing to live under my roof."

She jolted back to awareness. "Wait. What?"

"You heard me, young lady," her grandmother said, sounding more like Amber's mother than she would probably care to admit. "We're allowed to have visitors for up to thirty days at a time, but we have to pay for a guest pass. You can either find that tortoise or agree to be on my podcast. Cash is also an option if you'd prefer."

Amber thought about the sad state of her bank account and winced. Unless the going rent in a place like this was under a hundred bucks, her options were limited—a thing she felt fairly certain her grandmother knew. Thirty-one-year-old women didn't go running to their estranged elderly relatives without a word of warning unless necessity demanded it.

"Grandma, are you *blackmailing* me?"

Her grandmother tsked. "It's not blackmail, child. It's extortion—a thing any good investigator should know for herself."

Amber couldn't hold back her sudden shout of laughter. That sounded so much like something Horace Horatio would say on *Death Comes Calling* that she was almost tempted to agree to the podcast right then and there. But she wasn't ready to make that kind of commitment—or *any* commitment, really—which meant the tortoise was the only way forward.

Despite her reservations, Amber didn't hate the idea of earning her keep. She *wasn't* a PI, and unless she wanted to start her three years of training all over again, she never would be. Eventually, she'd have to get her life in order enough to find a job and a place to live, maybe even fake a new identity so she could put this whole Bones business behind her once and for all.

For now, however, she just needed a place to rest and lick her wounds, a too-cold condo, and enough bribery croissants to keep her belly full.

Besides, finding a missing tortoise was right in her wheelhouse. In fact, it was her first official case of her own, and she wanted to kill it.

Figuratively speaking, of course.

4

ONE OF AMBER'S PRIMARY JOBS as the unofficial assistant of a Seattle private investigator had been to conduct all the background research he couldn't be bothered to undertake on his own.

Bones was a man more of action than intelligence, preferring long stake-outs and entire days spent following his targets to the more boring (and, in Amber's mind, more rational) act of sitting in front of a computer. For example, if he was tasked with finding a skipped bail—one of the more common jobs to fall on his plate—he'd locate the target's girlfriend/sister/mother/wife and sit outside her house until his quarry appeared.

Trust me, babe, he would say as they took up their position and prepared to wait. *When a man in is this kind of trouble, he always goes running to the most capable woman he knows. Nobody fixes a problem faster than Mommy.*

He'd been disconcertingly correct about that—and about a lot of things associated with weak men and their inability to handle problems on their own—but Amber had preferred her own approach. She called doctors and dentists to find out when the target had appointments lined up. She scoured social media for background images that gave clues as to regular haunts and hideouts. She dived deep into forums to find out where they got their tattoos and their opinions on which bars had the best happy hours.

Which was why she started her tortoise hunt by seating herself a bench by the pickleball courts and opening a Nextdoor account.

The gentle, rhythmic pinging of the plastic balls back and forth set a strange backdrop for her search, but it was no stranger than watching her grandmother get a vitamin IV infusion while she and her friends discussed death betting pools. At least this way Amber was getting some fresh air.

"Okay, my little dinosaur friend," she said aloud as she entered her grandmother's address into the app and watched a map pop up. "Let's see what they're saying about your whereabouts."

As promised, the retirement community boards were full of long-running conversations about everything from sightings of the Admiral's missing tortoise to arguments over who was stealing the arugula from the garden plot of someone named Hannah. Amber almost laughed out loud to see how in-depth some of the discussions got. Soap operas had less convoluted story lines.

Did you ever stop to think that maybe the tortoise is the one eating all your arugula? asked one such thread.

I doubt he could stomach it. Hannah's arugula is so overwatered you can taste the rot taking hold.

MY ARUGULA IS DELICIOUS. STOP STEALING IT, PEGGY LEE, OR I'LL REPORT YOU TO THE ADMINISTRATION.

It's not me. I wouldn't eat your arugula if I was dying of hunger in the zombie apocalypse.

Ha! As if you'd last five minutes against the incoming hordes. I've seen you run. It's like watching a penguin try to cross the freeway.

Amber chuckled and kept scrolling, but although the discussions were entertaining, they weren't particularly enlightening. The tortoise had been sighted, in no particular order, frolicking in the garden plots, escaping through the iron-spiked fence, dumpster diving at three of the six restaurants, and once, with an accompanying blurred photo, enjoying a brief dip in the hot tub. He appeared to be elusive to an alarming degree, and it didn't take long before Amber realized he was something of a Bigfoot around these parts—often sighted, never substantiated, and largely apocryphal.

She was just about to give up and tuck the phone away when a different thread caught her attention.

Jade McCallan was out sunbathing topless again.

Tart.

Rude tart.

Evil rude tart.

Cut it out, ConcernedCitizen1443. It's her own back porch. She's not hurting anyone.

Tell that to all the grandkids running around. She's indecent. This place has gone downhill ever since she moved in. Are we getting anywhere with the petition to have her removed?

Amber's brow furrowed as she scanned the lines. While it was obvious that most of the residents used the app as a way to air petty grievances and take passive-aggressive jabs at one another, this particular attack seemed different somehow. *Meaner.*

A pickleball whizzed by her head before she could investigate further. The plastic ball pinged off a white-budded tree behind her, accompanied by a chorus of groans from the direction of the court. Laughing, she sprang up from the bench.

"Don't worry," she called. "I'll grab it for you. That was some hit."

"You can blame Wallace," returned a woman being held together by so much athletic tape that her skin was barely visible. "We keep telling him this is a gentle game, but he seems to think we're vying for a place at the Olympics."

"If you're not playing to win, what's the point of playing at all?" he countered.

Amber found the ball and tossed it back to the players, taking a few seconds to poke among the leafy fronds in case there might be a tortoise hiding underneath. There wasn't, but the sound of a nearby voice proved just as—if not more—interesting.

"It's gone. Missing. *Stolen.* What part of that don't you understand?"

Straightening, she turned in the direction of the voice. Sweat dripped down the nape of her neck and seeped into her sleep tank, which she hadn't yet had the time or inclination to change out of.

"I'm telling you, that ring is a family heirloom. An antique. I demand that you find it at once."

The voice continued even louder and angrier than before. Drawn to it the way a private investigator was drawn to, well, other loud and angry voices, Amber started to move in that direction. Where there was smoke, there was fire, and where there were heightened emotions, there was almost certainly something she wanted to see.

She stopped at the edge of the small park, where the first line of condos rose up in a tidy row. The one on the end boasted a potted plant hanging from the porch, the leaves looking wilted and unkempt as they brushed against the heads of the three people gathered underneath it.

Two of the people were known to her, their police uniforms darkened with sweat in the several hours since she'd last seen them. Officer Peyton, in particular, looked as though he'd have rather been *anywhere* else in the world.

Which, considering the nature of his next words, was understandable.

"I'm sorry that you weren't able to find what you were looking for, Ms. Vincent, but that's not what we're here to discuss. As I said before, your father—"

"Would never let that ring out of his sight. I don't think you understand just how valuable it is."

"Be that as it may, we didn't see any signs of a break-in here at the house. The podcast studio, however—"

Amber stumbled on a cactus, but any sounds she might have accidentally made were swallowed by the shout rising up from the condo's front porch. "My father is *dead*, Officer. Murdered at a retirement community where he was supposed to be looked after around the clock. Do you really want me to believe that our family's most cherished heirloom—an heirloom that was recently appraised for three million dollars—just so happened to go missing at the exact same time?"

"Well, now, Ms. Vincent. Until the autopsy report comes back, we don't know for sure that your father was murdered. We only suspect—"

It hadn't been Amber's intention to make her appearance known, but a low cough and a murmur from the porch indicated that someone had seen her.

"Who's there?" the shrill woman demanded. "Who's spying on us? I demand that you show yourself at once."

Amber's first instinct was to flee, but she tamped the feeling down as far as it would go. *Of course* this woman was loud and unpleasant, and *of course* she was ready to lash out at the first person to get in her way. Jade McCallan might be so familiar with death that she could treat it as nothing more than a blip in an otherwise sunny day, but this woman had just lost her father.

And if what the police are saying is true, she lost him in a singularly unpleasant way.

"I didn't mean to cause any trouble." Amber stepped forward, her hands up as if in surrender. "And I didn't mean to eavesdrop. I'm just out here looking for something."

"Not a ring, I hope." The woman stood in a wide-legged stance, her arms crossed and a frown creasing the thin, arched brows that Amber could have sworn were tattooed on. Her brindled hair was cut in a sharp bob around her chin, and a cashmere cardigan was draped over her shoulders despite the heat. "Because if you find it, it's mine. It belongs—I mean, belong*ed*—to my father. He's dead."

Amber winced. "I know. I'm so sorry about your loss. I'll be on my way. Unless, uh…" She hated to bother this woman any more than she already had, but one of the many things she'd learned on the job was that a good PI seized every opportunity with both hands.

Also that the best place to find missing things was often the most obvious one.

"You haven't seen your dad's tortoise anywhere around his condo, have you?" she asked. "Or signs that he's been there recently? Droppings or half-eaten vegetables or anything like that?"

"His *tortoise*? Are you serious?"

"Yes, actually," Amber said apologetically. "He's been missing for a few weeks, and some of the residents are really worried about him."

The woman whirled on Officer Peyton as if he were solely responsible for Amber's lack of tact. "Officer, are you going to stand back and allow this woman to creep around a crime scene?"

"Whoa, whoa, whoa." Amber kept her hands up as she started backing away. She felt pretty sure her earlier flirtation had turned the mustachioed officer into a friend instead of a foe, but she didn't like the way the woman was looking at her—and not just because her eyebrows had yet to move. "I didn't mean to get in the way of your investigation. I just thought the tortoise might be trapped somewhere inside the house without access to food or water. I wanted to make sure he's not suffering, that's all."

Officer Peyton nodded at Amber in a way that felt like approval. "And as I said before, Ms. Vincent, this isn't a crime scene. Not officially. You're welcome to search through your father's things and file a police report if you can't find the ring, but there are no signs of forced entry or other kinds of foul play. If the item was insured, then maybe you could—"

"You can't insure family history," she interrupted. "That ring is *irreplaceable*."

Amber was just about to make good her escape when the woman snapped her fingers. "You. Snooping girl. Come here for a second."

It was on the tip of Amber's tongue to inform her that she was a snooping *woman*, thank you very much, but sympathy and the uneasy suspicion that she was very much in the wrong allowed her to swallow the insult.

"I really am sorry for your loss," she said as she made her way up the porch steps. "And for intruding on such a painful moment. I can't imagine what you must be going through."

The woman batted the condolences aside with a wave of her hand. "You're not old," she said.

"Uh...thank you?"

She waved harder. "No, I mean you're a young person. In an old person's home."

"Oh. Um. Yeah. I'm staying with my grandmother for a little while. She was a friend of your father's. In fact, it was her—" Amber cut herself off before she could make the mistake of mentioning her grandmother's podcast studio in connection with the death. "Her request that I find the tortoise," she said instead. Since mentioning the death bet seemed callous in the extreme, she added, "Everyone here seems to really love the little guy. They have a whole Nextdoor thread about trying to find him."

This didn't appear to soften the woman by so much as an inch. "And what on earth does that have to do with you?"

"Nothing except that I have some experience with investigating. The residents asked me to put my skills to use while I'm here."

"What *kind* of experience?" the woman asked, and with such a hard stare that Amber felt herself growing flustered. Bones had often used a similar approach when trying to get answers out of people—a sort of bullheaded, no-bullshit way of acting aggressively without actually threatening anyone, so she should have been able to counteract its effects.

But it was hot, and she was wearing the same clothes she'd slept in, and none of this was going according to plan.

"I'm a PI," she said, since it was close enough to the truth to count. "And I—"

She was cut off by the screech of tires as a white sports car pulled up outside the condo. The car looked sleek and expensive, as did the woman who stepped out and immediately began stalking toward them in heels that teetered on four spiked inches.

The grieving daughter practically fell into the woman's arms. "Geerta, thank goodness you're here," she said. "You won't believe the things these police officers are saying about Dad."

"Don't say another word, Michelle," Geerta replied. For reasons Amber couldn't even begin to fathom, this woman *also* wore a cashmere sweater, and without a sign of sweat or heat exhaustion in sight. Amber wondered how it was possible—if women of a certain income level had a way of removing their sweat glands for aesthetic reasons—but she didn't dare ask.

Geerta turned to the officers with her hands on her hips. Her hair was an indeterminate shade of white that could be either blond or gray, her face layered with thick makeup that didn't quite conceal the vast array of freckles underneath. "I'd like to know on whose authority you're here conducting an investigation. This is private property."

Officer Peyton became all mustache again, his associate all belly. "Yes, ah. About that. I'm afraid there's been an incident, and we received an anonymous call to check it out. You must be—"

"The director of this facility?" The woman held out her hand, keeping it perfectly level until the officer had no choice but to shake it. "Geerta Blom. I'd like to know why I wasn't notified *the moment* the call was put in."

Officer Peyton winced. "We were only following protocol."

The daughter—Michelle, apparently—gave an inelegant snort. "Protocol to lose valuable pieces of jewelry and bring in outside private investigators, you mean."

For the first time, the blond woman appeared to notice Amber standing there. If she approved of what she saw, it wasn't evident in the way her nostrils closed to tight pinpricks. "And just who are you supposed to be?"

Amber liked to think she was brave for someone who only stood five feet two inches tall, but that woman's glower was almost her undoing. She found herself wishing for a few rolls of dimes just to be on the safe side.

"I'm, um, Amber?"

"Well, *Um Amber*, I don't know how you got in here or why you're snooping around, but I'm going to have to ask you to leave the premises immediately. In fact, why don't these two police officers escort you out? We might as well put them to use after they've come all this way."

"Yes, ma'am. Of course, ma'am. Only—"

Geerta turned her glare on Officer Peyton. "Only what? From what I understand, one of our elderly residents passed away in the retirement community where he has lived and been cared for over the past five years. I hate to break it to you, but that is precisely what this place is *for*." She turned her back on the man in a gesture that would have been rude in every country on the planet. "Please see to it that you and your investigators don't trespass here again."

Instead of causing Officer Peyton to slink away in shame, as Amber expected, he rose to the occasion.

"I'm afraid that's not how this works," he said. When he caught sight of the way the woman's face froze, he coughed and amended this with, "What I mean is, leaving isn't within our power. Asking us to leave in the middle of an open investigation is like asking someone to unring a bell. A call suspecting foul play was put in. We answered it and found a dead man. We have no choice but to see our investigation through to the end, or it's my job on the line. And Officer Katz's, of course."

The second officer nodded miserably. "Fishy business," he said, echoing the same words he'd said to Amber before. "Mighty fishy indeed."

Geerta seemed to be rapidly reaching the end of a rope that didn't seem all that long to begin with. "And this person?" she asked with a hard stare at Amber.

Support came from an unlikely source.

"She's a PI," Officer Peyton explained. "Apparently, she was hired to find the deceased's missing tortoise."

"Indeed?" Geerta asked in glacial tones. She turned to Amber with a curt nod. "In that case, I'd like to see some credentials."

"I don't exactly have any."

"No? A badge? A license? A website?" Geerta shot the words out like the rapid fire of a machine gun. "I thought not. You look like you're barely capable of paying a parking ticket, let alone solving crimes in an official capacity."

Since this was perilously close to the truth, Amber kept her lips clamped. The last she'd checked, she had three unpaid parking tickets—all of which had been acquired in the line of duty, and all of which Bones had promised to take care of as soon as he got around to it.

"Now." Geerta dismissed Amber with no more than a blink. "What's this nonsense I hear about murder, and how quickly can we get this matter resolved?"

Amber would have liked to hear the conversation that ensued between the apologetic officers and the irate facility director, but her sense of self-preservation was strong. After quickly sweeping the porch for any signs of the tortoise—of which she found none—she trotted down the stairs and out of view.

"I told you it wouldn't make a difference where the Admiral's family heard the news," a woman said. Amber gasped and whirled to find a pair of eyes watching from the other side of a shrub. The vibrant red wig the woman wore matched the flowering plant so well that she was practically invisible.

"Peggy Lee!" Amber gasped, her hand on her chest. "Were you watching us the whole time?"

"I saw enough," Peggy Lee answered. "And I was right, wasn't I? That daughter of the Admiral's is a nasty piece of work. The son's even worse, but he has to fly in from New York. We have a few days before he descends on us and makes all our lives miserable."

Amber blinked, taking a moment to absorb the information. "You seem to know an awful lot about what goes on around here."

"Bless your heart. Of course I do. Why do you think I work at the front desk? For the paycheck?"

Amber didn't answer. When it came to people like Peggy Lee, she knew she didn't have to. In the private investigative world, gossips were one of the most valuable resources in existence—especially gossips in a fishbowl like this one.

Peggy Lee's next words proved it. "I know about *everyone's* family, thank you very much. Lincoln's kids are a delight. Raffi's don't visit as much as they should. Camille doesn't have any, and as for Jade's…well." She tapped the side of her nose. "I expect you know more about the things Effie has done than the rest of us combined."

This time, Amber didn't answer for entirely different reasons. Truth be told, she knew very little about the estrangement between her mother and grandmother. They had vastly different personalities, obviously, and neither one was the sort to forgive and forget, but there was a difference between keeping your family at arm's length and cutting off the arm altogether.

"And the Admiral's kids?" Amber ventured instead. "What's wrong with them?"

Peggy Lee blinked. "You mean other than that they're greedy, self-absorbed monsters who never gave two licks about their father's health and well-being?" She practically cackled as she started to make her way back toward the nursing home. "All they've ever wanted is to get their hands on that ring. In fact, I wouldn't be surprised if they're the entire reason he's dead."

5

"I'm Horace Horatio, and you'd better hope
that death doesn't come calling for you next."
—*DEATH COMES CALLING*, CLOSING CATCHPHRASE

JADE MUST NOT HAVE EXPECTED the tortoise search to yield results right away. As Amber slunk into the condo with her figurative tail between her legs, she found her grandmother sitting in the living room with a police file in front of her and a look of intense concentration on her face. The tortoise—if she remembered his existence—appeared to be the last thing on her mind.

"That's exactly my point." Jade flipped over the page and scanned it. "The kidnappers *had* to have left a ransom note. Otherwise, what would be the point—"

She cut herself off as soon as she noticed Amber surreptitiously removing her flip-flops and trying to sneak down the hall.

"Excellent timing, child. You're needed. Come take a look at these police files and tell us if anything seems off."

Amber noted the use of the plural *us* but failed to see another person in the living room. She hoped it was a royal *we* situation rather than a sign of early mental decline. "If this is about the podcast, Grandma—"

Jade patted the couch cushion next to her. "Of course it's about the podcast. We're supposed to record an episode for Friday, but the police closed off the studio and won't let us in. We're holding a discussion in here instead. Come tell us what you think."

Amber gasped aloud as her grandmother's oversized rocker turned toward her. There, ensconced in the plush beige fabric, sat a slight, cherubic man with one of the worst toupees she'd ever seen. When the man grinned at Amber, it was to showcase a row of teeth so white and uniform that she knew she had to be looking at a set of dentures.

"Ah. You must be Amber. The granddaughter. So much fertile beauty could only exist in one family's tree." As he spoke, he struggled to his feet. Amber wanted to beg him not to bother—to save whatever elasticity remained in his knees for someone more worthy—but she had the feeling her worries wouldn't be appreciated. Especially when the man took Amber's hand and lifted it to his lips. "Jade's description didn't do you justice."

He cast a mischievous look over his shoulder. "You said she looks like she knows how to survive a street fight, but you were wrong. This girl looks as though she *starts* them."

This time, Amber really did gasp, but not with outrage. Her feelings contained nothing but delight. She'd listened to this man's low, deliciously ragged voice for so many hours that she felt as if she already knew him.

Granted, in her head, he'd been a good foot taller, fifty pounds heavier, and dressed in pretty much anything except a three-piece tweed suit and bow tie, but that didn't change her feelings in the slightest. If anything, the discrepancies only made this whole situation better. *Of course* the real Horace Horatio would be a dapper scrap of a man doused in so much leather and sandalwood cologne that it felt like she'd just wandered into a commercial for equine sporting equipment. A surly, burly retired detective would have been so obvious.

She allowed herself to be pulled forward as Raffi brushed a kiss on either of her cheeks, transferring a healthy portion of leather and sandalwood as he did.

"I'm Raffi Badir, but I'm sure you've already guessed that," he said with a twinkle. "Please, sit down. We've hit something of an impasse and need a fresh perspective."

If her grandmother had been the one doing the asking, Amber might have made her excuses and fled, using the tortoise hunt as a shield. As it was, she took the chair Raffi offered, still warm from his seat, and tucked her feet underneath her.

He handed her the police file her grandmother had been holding.

"Jade tells me you're a private eye," he said as he hitched his slacks and sank into the couch cushion next to Jade. "How fascinating."

For once, Amber didn't bother explaining the rules and regulations related to the industry—that in most states you had to have three years of training before you could become licensed; that in order for the training to count, your supervising PI had to actually fill out and sign the paperwork; that she'd done everything short of getting on her knees and begging Bones to make her position official.

"It's a living," she agreed blandly. "Or it *would* be, if I hadn't recently quit."

He waved this off as if running away from home was a blip rather than an upheaval of everything she knew and was. "Good for you. I imagine people underestimate you and tell you their deepest, darkest secrets all the time."

Amber blinked, once again at a loss to understand how everyone in this retirement community was able to see right through her. "What makes you say that?"

"Because I'm about to tell you mine," he said without losing his smile. However, he did drop his voice to a conspiratorial whisper. "The truth is, I'm a *terrible* detective. Before your grandmother found me and strong-armed me into reading her scripts, I never gave crime a second thought. I taught high school. Physics, mostly, with a touch of chemistry on the side. Kids hate physics. Chemistry too, but they always enjoyed the prospect of blowing up the lab with a Bunsen burner and a leaky hydrogen valve."

Nodding as though everything he'd just said carried no more importance than a discussion of the day's weather—another hundred-degree scorcher, by the way—he nodded down at the file. "Well? What do you think?"

"My working theory is that either the police or the family *did* get a ransom note," Jade said before Amber could get a word in. "According to the reports, no note was ever received, but I believe it was a cover-up. Either the police bungled the handover, so they pretended there was no ransom demand to save their own necks, or the family didn't want word getting out. Most of their fortune came from home security systems. It wouldn't look good if their own daughter was taken and held hostage for a hefty payout. Who on earth would hire them if news like that got out?"

With that, Jade sat back in her chair and took a sip of what looked like ice water but Amber suspected was straight vodka.

Amber fingered the police files in her lap, her skin practically itching with the urge to flip through them. She didn't though—not right away. She had the feeling that her insight might be the only bargaining chip she had in this situation.

She placed her palm flat on the top of the file. "About the podcast studio…did I hear you say they won't let you inside? The police, I mean?"

Her grandmother's shrewdly narrowed eyes told Amber that she was on to her tricks, but Raffi sighed and folded his hands over his lap. "Alas, poor George. One has to wonder what he was doing in the studio all alone that late at night." His melancholy *tsk* carried more weight than all her grandmother's earlier histrionics. "I expect he was trying to sneak in some extra research. I may lack the suspicious mind needed for this kind of work, but the Admiral lived and breathed the podcast. He'll be sorely missed, won't he, Jade?"

Her grandmother nodded with a solemnity Amber didn't trust for a second. "Lucky for us, the good Lord sent a replacement before we got too far behind on our deadline."

Amber thought about the anonymous call to the police and the missing heirloom ring, the way Peggy Lee was skulking in the bushes and her own uneasy suspicion that there was more to the Admiral's death than met the eye.

"Exactly how many of you work on the podcast?" she asked.

Raffi lifted a hand and started ticking off fingers. "Me and your grandmother, of course. George—the Admiral, that is—does most of our research. Lincoln has been instrumental in keeping us fed, Camille does all the distribution and PR, Julio keeps the books, and Peggy Lee is our tech guru. So…seven?" He frowned as he considered the events of the past twenty-four hours. "Or six, I suppose I should say. It won't be the same without George."

"We'll be fine," Jade said firmly. The glance she cast at Amber was even firmer. "Amber can fill the gap the Admiral left behind. Can't you, dear?"

Amber sighed and gave in. She wasn't even sure what she was trying to accomplish anyway. To see her grandmother exhibit a sign of grief, perhaps? Or to get an admission that her friend's death—or maybe even *murder*—was taking up more of her heart than she was willing to let on?

As much as she hated to admit it, Amber wasn't owed anything from her grandmother. Not a square meal, not a place to stay, and definitely not an explanation as to the inner workings of her heart. They were strangers, when all was said and done. She should content herself with the first two and call it a win.

Unfortunately, the driving urge to get to the bottom of things wasn't something she could just run away from. Believe her. She'd tried—was, in fact, actively, *desperately* trying.

She opened the file. Sure enough, it contained a police report about the kidnapping that the *Death Comes Calling* podcast was currently investigating. The case was an older one—from 1988, if she remembered the last few broadcasts correctly—and was officially considered unsolved.

None of this was particularly unusual. Most true crime podcasts dealt with older cases rather than ongoing investigations for the primary reason that many of the original files had been unsealed and the statute of limitations had passed. Although things like capital murders and kidnappings could still be prosecuted, the smaller, less heinous crimes wouldn't. This meant that anyone who may have been protecting themselves at the time—say, for petty theft or willfully withholding evidence—might be more open to discussing their part in the investigation.

What *was* unusual about this one was that the murder involved was only speculation. The body of the kidnapped girl—woman, really, since she'd been eighteen at the time of the incident—had never been recovered. Just a whole lot of blood, a grieving family, and thousands of missing posters that were eventually buried under band posters and pizza delivery discounts.

"Okay, so what am I looking at?" Amber asked as she lifted the top photograph. The question was a rhetorical one since it was obvious this was a crime scene photo. She'd been following along with Horace Horatio's investigation closely enough to know that the blood type found pooled in a remote cabin in Idaho had matched that of Sharon Schmidt, the missing girl, and that the sheer amount of it had prompted investigators to halt their search. No one, they'd claimed, would have been able to lose that much and live to tell the tale. Several promising suspects had been investigated at the time, including a boyfriend a decade older than her and a handyman who had clear and easy access to the family estate, but none of the evidence was strong enough to support an arrest.

In other words, it was the ideal case for a sensationalist murder podcast three decades later. And for the frenzy of conspiracy boards that had been coming up with theories and sightings for years.

"I'm not going to ask where you got these photos, since I'm pretty sure you aren't supposed to have access." Amber paused to give either of them a chance to refute her, but all they did was nod and smile. Since she'd flirted, cajoled, and once, in a *minor* breaking-and-entering incident, cheated her own way into looking at several police records, she didn't question them further. "But I'm not sure what you hope to gain by looking at them. If you really think there was a ransom note—"

This time, her grandmother did speak up. "I've been emailing back and forth with the brother for the past few months. I'm *this* close to getting him to admit that his parents were hiding something, but I'm running out of time to work on him. The narrative is getting stale, and our recent numbers prove it. I suspect those bungling cops have known all along exactly who did this, but they won't give me access to any evidence that proves it."

"What we want to know is what went wrong that day at the cabin," Raffi added. He gestured at the photo. "Even if the kidnappers were annoyed at the delay in their payment, this kind of bloodbath seems…extreme. Especially since the kidnappers no longer had a chance to get paid. It wouldn't make any sense for them to kill their bargaining chip before they got a whiff of money."

"'The motivation for every criminal activity can be boiled down to one of three things,'" Jade said, quoting an oft-cited line from the podcast.

Raffi finished it for her with a wink and his signature Horatio rumble. "'Sex, power, or money. And since money can easily buy the other two, I think we have our answer.'"

Amber fought the urge to roll her eyes. She'd always found that refrain to be a vast oversimplification of the things that drove people—what about fear? Revenge? Passion? *Love?*—but she didn't say as much out loud. She was too busy scanning the image, her brain working a mile a minute as she looked—not at the sticky blood spread across the kitchen floor or the over-turned table, the pots and pans scattered at random, but at everything else.

Or rather, at *nothing* else.

"Actually, I think your answer might not have anything to do with money at all." Amber tapped the photo. "Didn't you say in one of the episodes that Sharon Schmidt didn't get along with her parents? That several neighbors went on record about their late-night arguments?"

"Ah!" Raffi rubbed his hands together, filling the air with the crackle of dry skin. "You think she sent the ransom note herself, yes? We've considered that angle, but what went so wrong that the plan ended in bloodshed? And who was her accomplice?"

"If I had to guess, I'd say it was that friend you mentioned in—what was it?—the second or third episode. The hairdresser. The one who was super into punk and ran away a few months later to become a groupie." Amber handed the photo back to her grandmother. "In the upheaval, someone spilled a bowl of walnuts all over the kitchen. See them?"

Her grandmother barely glanced at the photo, her gaze instead fixed on Amber's face.

"Walnuts," Raffi echoed before whipping out a pair of readers and perching them on the end of his nose. "Yes. Yes, I see them. What do they mean?"

"Well, there's no other food or garbage spilled anywhere you'd expect to find that stuff, especially if there was a struggle. It's as if the culprit was care-ful to clear away any incriminating items before he or she started throwing things around. But the walnuts stayed, see?"

Both her grandmother and Raffi nodded.

"My guess is that they used the shells to dye Sharon's hair—I had tons of friends do the same thing during our middle school Panic! At the Disco phase." She saw that the name of the band had little to no impact on either of her listeners, so she went on. Some generations would never understand the deep bond that she and six million other tweens had formed with emo pop. "Sharon was a blond, right? She'd have been easily visible during that time since her story got such wide publicity. I'd say they lay low for a few days, changed her appearance with whatever they could find out in the forest, and then staged the scene to look like a bloodbath. Unless they tested the blood for DNA, it could have come from both of them. Did anyone think to check the hairdresser's blood type? Or ask what became of her after she ran away to follow Van Halen?"

The stunned silence that followed this pronouncement filled Amber with a sense of pride that had her sliding her legs out from under her and sitting tall.

"It's not possible," Raffi murmured.

"On the contrary—it *is* possible. A bit of a stretch, obviously, but that's our specialty." Jade's posture suddenly rivaled that of Amber. Her voice took on a lilting tone that, as she'd admitted herself, sounded too much like a frail old lady to carry the same impact as Horace Horatio's grizzled baritone. "Tired of the gilded shackles that bound her to a family who didn't understand her, Sharon and her best friend—or maybe even her lover?—came up with a plan to release her. Not for money or for power, but for freedom. To live life on her own terms, to make her own way in this world. Oh, yes. We can sell that. We can *absolutely* sell that."

Amber barely had time to wonder what she'd done when she felt her cheeks being pressed between two strong hands as her grandmother pressed a kiss on her lips.

"You beautiful, brilliant girl," she said. "It's the perfect ending. We'll ask our listeners to respect Sharon's wishes and close the conspiracy boards so she can continue to enjoy life on her own terms. They won't, of course, but that won't be our problem. That's the beautiful thing about podcasts. We just have to sell a convincing story; it's up to law enforcement to actually *do* something about it. What do you think, Raffi?"

Raffi stroked his chin thoughtfully. "It's not the worst finale we've ever come up with, and the rest of our leads haven't gone anywhere promising..." He appeared to be deep in thought as his voice trailed off. Amber wondered exactly where he'd disappeared inside his head—or how long it would take him to come back again—when he nodded. "I approve. Put it to paper, Jade, and I'll record it first thing tomorrow. Unless…"

This time, the trail of his voice led to a place all of them could easily follow.

"I'm sure they'll let us into the studio by then," Jade said. "Last spring, Gerald keeled over in the swimming pool, and they only closed that off long enough to give it a chlorine shock before throwing the annual luau."

There were so many things wrong with that statement—not the least of which was the fact that they didn't even *drain* the pool after a man died in it—but Amber didn't allow herself to be distracted this time.

For distraction she felt sure it was.

"I think it might be more difficult to get into your studio than you think," Amber said without a hint of a smile. "There's more to George Vincent's death than the cops are letting on."

The fact that she used the Admiral's real name did more to sober the two people facing her than anything else she could have said.

"How did you…?" Raffi began.

"I ran into his daughter, Michelle," Amber explained. "And the director of this place, Geerta Blom. She had quite a bit to say about the fact that the police were called instead of the facility following the usual protocol."

Raffi's eyes widened in surprise, but her grandmother tsked and shook her head. "My, but you *have* been a busy little bee, haven't you?"

Amber fixed her stare on her grandmother's face, but despite the familiar lines she saw there—the melting chocolate eyes they shared, the wide-angled cheekbones that turned both their faces into a heart, her mother's slightly upturned nose—she had no idea how to read the other woman's expression.

If Jade McCallan had been the target of one of her private investigations, Amber might have spent a few days researching how to best slip under her radar, worm her way into the woman's good graces and pounce when her guard was down. But this was her grandmother. Her blood. The only member of her family who shared even a fraction of the freewheeling, free-dealing outlook that had gotten her into trouble so many times in the past.

"Someone called in an anonymous tip late last night," Amber said without once moving her eyes from her grandmother's face. "And when the police arrived at the podcast studio, they found it in complete upheaval. They're waiting on an autopsy before they make an official statement, but his daughter is crying foul play. Apparently, there's a missing family ring she claims is worth a lot of money."

Not by so much as a blink did Amber's grandmother show signs of surprise.

"Interesting," Jade said, drawing the word out until it practically grew legs and stood up in the center of the room. "And have any of these so-called experts considered the possibility that the Admiral was an old man whose time had merely come?"

There was little Amber could say in response except, "That theory is on the table, yes."

"Then there you have it. The whole thing is a tempest in a teapot, if you'll excuse the trite expression." Her grandmother turned to Raffi as if there was no more to say on the subject. "I'll get to work writing up the last episode, but we're going to need to find a way to break into the studio."

It was almost too much. "Grandma, you can't just break into a crime scene! A man is dead. If you just wait a few days—"

She may as well not have spoken for all the attention the other two paid her.

"We can always record the final episode in the bathroom, but all our case files are in that studio. If we want to get a jump start on a new season, we need to find a way in." Jade tapped the center of her chin with her forefinger. "Have you been by to see what kind of security they've put up, Amber?"

She blinked. "Of course not. But I'm sure—"

"Raffi and I will create a distraction so you can slip in. The files are in boxes along the back wall. Just grab a few, and we'll start sorting through to find the most promising. There's a lovely one about an underground fighting ring and a missing giraffe at Zoo Atlanta that's been bothering me for years."

"A distraction," Raffi mused. "Yes. Yes, I know just the thing."

Amber made one last valiant attempt to save herself. "But I'm already doing the tortoise thing, remember? You said I can skip the podcast as long as I find him."

As before, her words had virtually no impact. She was starting to wonder if they ever would.

"I said you don't have to appear on the podcast, child, and I meant it," Jade said in a tone that brooked no argument. "But it would be a shame to waste a mind like yours on something as silly as a missing pet. Anyone who can come up with walnut hair dye to solve a case thirty years in the making is worth her weight in gold. Consider yourself officially on the research staff."

6

*"If you knew how many crimes go unreported in
this country, you'd never leave your house again."*
—DEATH COMES CALLING, SEASON 2 EPISODE 12

MUCH TO AMBER'S RELIEF, THEY didn't have an opportunity to break
into the podcast studio that night. The flesh was willing—for the most
part—and the flimsy bit of yellow tape across the door of the converted
garden shed looked easy enough to bypass, but her grandmother had made
reservations for dinner and had no intention of missing them.

And because dinner in a place like this took place at four-thirty in the
evening, Amber barely had time to shower and dress before she was being
pushed into a golf cart for the half-mile jaunt to the steak house.

Her grandmother angled the golf cart into a narrow parking space out
front, casually disregarding the scrape of the passenger side against a brick
wall and the fact that she'd given Amber exactly zero inches in which to step
out. Amber had to clamber over the driver's-side seat and, since she was
wearing a gauzy, flimsy sundress that she'd been forced to borrow from her
grandmother, she had to do it without the least bit of panache.

Her grandmother reached out and straightened the dress, which boasted
tropical flowers the size of small planets and a slit that went so high up one
thigh that Amber had been forced to safety-pin it closed.

"They prefer semiformal for this place, but you'll have to do," Jade said.
She tucked a wayward strand of Amber's hair behind her ear. It was such an
easy and loving touch that something in Amber's chest clenched. That kind

of mechanical affection had never been something her mother excelled at; hugging her felt like embracing a statue of the Virgin Mary whose arms were already full. "Also, I should warn you that my friends are all desperate to spend time with you, so I've had to parcel us out a bit. We'll start with drinks in the bar with Camille and move on to dinner with Julio. And I tried—with all my heart I tried—to shake Peggy Lee, but she's determined to join us for dessert and postprandial libations. I hope you can hold your drink."

Amber felt certain that although she could hold her own with her contemporaries, there was no way she was keeping up with this crew.

Even though it was absurdly early, the steak house was abuzz with activity—most likely because the interior was dimly lit and hung with heavy red curtains that made it appear a much more reasonable hour in which to dine. Camille was waiting for them at the wood-topped bar, swathed in an exquisite camel-colored wide-legged suit that Amber suspected hadn't come from a department store. Her short gray hair was brushed up in a chic faux-hawk, and she wore a pair of dangling gold earrings so long they touched her shoulders.

"As you can see, Camille, I've brought you a present." Jade settled herself on one of the low stools—fully cushioned and with an orthopedic backrest— and raised a finger. The bartender immediately started shaking out a martini. "You may ask Amber exactly three personally invasive questions before we're moving on to less fraught waters."

Amber was so dazzled by the woman's beauty that she didn't understand what her grandmother had said until it was too late. "Um…three what, now?"

Jade laughed and accepted one of the chilled glasses the bartender slid in front of them. "Camille ran the entire marketing department for a chain of hospitals back when women were only considered fit to be nurses. We have to give her at least three straightforward answers up front, or she'll hammer away at you for the rest of your stay until she has your whole life story in her back pocket. Believe me when I say it's much better this way."

Amber clutched her own martini with a gulp. If she'd ever wondered how a woman in her seventies and living in a retirement community could manage to pull off a podcast like *Death Comes Calling*, those thoughts were now laid to rest. This place was a veritable fount of experience and wisdom.

"Exactly how long is the 'rest of your stay'?" Camille asked in a lightly accented voice that made Amber think of elegant Parisian drawing rooms and ballrooms composed entirely of mirrors. "And yes, Jade, I am aware that counts as one of my questions, so you can sheathe the dagger. I need to set a basis for my timeline."

Amber was almost afraid to ask. "Your timeline for *what*?"

Camille tsked lightly. "Not so fast, dear girl. I asked first."

Since this question seemed much less ominous than the myriad others a woman like this might ask—and that Amber was desperate to avoid—she answered. "I don't know how long I'm staying. A lot of that depends on my grandmother. I'm sort of...lying low for a while."

"She's coming off a bad breakup," Jade explained. She polished off the rest of her martini and signaled for another. "Her ex-boyfriend was a private investigator up in Seattle, but things didn't end well. I expect she's on the run. She wouldn't have come to me otherwise. That's Effie's doing—she's done her best to paint me as the worst sort of monster to my grandkids."

"Grandma!"

Her grandmother reached over and patted Amber's hand. "Don't worry, child. I don't blame you for your mother's actions. You can stay with me as long as you need."

This was such a generous offer that Amber *almost* forgave her for spilling way more of her secrets than she'd intended. Camille must have been able to read these thoughts on her face because she released a low, throaty laugh.

"See what I mean? Timeline established." She winked. "I'm rather good at this, aren't I? For my second question, I'd like to know what the ex-boyfriend did to instigate such a precipitous flight. And I warn you right now—if the answer is violence, I reserve the right to seek vengeance through any means necessary."

Amber turned toward her grandmother, certain that she was the one responsible for this line of questioning. There was no reason why a perfect stranger—especially a perfectly dressed one—would be interested in *her* life story. She was a thirty-one-year-old woman sitting in a retirement community steak house in her grandmother's borrowed sundress, for crying out loud. Clearly her life decisions to date hadn't been great ones.

"It wasn't violence," Amber was quick to say, since the last thing she needed was a posse of senior citizens descending upon Seattle en masse. "Bones isn't like that."

"Bones?" Her grandmother's eyes practically lit up. "I thought his name was Charles."

Not for the first time since she'd arrived, Amber felt a sense of growing unease. Bones's real name *was* Charles—Charles Fuller III, to be hilariously exact—but that wasn't the sort of pedigree that loaned itself to skulking around in seedy bars and exacting information from the unwilling. He'd eschewed his name and the trust fund that fueled it when he'd become a Navy SEAL and, to the best of her knowledge, intended to carry that secret with him to the grave.

In fact, when Amber had stumbled across his real name—honestly, what had he expected when she was as much of an investigator as he was and he'd left the IRS paperwork in her hands?—he'd all but begged her not to tell anyone. It would ruin his reputation. Put him at risk for extortion or blackmail. Make the other guys at the bar look at him funny.

But her grandmother knew. Her grandmother *had already known.*

"He goes by Bones," Amber said cautiously. "And he'd never do anything to hurt me. We had a…slight disagreement about one of the cases we were working on, that's all."

When Camille cast a fleeting, almost imperceptible glance at her grandmother, Amber realized she was going to have to say more or risk Jade doing it for her.

"A few months back, I got a bad feeling about one of our clients. It was the usual stuff—a rich older guy who married someone way younger than him, suspected her of cheating and wanted to catch her in the act, yadda yadda." Amber sighed as she recalled how many hours she'd spent in spin classes and spas, keeping a close eye on the twenty-six-year-old woman for the usual signs of infidelity. That sort of task often fell to her, especially in spaces where a man like Bones would have stood out like an enormous, throbbing thumb. Those endless spin classes were the main reason she was in such phenomenal shape. "But she wasn't doing anything out of the ordinary—not that I could tell, anyway. Her life seemed kind of sad, if you asked me. She didn't have many friends, and she rarely went anywhere that wasn't related to the maintenance and upkeep of her body. But the guy was *obsessed* with catching her in the act. He even asked Bones to set up a honey trap for her. A honey trap is when—"

Both Camille and her grandmother gave a sharp, sudden crack of laughter.

"Bless you, child. We know what a honey trap is," her grandmother said.

Camille nodded. "They're one of the few things in this world that's been around longer than we have."

Amber flushed but continued. She'd once tried explaining the phenomenon to her mother—*It's a thing PIs do all the time, Mom. No, not prostitution. I don't actually sleep with the guys. I just gauge their willingness to cheat if the opportunity presents itself*—but that had been a mistake. She was pretty sure her mom had joined an online support group for parents of sex workers after that.

"Bones put him off for a while, but we found out the guy hired a second PI firm to catch anything we may have missed. I never liked the job to begin with, but that got me thinking. It was almost like the guy *wanted* her to be cheating." She plucked one of the olives out of her drink and popped it in her mouth. "So I looked into his background, flirted with a few law clerks, and got my hands on their prenup."

Camille snapped her fingers. "There was an infidelity clause, wasn't there?"

"Bingo." Amber was grateful to find that Camille had such a ready understanding of the situation. "I wanted Bones to drop the client after that. The guy was obviously looking for a cheap way out of his marriage, and he was willing to go to any lengths to get it. Bones kept saying we needed to wait for more evidence before we gave up on the job, but I didn't trust that other PI firm. They have a reputation for stepping outside the lines. So I introduced myself to the woman one day after Spin Cycle and told her everything."

"You told her," her grandmother echoed.

Amber nodded, feeling even more flushed now that she'd admitted her culpability. "Bones was furious. He said I broke every rule of private investigation and that I'd made him a laughingstock—that no one would ever hire him again if they knew he had a secretary who couldn't be counted on to keep her mouth shut. That was when I snapped."

Amber closed her eyes and thought back on that day—so certain that she'd been in the right and even more certain that she could no longer continue working by Bones's side.

"His *secretary*," she repeated, the word still stinging like a thousand paper cuts. "I'd been training under him for three years—sitting next to him on all his stakeouts, running investigations for him, cycling about a thousand freaking miles on those exercise bikes. All he had to do was sign the paperwork, and I could've had an investigator's license of my own. But he refused. He said he couldn't attach his good name to someone who would let her *emotions* get in the way of the job."

"Oh, dear," her grandmother murmured.

Amber opened her eyes again. It would have been too much to say that she literally saw red, but the edges of her vision were blurred with hot, angry tears. "So I left. I packed up everything I owned and drove off. Only before I did, I took his…" As her voice trailed off, she bypassed the second olive and went straight for the gin.

The fiery burn of it hit her throat, causing it to tighten even more. She could tell that both Camille and her grandmother were on tenterhooks to hear more, but her phone buzzed before she could find the strength to continue. She could practically taste their combined disappointment as she reached for it.

And then when all three of them saw the name flashing on the screen, their disappointment turned to interest.

"'The Rat Bastard,'" her grandmother read aloud. "That's him, isn't it?"

"You'd better answer it," Camille added. "Unless the thing you took is a vital portion of his anatomy, in which case I suggest you throw that thing in the koi pond, and we'll all make a run for Mexico."

Amber choked on a laugh as she sprang to her feet. "He's still intact, I promise. But I should answer this. He might be reaching out to…"

She let her voice trail off, unsure how to finish. He might be reaching out to *what*, exactly? Apologize? Beg her to come back? Rant and rave in a fury that could only belong to a man with a roman numeral after his name?

She could sense the women's disappointment as she ducked out of the restaurant without finishing her sentence. She was also fairly certain she heard Camille say, "Don't forget that I still have one question left," as she stepped into the bright light of the afternoon.

"Hey," she said, trying not to wince as the call came through. "What's up?"

"Are you fucking *kidding* me right now?" The voice on the other end—rough and gruff and once capable of sending thrills down her spine—left little to the imagination. "Where is it?"

Ah. And there it was—not an apology and not a plea, but a demand. *Typical.*

"Where is what?" she asked in a tone that oozed innocence. The jack-hammering of her heart made it difficult to maintain her calm, but she was determined to do it anyway. "Your dignity? Your sense of ethics? I'm not convinced you had either of those to begin with."

"Not funny, Amber. You know what I'm talking about. Burglary—that's what you did. You're lucky I don't call the cops and have them drag you in. Sergeant Gates owes me at least six favors for that missing persons case I solved for him last year."

"Ha! You mean the missing persons case *I* solved for him last year?"

It was the wrong thing to say. While *she* had done the bulk of the leg-work on that case, and it had been *her* idea to scan the animal shelters in search of the easily identifiable three-legged Chihuahua instead of a runaway teen who had no desire to be found, Bones was inordinately proud of the full-page local hero story that particular case had elicited.

"I want it back, and I want it back now. You know it's my lucky talis-man. I haven't been able to solve a single case since the night you stole it out of my car."

She snorted, all attempts at maintaining her calm at an end. She paced the strip of Astroturf along the side of the steak house, her feet scrap-ing against the fake grass with a satisfying *swish-swish*. "It's not a stupid dashboard hula girl that helped you solve your cases all those years, Bones. It was me."

She could practically hear his teeth grinding over the phone. "Give me Tatiana back."

"Not on your life. She's mine now. Buy a replacement—or better yet, come and get her." She laughed, reveling in a bit of irony that she felt sure her grandmother would appreciate. "Oh, wait. You don't know where I am—and you can't find anything unless you have your lucky charm to help you. Or should I say, your silly little *secretary*?"

"Amber—" he began, but she clicked the phone off before he could say more. She also immediately blocked his number. Although she was pretty sure she could investigate circles around him, one of the things he actually was good at—other than his intimidating size and dangerously charming smile—was persistence. Where logic and reason failed, his monumental patience would succeed.

"*Ugh.*" She blew out a long breath and eyed the door to the steak house with misgiving. It was easy enough to push a button and make Bones disappear, but Camille and her final question were still waiting for her inside. There was no doubt in her mind that the elegant, terrifying woman would want to know what the phone call was about and why it had whipped Amber into such a frenzy.

Which was why she sank down onto a rock and gave herself a moment to gather her thoughts. She wasn't *opposed* to telling Camille and her grandmother about the childish stunt that had propelled her to wait until Bones was sound asleep, snag his keys from the hook by the front door, and steal the hula girl from the dashboard of the early-2000s Lexus that he drove to "keep a low profile on the job," but she was trying to pull herself together over here.

Not resort to petty theft and then goad her ex into tracking her down in the desert oasis where she'd hidden herself away.

She wasn't sure what alerted her to the sound of movement behind her. It wasn't a rustle of plants, since there weren't any nearby, and it wasn't a slow, methodical plodding either. All she knew was that one moment, she was wondering how on earth a fully grown woman could make such a mess of her life, and the next, she was staring into the beady eyes of an ancient pint-sized tortoise who looked as though he could teach her a thing or two about survival.

"It's you!" she cried as she dropped to her knees and held out a hand. The tortoise blinked a few times, his tongue darting out and back in again before he decided there wasn't anything to interest him. He began to slowly turn back the way he came. "No, wait—don't go, little guy. The residents have been looking for you everywhere."

Even though his movements were slow enough to merit the term *glacial*, Amber was quick to scoop him up into her arms. She had no idea how he'd managed to escape capture for so long, but she wasn't about to lose out on her first big win. The tortoise's stubby arms and legs wriggled helplessly for a moment before he settled down and let her cradle him.

In terms of all the cases she'd solved in her life, this one barely counted as a blip. The tortoise had found *her*, not the other way around, and the mud caked on his legs was likely to ruin her grandmother's sundress forever, but she needed this—more than she was willing to admit to herself and definitely more than she'd ever admit to Bones.

"Maybe Tatiana really is lucky," she said, thinking of the slightly squashed hula girl currently inhabiting the bottom of her backpack alongside seven days' worth of underwear and very little else. "Maybe she's been the secret to Bones's success all these years."

In which case her luck was about to take a drastic turn for the better.

It's about freaking time.

7

"Strangers—especially those of the tall, dark, and handsome variety—should never be trusted."

—*DEATH COMES CALLING*, SEASON 3 EPISODE 8

AMBER'S SECOND NIGHT OF SLEEP wasn't nearly as restful as her first.

After hours of tossing and turning and dreams about hula girls endlessly swaying in the distance, she awoke the next morning well before six o'clock. Today, it wasn't the scent of coffee and croissants that drew her toward the living room but a triumphant male voice making no attempts to keep his volume down.

"Six thousand… Seven thousand… Eight thousand. Voilà!" Julio slapped a stack of bills on the coffee table in front of Jade, beaming as only a man in starched polyester at this hour was capable. "Paid in full. I expect a nice birthday present this year. For once, you can actually afford it."

In terms of physical size, eight thousand dollars wasn't much in the way of cash—just a small stack of bills that could easily fit inside an envelope. Throughout the course of her career, Amber had learned that many such things were disappointing in that way. Gambling debts were settled inside the living rooms of perfectly ordinary people, and unless you only carried singles, those debts could be carried away in your purse.

Still. She rubbed her eyes as she took in the sight of that neat stack of hundreds. That was an *awful* lot of money to earn from a man's death. Any amount was, when she thought about it.

"Those must have been some seriously long odds, Grandma," Amber said as her grandmother scooped up the money and tucked it into her bra. "Are you sure you should accept your winnings? Maybe we should use it to buy a habitat for the tortoise or you could give it to the Admiral's kids for funeral expenses or something."

"The Admiral would want me to have this money." Jade patted her left breast. "And as for the tortoise, he seems perfectly happy in the bathtub. I'm almost certain he winked at me when I was putting on my face this morning."

"Grandma, you can't keep him in a bathtub forever. It's animal cruelty."

Julio ranged himself on her side—both metaphorically and physically, his gait as bowlegged and his breathing as heavy as always. "It does seem a pity for the poor guy to be trapped inside a porcelain tub for the rest of his life. Are you going to keep him, Jade?"

"*Moi?*" Her grandmother couldn't have looked more shocked if Julio had asked if she planned to throw the tortoise out a window. "Don't be absurd. I'm far too old to be saddled with a reptile who might live well into the next century. The last thing I want is a creature like that reminding me of how quickly I'm marching to the grave. My gorgeous young granddaughter is already doing her fair share of that."

Amber saw this compliment for exactly what it was. "Is this your way of getting me to offer to take him? Because it'll never work. I don't think he's going to want to hitchhike his way across Arizona with me until I find someplace permanent to live."

Her grandmother reached over and patted her knee. "I'm in no rush to lose you, child. Don't make any hitchhiking plans just yet."

Once again, Amber felt that glow of approval—a warm, unfamiliar sensation of comfort and belonging. Her throat grew thick with sentiment, leaving plenty of room for her grandmother to continue.

"Now that the mystery of the tortoise is solved, it's time for us to move on to greener pastures. More specifically, what we're going to start investigating for the next podcast." Jade nodded at Amber in a way that was both decisive and terrifying. "And I think we should start tonight. Have you decided how you want to break into the studio?"

Amber's gaze slid to Julio. "Are you sure we should be discussing this in front of the facility's security guard?"

That set her grandmother off in a ripple of laughter—one that Julio joined with his low, raspy cough. "You mean his whole stand-guard-and-swagger-at-the-gate routine? With the big red button?"

Julio gave an exaggerated groan. "Don't tell *all* my secrets, Jade. A man needs some mystery."

"Wait." Amber looked back and forth between them. Nothing about their expressions led her to believe they were taking any of this seriously—not the fact that there was a living, breathing creature that had the potential to live for decades in the bathtub, not the fat stack of cash currently nestled against her grandmother's bosom, and definitely not that breaking into a crime scene carried a lot more repercussions than the mild slap on the wrist they seemed to expect. "What do you mean about the big red button? Like the one that's at Peggy Lee's reception desk too?"

As before, her grandmother seemed more approving than surprised at Amber's attention to detail. She clapped her hands. "Very good, child. You clocked the security first thing, didn't you?"

That seemed like an awfully theatrical phrase for what had, essentially, been a minor blip of attention, but Amber nodded. "I'm not sure I understand your exact role, Julio. Are you an employee or a resident here?"

Her grandmother answered for him. "Both. Lots of the residents here find the extra time on their hands a little wearing. The director—that's Geerta, the woman you met earlier—created a few part-time jobs for those of us who want to do something more constructive with our days."

It didn't take long for Amber to reason her way through this. "Wait. So the entire front gate security boils down to a part-time retiree whiling away his leisure hours?" She wrinkled her nose. "No offense, Julio, but that doesn't sound very reliable."

Julio puffed his chest. "That's because you're forgetting my clipboard and general air of authority."

"And the reception desk security is the same…just a little old lady and her telephone?"

"Never underestimate the power of a little old lady and her telephone," her grandmother chastised with a *tsk*. "Why do you ask?"

Amber bit down on the reply that automatically rose to her lips: *Because that seems like a question the police are going to ask if they're investigating the Admiral's death. Because you're hiding something, and I don't like it.*

Instead, she curved those same lips into a smile and gave every appearance of someone as carefree and irreverent as the residents here seemed to be.

"Curiosity, mostly. But if you also work on the podcast, when do you find the time to, you know, be retired? Isn't that the whole point? To live out your golden years in peace and quiet, enjoying the spoils of a lifetime of hard work?"

Julio and Jade shared a quick glance. In anyone else, such a look might have been taken for amusement at the follies of youth, but Amber had the sinking suspicion that peace and quiet were two things that her grandmother had absolutely zero experience of.

"Retirement is more than just golf and happy hour," her grandmother said.

Julio nodded. "And a lifetime of hard work doesn't always go as far as it should. Especially in a place like this."

Amber thought of the bill from last night's dinner, the slip of paper that her grandmother signed without looking at it. Tight finances were a thing she could readily—and unfortunately—understand, but nothing about Jade's lifestyle hinted at pecuniary distress. She'd wagered a thousand dollars on her friend's death as though it meant no more to her than tipping for a pizza delivery. The slide sandals she was currently wearing boasted the encrusted crystals of a bona fide pair of Manolo Blahniks, and Amber had pulled a bottle of Beluga vodka out of the freezer yesterday that she was pretty sure retailed for around three hundred bucks a pop.

She opened her mouth to ask exactly how much money the podcast made—since Julio, being the bookkeeper, was in a good position to know—but something stopped her. Maybe it was the way the two of them shared another knowing glance, or perhaps it was the fact that Amber had no right to demand answers of a woman whose generosity was the only thing keeping a roof over her head.

Either way, she only shook herself off and got to her feet.

"I'm going to take the tortoise for a walk," she said. "He and I could both use the exercise."

"An excellent idea!" her grandmother said with more enthusiasm than the situation warranted.

"I'll walk you out," Julio agreed as he followed her to the door. "In the meantime, start thinking about your B and E plans for later tonight. Those files aren't going to search themselves."

Amber sighed. "Are you sure you don't just want to wait a day or two until the police open the studio back up again? There's no real rush to get the podcast started, is there?"

Her grandmother's trilling laugh rang out. "At our age, child, waiting is a death sentence. There's no saying when the Reaper will come calling."

Julio winked. "But if you want to place odds on the possibility, you know who to ask."

If Amber expected early morning tranquility and somber time for reflection during her walk, she'd come to the exact wrong place.

"Morning, Amber!" called Peggy Lee as she speed walked along the bicycle path in a nylon tracksuit in a shade of garish teal that clashed with her hair. "Can't slow down to talk—I need my two thousand steps before breakfast."

"Good to see you out taking the air," Lincoln said with a smile and a nod as he sat sipping a cup of coffee by the pool, a book of large-print crossword puzzles in his lap.

"At that rate, darling, it'll take you three weeks to get anywhere," said Camille, who paused in the act of doing laps across the pool in a floral swim cap that looked like something straight out of a 1950s *Vogue* magazine. "But it's sweet of you to take that tortoise out. He looks as though he has a touch of ennui, don't you think?"

The tortoise did, in fact, look depressed, almost like one of those killer whales in captivity for so long that their fins started to droop. Amber had done her best to tempt him with various tidbits from her grandmother's kitchen—lettuce and cucumber and even one of the dark red maraschino cherries from the bar cart—but instead of eating, he'd merely rolled his eyes at her and sighed.

Until yesterday, she hadn't even known tortoises *could* sigh.

"Did the Admiral ever give him a name?" she asked as she set the tortoise down and let him poke around a leafy frond near the tiki bar. She'd affixed a piece of twine around his midsection and held it like a leash, but she needn't have bothered. He didn't appear to be in much of a hurry to get anywhere. "It seems weird to just keep calling him 'that tortoise.'"

Camille propped her arms on the pool's edge and lazily kicked her legs as they chatted. "I believe he's had six or seven different names throughout his lifetime, poor love. That's the downside to outliving every single one of your owners. The Admiral thought it would be cruel to give him another name just to have to change it again someday. He was like that, you know—sensitive, sentimental. Always putting everyone else first."

Amber thought she detected something more than just sadness in the woman's voice, but Camille moved on before she could plumb its depths. "But if you're the one adopting him, you can give him his final name. A healthy young thing like you? I'm sure you'll be the one to see him through to the end."

That was the second time it had been hinted that the tortoise was her problem now, and she didn't like it any more now than she did when her grandmother suggested it.

"Why does everyone keep assuming I want a ninety-eight-year-old tortoise?" Amber asked with a shake of her head. "I can't keep him. I don't have an apartment. Or a car. Or even a change of shoes. It would be like giving a human baby to a pack of wild turkeys to raise."

Camille smiled but didn't say anything. Instead, she turned and kicked elegantly off the wall, her arms cutting smooth arcs in the water as she headed in the opposite direction.

Lest the tortoise get the wrong idea, Amber scooped him up and stared at him. "I'm sure you're a very nice reptile, but you can't live with me. My entire existence is a wreck—a disaster. There's no structure to my days and even less to my life. What would I do with you? Carry you around in my backpack next to Tatiana?"

The tortoise emitted a clicking sound. It didn't sound like an *unhappy* clicking noise, but what did she know about the inner lives of reptiles?

"Do you like backpacks?" she said, emphasizing the last word. When the tortoise only blinked, she tried again. "Or is it Tatiana that you're drawn to?"

CLICK.

There it was again. A little snap, almost like approval. Amber would know; she was deeply attuned to the hint of anything even *approaching* approval. Two years ago, her parents had given her a package of ten therapy sessions for Christmas—a thing she'd neither asked for nor wanted—and that had been the doctor's primary takeaway.

You keep falling for men like Bones because he makes you work twice as hard to earn his affection as someone in a more functional relationship. Does that seem like a healthy choice to you?

I don't know, had been Amber's annoyed response. *My parents gave both my brothers and their families a time-share in Maui for Christmas, while all I got was ten hours with you. Does that sound like people who raised me to feel like I deserve nice things?*

She'd won that particular round in therapy. She won most of the rounds, actually, though her therapist's parting wisdom had been that trying to win at mental health rendered every breakthrough null and void.

"Ta-ti-an-a," she said now, her gaze intent on the tortoise as she carried him down the path without paying much attention to where she was going. She'd clocked the entire grounds yesterday and found the whole thing to be around two hundred acres—similar to an eighteen-hole golf course—so she didn't fear getting lost. "Tat-i-ana. Tatiaaaaana."

With each croon of the name, the tortoise seemed to perk up more. She rubbed her finger under his chin.

"Fine. I'll call you Tatiana, but that doesn't mean I'm keeping you. I'm just holding you until I run into the Admiral's daughter again. I'm sure you'll be very happy with her. She seems...lovely."

She ignored the pang of guilt that assuaged her at the thought of leaving Tatiana with a woman like Michelle Vincent, who probably ate things like turtle soup and those cute little Parisian birds whose bones you were supposed to crunch like a giant eating the young. The tortoise had survived ninety-eight years on this planet. He'd be fine no matter what he ended up calling home. *She,* however, would—

"Unnnghhhhh."

Amber gasped and jumped back as she made contact with a warm body and a pair of not-warm metal bars that extended out in front of it. She was so worried about keeping hold of the tortoise that she didn't realize what was happening until the man—and the walker he was attached to—started to go down.

"Nancy, quick! I can't—"

"I'm here, Ethan. I've got you. Whoa, there."

Amber watched as a woman in kitten-covered rainbow scrubs wrapped her arms around the man behind the walker. Since the woman in question was six feet tall and seemed to be built like a lumberjack, she had no problem holding him up until he managed to right himself. Especially since he wasn't nearly as tall as she was. He was...five foot eleven? Ten? Six?

Gah. Why was it so hard to make any sense of that man?

"Do you always run down the sidewalk without looking where you're going?" As soon as the nurse stabilized her patient, she turned to Amber with arms akimbo and a glower that made her wish that turning to stone was a real thing. "You could have seriously injured someone—in fact, until we get Ethan here into an X-ray, we can't rule out any permanent damage."

"It's fine. I'm fine." The man, Ethan, who was leaning heavily on the walker with a strained expression on his face, winced as he adjusted his footing. "I don't want an X-ray. I just need a second to catch my breath."

Instead of taking comfort from this, the nurse doubled down. "You're lucky I don't call security and have them kick you out. What do you think you're doing here at this hour? And with *that* creature? All pets have to be approved ahead of time. It's policy."

As the woman shot off her criticisms, Amber started taking small steps backward. She suddenly understood her grandmother's references to "Nasty Nancy." Despite the cheerful scrubs and the fact that she wore bright pink Crocs, the woman looked *exactly* like the type to miss someone's vein on purpose. She was in her mid- to late fifties, with short, permed hair in tight coils against her head. Her eyes were heavily made up behind a pair of cat-eye glasses, the lines of her face etched into a permanent frown.

"No need to go all white knight on my account, Nancy," Ethan said.

He no longer looked like he was going to pass out, but he was clutching the walker in front of him as if it were the only thing keeping him standing—which, Amber was soon to realize, it *was*. Although his age was as unclear as his height—twenty-five? thirty-five? *forty*-five?—he wasn't even remotely close to the average age of the residents here.

His features were also just as difficult to pin down now that Amber was looking at him in close proximity. It was like seeing a platonic ideal of a cisgender white man. Every feature was well-formed and accounted for, but there was nothing remarkable about any of them. Hair and nose and face were all just...there. She couldn't help but feel that a guy like this would make a perfect PI. He could slip into any room, stand watch over any stakeout, and no one would ever remember he was there.

"Besides," Ethan added, an ironic, almost malicious gleam in those gray-green-brown-blue eyes. "Unless I'm mistaken, that's the Admiral's missing tortoise—or, er, formerly missing tortoise, I should say."

"His name is Tatiana," Amber said. She had no idea why those particular words escaped her lips, but there was no taking them back once they were out. "I'm watching him until we figure out the chain of title."

Neither party seemed charmed by the whimsical name. Nancy—was it too soon to call her Nasty?—looked as though she wanted to wrest the tortoise out of her hands and stomp him underfoot. "That doesn't answer the question of you who you are and what you're doing here," she said.

Amber opened her mouth to defend herself, but Ethan beat her to it.

"This is the woman I was telling you about," he said. "Jade's granddaughter."

"I'm Amber," she said tightly, but she may as well have stayed silent for all the attention the two paid her. Nancy's flared nostrils and expression of utter disdain told Amber everything she needed to know about that woman's opinion of her—and Ethan's lack of any expression at all did the same.

Especially when he added in a flat voice, "She's the one who was flirting with the cops yesterday to try and wheedle information out of them."

"And it worked?" Nancy asked with a sweep of her gaze from Amber's vaguely see-through tank to the same pair of cutoff jean shorts she'd worn the day of her arrival. "How? She's so...obvious."

Amber thought she detected the pull of a smile at Ethan's mouth. It had the potential to transform him into someone with an actual expression, but he suppressed it before it had a chance to escape.

"Now, Nancy," he chided. "Be nice. What happened to your resolution to find one generous thing to say about everyone?"

"Fine. She seems *exactly* like her grandmother."

Nancy said this with a curl to her lips that dashed any of Amber's hopes of a compliment. Unfortunately for the nurse and her walker-clutching companion, this kind of hostility only made Amber double down on her determination to beat them at their own game. It was the same perverse nature that had made her sneak into Derek's house one night and hide all those stupid Chanel hand towels; the same one that drove her to steal a cheap plastic hula girl from her ex-boyfriend before she fled into the night.

It was also the same perverse nature that made her parents so disappointed in everything she said and did and *was*.

"Are you upset because I was flirting with the cops yesterday instead of you?" she asked Ethan *flirtatiously*. There was a batting of eyelashes and a purse of her lips, that subtle shift in stance that always seemed to make men feel a driving urge to protect her. "Because I totally can if you think it'll help. Let's see… The way you hunch over that walker really does it for me. Like the old man from *Up*."

There was that almost smile again. "Joke's on you. The old man from *Up* had a long, healthy relationship with the love of his life. We should all be so lucky."

Nancy didn't appear to appreciate a conversation that didn't include her. "If you're done trying to run over my patient, we'll continue with our physical therapy session now. Come on, Ethan. You promised me you'd make it to the end of the garden today." A glimmer of genuine concern flickered behind the cat-eye glasses. "Unless that knock took more out of you than you're willing to admit."

"I can make it," Ethan said grimly. He paused long enough to look back in Amber's direction—not at her, but at the tortoise squirming in her grasp. "By the way, if you're going to carry him around like he's your newborn baby, get him a sling or something. Tortoises don't like it when their legs flail around."

And then he turned and started slowly making his way along the path, Nancy hovering nearby and murmuring words of encouragement. Amber blinked down at Tatiana, who merely blinked back.

"Well, *that* didn't work," she mused aloud as she tucked the tortoise more securely under her arm. True to Ethan's words, Tatiana instantly calmed down. "I must be losing my touch."

A small voice nagged that her touch had never been all that much to begin with, and that her tricks were getting as old and tired as she was, but she ignored them. It didn't matter whether or not she was a skilled investigator anymore.

She was done with that life. Retired, in a way.

From now on, she was just a carefree granddaughter. She didn't solve crimes. She didn't research true crime podcasts. She lived a perfectly ordinary life, and as soon as she finished taking her century-old pet tortoise named Tatiana for a walk around the two-hundred-acre retirement community she currently called home, she'd prove it.

8

"Head wounds don't bleed nearly as
much as wounds of the heart."

—*DEATH COMES CALLING*, SEASON 4 EPISODE 4

BOTH AMBER AND TATIANA WERE ready to call it quits by the time they
made it back to the condo. Amber, because carting around eight pounds of
tortoise was a lot more work than it looked like, and Tatiana, because *being*
eight pounds of tortoise appeared to be equally burdensome.

"How did you go a whole month without anyone finding you?" she
asked the animal as the pair of them rounded the corner to the now-familiar
gray building they called home. And then she almost dropped the tortoise—
not because he was too heavy, but because a police car sat parked in the
driveway.

Despite her crash and burn with Ethan earlier—or perhaps because of
it—Amber gave her appearance a quick once-over in the reflection of the
driver's-side window before she entered the condo. She looked no better or
worse than she had the day before, so after biting on her lips for a few seconds and slapping her cheeks to add color to them, she trotted up the steps.

"I'm ho-ome!" she called in a singsong voice as she stepped through
the door. "I hope everything's all right. I saw that nice Officer Peyton's car
parked outside and thought—*oh*. Hello. You're here."

Since she (a) knew very well that the police officer was here and (b) had
said all of that with the sole intention of buttering him up, she had to feign
surprise at seeing him perched on the end of her grandmother's couch, a

pad of paper and pen in hand. Less feigned was her surprise to find not only Officer Katz in attendance but Geerta Blom as well.

"Ah, Amber. You're just in time to give me a character reference." Her grandmother patted the couch cushion next to her. Although Jade was smiling, Amber noted a tightness around her mouth that made the wrinkles on her upper lip fold like an accordion. "I'm being charged with murder and would like to get this over with as soon as possible. Tell them what a delight I am and how hard I have to struggle just to make it up the front steps."

"For the last time, Ms. McCallan, we're not charging you with anything." Officer Peyton cast an agonized and—dare she say it?—pleading gaze toward Amber. "We only want to know if you have the Vincent family ring in your possession. It's highly valuable, and given the current state of affairs, his family is eager to get it back."

Amber slid her gaze toward Geerta, who stood leaning against one wall with her cashmere-clad arms crossed over her chest and an equally warm scarf tucked securely around her neck. Given the current temperature inside the condo—and, for that matter, inside all the buildings around here—the extra layers were starting to make sense.

"You mean the missing ring? The one the Admiral's daughter was looking for yesterday?" Amber wrinkled her nose. "Why would my grandma have it?"

"Most likely because George offered to give it to me at least a dozen times. I never took it, but that didn't stop the blessed man from trying." Jade nodded at Officer Peyton, whose pen was running a mile a minute. "He wanted to marry me, but if I told him once, I told him a thousand times—I'm no Elizabeth Taylor. Seven marriages were enough for me."

Amber couldn't help but choke. "You've been married *seven* times?"

"Bad luck, that number," muttered Officer Katz from where he stood next to Geerta. "Seven and thirteen both."

Geerta lifted a hand to pinch the bridge of her nose. From the painful way her fingers dug in, Amber guessed that this interview had been underway for some time already—and that her grandmother had been enacting a high drama the entire time. "Ms. McCallan, please just give the officers a straight answer. Do you or do you not have the ring in your possession?"

"Of course not. What would I want with someone else's family heirloom?" In a loud-voiced aside to Amber, she added, "A hideous one too. White and yellow gold thrown together at random, diamonds and pearls like pustules growing all over it. I'll show you a picture later."

It was difficult to tell if Geerta's sigh contained more relief or disappointment at Jade's declaration of innocence. "And would you object to the officers searching the condo to make sure? Michelle is anxious to get her hands on the property, and the sooner we get this all sorted, the sooner—"

"Wait." Amber spoke up before the facility director could finish her sentence. She also set Tatiana down so she could give the conversation her full attention. The tortoise, sensing that things were about to get unpleasant, turned and ambled in the direction of the bathroom. "Are you accusing my grandmother of theft? Because if you are, I'll need to see a search warrant before any of you set foot outside this living room."

"So sorry," said Officer Katz with an embarrassed cough. "Due diligence."

Officer Peyton offered a more coherent explanation, though with equal embarrassment. "The Vincent family is eager to get this situation settled. We'll make it as quick and painless as possible, and you can accompany us every step of the way."

Jade waved her hand in the direction of the hallway. "It's fine with me. Make yourselves at home. I have nothing to hide."

Both officers looked to Geerta, who was clearly the person whose opinion carried the most weight. The icy control that woman had over herself— and, by extension, the whole room—was nothing short of impressive. "By all means, go ahead," Geerta said tightly. "I don't have time to stand around debating this issue all day. If you had any idea what this kind of publicity does to a place like this… First, you inform the chief that a perfectly normal death necessitates a murder investigation, and now this? I'll be lucky if the board doesn't fire me on the spot."

Amber didn't know enough about property ownership in a retirement community to say for sure that the director of the facility had the power to search the premises, but she *did* know that she didn't like where this was headed. A missing ring was all well and good, but that other word— *murder*—carried with it a weight that made a shiver move down her spine.

"No."

All four people in the room turned to stare at her, but Geerta was the first to speak. She did this with an arch to her brow that only made the shiver move back up again. "I beg your pardon?"

Amber tried to match the other woman's stare, but she felt herself being trapped by the sharp pinpoint of her pupils. She fixated on the center of Geerta's forehead instead, the dusting of freckles once again concealed underneath a spackled layer of foundation. "No, you don't have permission to search this house, and no, we will not be answering any more questions unless my grandmother has an attorney present."

Geerta narrowed her eyes. "You're that PI from yesterday," she said, as though just now realizing the connection.

Amber lifted her chin. "I am."

"The one who was poking her nose around George Vincent's house a few hours after his death."

"Also true," Amber said. Since Tatiana had only made it about three feet away by this time, she felt compelled to add, "As you can see, I found the Admiral's missing tortoise within record time. The family is welcome to claim their property whenever they're ready."

None of these concessions seemed to please Geerta, but they did impress Officer Peyton.

"Well, now," he said with a low whistle. "That's some good detective work."

"Handsome little guy," agreed Officer Katz with a nod. "Very…turtle-y."

The last thing Amber wanted was to be asked for her nonexistent PI credentials again—especially in front of the two officers—so she spoke up before Geerta could make her demands.

"This interview is over. I'm afraid I'm going to have to ask you all to leave." She flashed Officer Peyton her sweetest smile, hoping to palliate the severity of her tone. "Unless you'd like to take my grandmother in for questioning? If the request is an official one, we'll be happy to comply, but I'm afraid we can't let people wander around her condo without just cause. As a fellow officer of the law, I'm sure you understand."

As she'd hoped, her sweetest smile did the trick. Officer Peyton colored

all over—at least, the parts of him that weren't obscured by the mustache—
while Officer Katz began beating a hasty retreat to the door, his belly leading
the way.

"If it'll help your investigation, I could do a little asking around after
that ring," Amber offered as she followed them out. "Strictly off the books,
of course. Since I'm already staying here at the retirement community, it'll be
easy for me to make a few inquiries. I don't mind."

Officer Katz looked so relieved at this offer that he tugged a handkerchief out of his pocket and began dabbing at the sweat beading across his
brow. "Big help. Very kind."

"I suppose it can't hurt to have an extra pair of eyes," Officer Peyton
agreed. His gaze slid toward Geerta. Even though Amber couldn't see the
facility director from where she was standing, the officer's reaction gave her
a pretty good idea of how the woman must look right now. "We'll, ah, just
see ourselves out. So sorry for the intrusion. And if you find anything out
about that ring—"

"I'll call you straightaway."

Amber stood at the door and waved cheerfully at the officers, refusing to
move from the spot until Geerta took the hint and followed suit. The click
of her heels moved slowly across the tile floor.

"Very neatly done, Ms. McCallan," Geerta said to Amber as she brushed
past. Her perfume, an expensive combination of ambergris and jasmine,
wafted about her person like a cloud. "But it won't last. The police might be
willing to let this one go, but I answer to some very powerful people."

"It's Ms. Winslow, actually," Amber informed her—and not without
some pleasure at being able to put the woman in her place. "And I'll bear
that in mind. But my grandmother and I don't take kindly to threats or
intimidation, so I suggest you try a different approach next time."

Her grandmother started applauding before the door was all the way
shut behind Geerta.

"That. Was. *Glorious.*" Jade enveloped Amber in a hug that was tight
enough to bruise ribs. "Honestly, child. For a moment there, I thought I was
watching your mother. No one can reduce a grown woman to shreds faster
than Effie in one of her Karen rages. It was always one of her greatest gifts."

Amber stopped—partially because she was basking in the strength of her grandmother's hug, but more because of the casual way the older woman tossed her mom into the conversation. Her mother avoided the topic of Grandma Judith as though naming her gave her power, feeding a mythical beast who only grew stronger by the attention she gave it. Her grandmother, however, seemed to feel nothing but a casual regret that her daughter had turned out the way she had, like a loaf of bread that didn't rise quite as much as it was supposed to.

"How long has it been since the two of you talked?" Amber found herself asking.

Her grandmother's arms stiffened but didn't let go. "La, child. Who can keep track of the time anymore? She sent me a note when your brother Derek's baby was born—what did they name the poor thing? Meredith? Mabel? I remember it was one of those old-fashioned names that should've stayed in the past where it belongs."

Amber pulled back before she gave too much of herself away. Muriel—whose name was, alas, a burden on them all—was a bouncing eleven-year-old with braces, an epic Pokémon card collection, and a determination to become the next big TikTok star. Since the date of that note's being sent, both Derek and Mikey had become fathers to two more children each.

Which meant that her grandmother had a total of five great-grandchildren, four of whom she didn't know existed, and all of whom existed in a world where the name Jade McCallan meant nothing.

This vibrant, glorious woman was a stranger to them. A nobody. A piece of family history they were happy to pretend had never happened.

"Muriel," Amber said quietly. "She goes by Muriel."

The rest she kept to herself. She also refused to let her grandmother slip down the hall as her sudden jerk in that direction indicated. "Not so fast, Grandma. I want to know what that was all about."

Her grandmother blinked in a slow, purposeful way designed to make her appear innocent. She wasn't, but the expression was convincing. "What do you mean? You heard those nice officers. The Admiral's ring is missing. Since the police were already here taking care of his unfortunate passing, the family asked them to look into it. I'm only sorry I couldn't help them more."

She paused a beat, her gaze never wavering from Amber's. "Don't tell me *you'd* like to search the house for the ring too?"

Amber set her mouth. If that ring was in the condo somewhere, she had the distinct impression it would be hidden somewhere no mortal could find it. "No, Grandma. I don't want to search your house. But what I do want is a few answers. *Now.*"

―――――――――

Interrogation had never been Amber's strong suit. Not only had Bones been gifted with a build and demeanor that could make any living human being quake with fear, but he was also capable of being so charming that all a person wanted to do was draw a single *good girl* from his lips before surrendering everything.

Unfortunately, Amber had neither of those qualities. Especially when the person being interrogated was clearly a master at giving nothing away.

"Grandma, you're not taking this seriously." Amber stopped just short of stomping her foot in frustration. Her grandmother sat at the dining room table, a glass of white wine in her hand and a *Senior Living* magazine open in front of her. She flicked casually through the pages, a moue of distaste on her signature coral lips as she skipped over advertisements for discount medical supplies and luxury golf clubs. "You run a murder podcast. You know how big of a deal it is for the police to search your house. They don't ask that of innocent people."

"Of course they do," her grandmother returned without a flutter of her eyelashes. "There was a recent study that found six percent of all arrests in the United States are made falsely. Considering the police make around ten million arrests per year, you do the math."

Amber tried not to, but the numbers swam before her eyes.

"It's six hundred thousand," her grandmother answered for her. "Julio has always been good with numbers. Before he was forced into retirement, he was an accountant for one of those big, boring corporate places—you know the type, all cheap suits and pension packages."

"So you don't have the ring?"

"Of course not. Like I said—the Admiral would have happily bestowed both it and all his worldly possessions on me, but the last thing I wanted was his pair of scavenging children descending upon us with their lawyers and declarations of incompetence. You know what I mean. You met the daughter. She'd have been a nightmare."

Amber couldn't help but agree. Michelle Vincent had seemed like the *exact* sort of person who would resent her father's remarriage to such a degree that she'd make every aspect of their lives a misery. One thing, however, nagged at her…

"Wait." She dropped to the chair opposite her grandmother and pushed the magazine out of the way. "Was that the only thing standing between you and marrying the Admiral? Not someone else? Not…Lincoln?"

"Lincoln?" Her grandmother's rich peal of laughter filled the air. "And me? Bless you, child. That man loves his wife so much it's like a watching a Hallmark movie on steroids."

"His wife? What wife?"

This question was treated as cavalierly as all the rest. "She's staying with one of her sisters right now, I believe. In Malibu? Or is it Santa Cruz? I promised to keep him occupied while she's gone, which is why you got all those croissants the other morning. They take eight hours to make. We'll need something else to busy him soon. A beef bourguignon should do the trick."

Amber refused to let her grandmother draw her off track. "So you loved the Admiral?" she persisted. "Enough to want to marry him?"

"I've married several men that I loved less than him, yes."

It wasn't an answer, but it wasn't *not* one either. Amber slid her hands across the table and gripped her grandmother's soft, smooth palms. The knee-jerk reaction that had her grandmother trying to pull away said more than her words ever could.

"I'm sorry about your loss, Grandma," Amber said. There was no trace of irony in her voice, nothing to hide the fact that she was genuinely grieved about what her grandmother must be going through. "And I'm sorry that you think you have to hide your feelings from me. But if and when you're ready to talk about it—about *him*—I'm here. It's the least I can do after everything you've done for me."

Her grandmother took her hands back and turned away, a surreptitious wipe at her eyes the only indication that anything had passed between them.

"You know, if we *really* want to keep Lincoln busy, what we need is a new case to work on," her grandmother said. Her tone was a little too bright, almost sharp in its brilliance, but Amber let it pass—even though she knew very well what the next words out of her grandmother's mouth were going to be. "It's too bad those case files are locked up in the podcast studio. If only we had someone young and strong to get in for us…"

Amber groaned, but she knew when she'd been beaten. In fact, she was starting to suspect that she'd been beaten the moment she walked through Julio's less-than-secure security gate.

"Fine," she said before her grandmother could start laying an assault on her defense. "We'll go tonight. But if the police try to arrest me for tampering with a crime scene, you have to promise to bail me out afterward."

Her grandmother brightened to such a ridiculous degree that Amber thought she might have promised a lot more, if only to bask in that smile a few seconds longer.

"I'll bail you out of anything you want, child, but take it from me. The police will never hear a peep about what we're doing in the studio. That's a Jade McCallan guarantee."

9

"All it takes to be a police officer is guts,
grit, and a whole lot of grumbling."
—*DEATH COMES CALLING*, SEASON 1 EPISODE 11

RAFFI DRESSED FOR THE BREAK-IN in a pinstriped suit and bow tie, his toupee whipped up into a dark froth atop his head.

Amber had become so accustomed to the eccentricities around this place that she barely batted an eye as he dragged a pushcart up to the podcast studio door as though about to pull off a heist of James Bond proportions.

"Does one cut the police tape with ceremonial scissors when embarking on a crime like this, or do we just duck underneath?" He blinked expectantly at Amber. "It's my first time, so I don't want to get it wrong."

"For Pete's sake, Raffi. Just use your key to unlock the door. I left mine back at the condo." Jade nudged Raffi with the tip of her shoe. Like her friend, she'd dressed for the break-in by donning a long black skirt paired with a black tube top that was doing *a lot* of heavy lifting. "Go on then. We don't have all night."

Raffi made a big show of patting down his pockets. He extracted, in no particular order, a gilded pocket watch, a leather notebook, two pens, and his wallet, but no key. "Oh, dear. I must have forgotten to grab it before I left the house. We'll have to call up one of the others and have them bring their copy."

Amber sighed. Although the podcast studio was tucked into a dark corner behind the vegetable plots, as befitted a converted garden shed, it was visible from the main pathway. The last thing they needed was yet another retiree dressed in head-to-toe black drawing attention to their actions.

"Just stand watch for a sec, would you?" she said as she fell into a crouch in front of the door. "If you see anyone coming, hoot like an owl."

Picking locks was yet another skill passed down to her via Bones's questionable hands. She usually preferred to rely on social engineering for this kind of thing—like, say, waiting until one's ex-boyfriend was sleeping before stealing his car keys—but needs must and all that. Amber pulled out the lock-picking kit he'd given her, cleverly disguised to look like a credit card, and started to work on the mechanism.

"It's a bit of a tricky one," her grandmother said after a few seconds of Amber's poking and prodding. "We can only get the dratted thing to lock from the outside." Then, "Aren't you a bright young thing? I didn't learn anything this useful in my twenties and thirties. You're going to be such a force to contend with when you're older. I can't wait to see it."

Amber was so flustered by this compliment and the prospect of a future with her grandmother that she didn't notice right away how easily the locking mechanism gave way. And by the time she realized that it must have been broken by the police when they came to investigate the anonymous phone call, the door had already swung open.

Since Amber had never been inside a podcast studio before, she couldn't say for sure what the standard style of décor was supposed to be. The soundproofing tiles on the walls seemed appropriate enough—even if she *did* wonder how, if they were as thick as they looked, anyone had heard enough of a ruckus to call the police the night the Admiral died. The recording equipment also looked right for the space, with microphones and headsets and a soundboard covered in so many colorful buttons that it looked like an overly complicated game of Simon.

But that was where Amber stopped feeling anything but a sense of unease.

The police had been right about one thing—a struggle had definitely taken place inside the studio. An overturned bar cart had shattered several bottles of vodka and gin over the floor, scenting the space with an oddly chemical tinge. Several chairs had been tipped on their sides, their adjustable backrests and arms at odd, broken angles, and notepaper had been torn from a pad and strewn about like confetti.

In fact, the only untouched parts of the studio were the boxes of files lining the back wall. A less suspicious woman might have accepted this as nothing more than coincidence, but Amber was instantly on alert. Especially when her grandmother gasped and came to a halt behind her.

"Oh, dear," she murmured. "This is not at all what I was expecting. Are the files still intact?"

Jade brushed past Amber, who remained rooted to the floor. She watched with a kind of detachment as her grandmother lifted the top off of one of the boxes and started rifling through the contents.

"Phew. I think we'll be okay. These seemed to have escaped the melee." Jade turned back toward the door. "Raffi? The handcart?"

Amber stepped forward to block his way. "Grandma, what exactly is in all those files?"

Her grandmother raised a delicate brow. "La, child. How should I know? I told you already that the Admiral was our primary researcher. He's the one who kept everything organized—old police files he happened to stumble upon, cold cases he dug up from long lost forums… You know how it is. These things just have a way of appearing out of nowhere."

If you asked Amber, these things most decidedly did *not* have a way of appearing out of nowhere. She'd spent the past three years dipping her toes into the investigative waters, and she'd never once "stumbled upon" an unsolved crime just waiting to be turned into a podcast. Finding a story that wasn't only interesting enough to carry a whole season, but also had enough evidence to actually *investigate* it required determination—and, unless she was very much mistaken, a casual disregard for the state of one's own skin.

How many of these files contained actual, verifiable evidence? And who, knowing that evidence was being held inside a tiny podcast studio in the middle of Arizona, would have gone to extreme lengths to secure it?

Everything that was wrong about this situation came rushing over Amber at once. This really was a crime scene. A murder really had taken place here. And the key to it all could be contained inside these boxes of files.

Before she could voice any of these concerns aloud, the police arrived.

Okay, so technically speaking, it wasn't the police so much as a large, uniformed security guard in a wrinkled button-down shirt and khakis, and he didn't *arrive* so much as knock politely at the open doorway, but the premise held.

"What's going on?" The guard poked his head into the studio, saw how crowded it was, and decided to question them from the outside. "You aren't supposed to be in here. The cops said it's closed off until further notice."

By this time, Amber's heart was practically in her throat, but her grandmother's calm could have withstood a hurricane.

"Oh, hello, Giles. I had no idea they put you on nights. How are the kids? And Patrick?"

The security guard smiled down at them. There was a gap between his front teeth, and his thinning hair showed a flaky scalp in desperate need of dandruff shampoo, but both seemed to work in his favor. "As well as can be expected when we're in the thick of baseball season. You wouldn't believe how many hours we spend sitting around packed diamonds waiting for tournaments to start. Patrick has taken up knitting just so he has something to do."

"Ah, yes." Raffi nodded. "The great American pastime. I know it well."

No one except Amber seemed to find anything odd about this exchange. Her grandmother even went so far as to solicit the security guard's help. "We're sorry to disturb you, but we were hoping to gather a few files for our next podcast. I don't suppose you'd mind giving us a hand with these heavy boxes?"

Giles narrowed his eyes. "Aren't those evidence?"

"If they were, wouldn't the police have confiscated them?" she countered. This was a fair question, but it wasn't until Jade smiled winningly up at the security guard that Amber realized just how far her grandmother was willing to go to get her way.

She's willing to go as far as it takes. Just like me.

"The truth is, we're all heartbroken about the Admiral's death and are hoping to distract ourselves by jumping feet-first into a new project." Her grandmother's smile dimmed. "I know it's not protocol, but we need this—something to sink our teeth into, something that keeps us busy. You understand that better than anyone, don't you, Giles?"

She couldn't have chosen easier prey. Something in the security guard's eyes softened. "I guess it can't hurt anything. Since the police just left them here and everything..."

"Excellent! I knew we could count on you." Jade put her hand on Raffi's back and started propelling him toward the door. The look she cast over her shoulder at Amber contained pure mischief. "Why don't you and my granddaughter chat about important security things while you load up the boxes? Amber is a PI, so I'm sure you'll find plenty to talk about."

Amber could have sworn she heard her grandmother laughing to herself as she and Raffi disappeared into the night, leaving the two younger members of the group to do all the hard work. For once, Amber didn't mind. While her hands were busy helping Giles load the boxes onto the handcart, her brain was even busier trying to make sense of everything that had happened.

Point 1: She was tampering with a crime scene.

Point 2: Was it technically tampering if the door was unlocked and the retirement community's security guard helped load the boxes?

Point 3: The retirement community had a security guard.

Point 4: A *real* one.

Point 5: And her grandmother knew about him long before she'd dragged Amber into this heist.

Of all the thoughts clamoring around inside her head, that last one rang out the loudest. Amber had made it a point to ask her grandmother about the security in this place, and she'd lied—told her that Julio and Peggy Lee were the only barriers to entry, that everything boiled down to a few red buttons and part-time workers more interested in socializing than preventing crime.

But *why* would she lie about something like that? And why, with so little regard for how it made her look, had she literally introduced Amber to the truth now?

"So." Amber pushed the cart out the door, her arms resting on the top as she waited for Giles to shut the door and slip the police tape back into position. "You were able to get here pretty fast after we got through the door. Did we trigger a silent alarm or something?"

"Silent alarm?" Giles scratched the top of his head, sending flakes of dandruff flying. "No, nothing like that. I was watching you guys on the cameras the whole time."

"Cameras?" Amber echoed. She scanned above her head for the usual signs—a bulbous black mass mounted on the pathway lights or a CCTV-style rectangle—but nothing caught her eye. "What cameras?"

Giles gave a rumbling laugh. She put his age to be somewhere near her own, but something about his mild demeanor made him appear older. "You're kidding, right? This place is watched closer than a federal prison. You can't walk five feet without your movements being recorded, logged, and backed up to the cloud."

"Really?" Amber felt a prickling sensation move over her. It might have been how quickly the temperature dropped once night fell in the desert, but she suspected the real cause was psychological in nature. "Isn't that, like, an invasion of privacy? I'm surprised the residents stand for it."

"They're the ones who demand it, actually. It's half the reason this place is able to charge such massive fees." Giles hooked his thumb over his shoulder toward the nearest line of condos. "The residents spend so much time in front of their TVs, absorbing twenty-four-hour fearmongering, that nothing will convince them the whole world isn't out to kidnap, rape, and/or otherwise cause them bodily harm."

Amber found this oddly comforting. If there really *was* security at this community, and that security had videos of all the comings and goings around here, then maybe there hadn't been a murder after all. Maybe the whole thing had just been a terrible misunderstanding.

"Were you working the other night?" she asked. "When the Admiral was in the podcast studio, I mean?"

"Nah. I was off that day—the kids had a baseball game, and I promised them I'd be there with orange slices." He eyed her carefully, as though trying to ascertain her motive in asking. Since she hardly knew the answer to that herself, she wasn't worried about what he'd find. "If it helps, I *was* there when the police came in the next morning. I gave them a copy of the footage, but

I'd be surprised if they found anything worth note. From what I understand, it was a pretty quiet night."

"Until the anonymous phone call," Amber pointed out.

He frowned. "Yeah, that was weird. Usually, the complaints come to us first."

Amber was burning to ask more questions—could she see the footage that the police took away? If he'd been at his kids' baseball game, who was in charge of security that night? What other kinds of complaints did they get?—but she had the feeling she was already pushing things.

"Thanks for helping me load up the boxes," she said. "And sorry again about this whole breaking into the podcast studio thing. My grandma isn't an easy person to say no to."

"No problem." Giles gave her a mock salute. "Just stay out of the studio until you get the official all clear, okay? My eyes are always on you."

This last part was said without threat, so Amber wasn't too worried as he turned around and headed back toward the main facility. Still, she kept her eyes peeled for signs of the cameras while she wheeled the cart of boxes down the path to her grandma's condo. She didn't like the idea that she was being watched—that she had been watched since the moment she arrived here—without her knowing it.

Then again, she also didn't much care for having a grandmother who turned every interaction into a riddle, but she was still here, wasn't she?

It's because I don't have anywhere else to go, she told herself firmly. *I'm only doing this because I'm desperate.*

Desperation could do strange things to people in that way. In the last week alone, desperation had sent a grown woman fleeing to the desert without a plan, drove an ancient tortoise into her reluctant care, and caused her to take up the cudgel in defense of an old lady who was almost definitely hiding something.

And sometimes—just sometimes—desperation even drove people to murder.

With any luck, this wasn't one of those times.

10

"When what to my wondering eyes should appear
but a mysterious clue...and a way to interfere."

—*DEATH COMES CALLING*, SEASON 2 EPISODE 7

AMBER AWOKE THE NEXT MORNING under the giant naked painting of her grandmother, surrounded by dozens of boxes of cold case files, and with a tortoise perched on the end of her bed.

Of these three things, the latter was the one that alarmed her the most.

"Tatiana?" She bolted upright and rubbed her eyes, certain she must be seeing things. That certainty wavered when she noticed a yellow Post-it affixed to the center of his shell. "Oh, geez. Grandma put you in here, didn't she?"

She plucked the Post-it and read it aloud.

"'I have Zumba at eight and bowling league at ten. I tried to feed the tortoise, but he refused. Will the two of you pencil me in for lunch instead? My treat. XOXO.'"

Amber felt a warm prickling behind her eyes. It was such a silly, unimportant thing—a woman leaving a quick note to her houseguest— but she couldn't help it. Especially considering what a terrible night's sleep she'd had.

At first, she'd blamed her inability to fall asleep on the early hour and the adrenaline of the podcast studio B&E. By midnight, she'd been forced to admit that the real problem was her thoughts revolving in an inescapable loop of motive-means-opportunity. By 3 a.m., she'd given up on sleep entirely and started pouring through the files in hopes of finding some sort of clue about what had happened to the Admiral and why.

"It turns out I'm just being paranoid about the whole murder thing," she said to the tortoise. She lifted the animal up and stared into his dark eyes. "There's nothing in those boxes but reams of old printouts and newspaper clippings from the eighties."

This was no more than the truth; she *had* taken the time to set aside a few of the more promising cases to show her grandmother. There was one in particular about a Russian ballerina-turned-defector in the height of the Cold War who got caught up in a land dispute that she thought might make for an interesting podcast.

Tatiana blinked at her.

"I know what you're thinking," Amber said as she swung her legs out of bed and set the tortoise gently on the ground. "You're sure I'm sabotaging this relationship with my grandmother because it's the first good thing to happen to me in a long time, but you're wrong. I'm only trying to help her."

Tatiana didn't move.

"It's not as easy as you think," she continued as she got dressed in the same tired, tattered jean shorts she'd been wearing all week. "There's more going on here than meets the eye. My job is to find out what. And why. And how. Every halfway decent detective knows that."

This time, Tatiana *did* move. He turned and started slowly ambling away as if unable to bear the lies coming out of Amber's mouth.

"Fine. You win. I'm doing this because I can't help myself. I'm as bad a snoop as Peggy Lee." She scooped up the tortoise before he made it more than a few steps. Mindful of what Ethan had told her about his flailing legs, she grabbed a throw from the foot of her bed and manufactured an impromptu sling with it. Weirdly enough, it worked. Tatiana settled against her chest like a baby being lulled to sleep by its mother's heartbeat. "But in my defense, the police *did* ask me to look into that missing ring. I'd be remiss in my duties if I didn't at least try to find it."

As soon as she said the words aloud, she realized how true they were. There was some mystery attached to that ring—one that involved both the

Admiral and her grandmother, and one that could very well settle what was going on around here.

And she knew exactly where to start her search.

As Amber tiptoed her way down the hallway, she was hit with a surge of paranoia that the retirement community surveillance system extended to the private condos, and that Giles was sitting in a booth somewhere watching her every move, but she forced the feeling down. *That* level of security was a bit much, even for a place like this. Besides, considering some of the activities her grandmother likely got up to, she was sure to have covered up, dismantled, or otherwise removed any interior cameras by now.

Careful to hook the chain on the front door so she'd hear her grandmother if she decided to come home early, Amber set about systematically searching the house for signs of the ring. She felt a twinge of guilt when she slipped into her grandmother's bedroom and started rifling through the jewelry box, and an even stronger one when she found an engraved silver locket containing a photo of her mother, but what could she say?

She was a PI. A detective. A woman whose only real tie of affection was to the tortoise currently dozing against her chest.

She had no idea how long she stood blinking down at the locket, her mother's much younger heart-shaped face looking sternly back at her. Even back then—at a time when her mom should have been a carefree teenager—she looked disappointed. As if she couldn't believe the audacity of the photographer in telling her to smile—or in her own mother having her pose for such a fleeting, self-indulgent moment.

Amber traced the familiar lines of her mom's face, her throat tight. For what was probably the first time, she felt a strong urge to pick up the phone and call the woman who'd given her life. *Who is the real Judith Webb?* she wanted to ask. *Is she the monster you've always made her out to be, or is she just a flawed human being you blame for every bad thing in your life?*

Or perhaps, most important of all: *Is the reason you've always disliked me because I remind you too much of her?*

Amber's fist closed around the locket, and it somehow made it into her pocket before she realized what she was doing. Amid all the baubles and bangles, the mess of tangled chains, she doubted her grandmother would even notice it missing. Not right away, at any rate.

There was no sign of the Vincent ring, so she moved quickly through the rest of the room. She was too scared to check the bedside table, and her grandmother's underwear drawer was equally off-limits, but she felt only a minor qualm as she ducked into the bathroom off the primary bedroom. Tatiana twitched as she entered the room, so she put a calming hand on the tortoise lest he fear he was about to be imprisoned in a bathtub again.

As expected, her grandmother's bathroom was a treasure trove of beauty and antiaging products that ranged from moisturizer made from the essence of snails to bulk-sized tanning lotion. The medicine cabinet also contained an array of pills and prescriptions to be expected from a woman in her eighth decade of life.

Atorvastatin for cholesterol, lisinopril for blood pressure, sildenafil for reasons she wasn't even going to begin to explore... When all was said and done, her grandmother appeared to be in fairly good shape for her age.

Until she found an empty bottle tipped on its side, its label hidden behind an enormous bottle of collagen pills.

"Hydrocodone," she read as she pulled it out. "Jade McCallan to take one pill as needed for pain. Do not mix with alcohol. If signs of respiratory depression occur, seek help immediately."

Amber wasn't sure why she tucked the bottle into her pocket next to the locket. She wasn't proud of her sudden descent into kleptomania, and she could come up with a dozen legitimate reasons why her grandmother may have needed pain pills, but she couldn't seem to help herself. Besides, she didn't trust the police not to come back with that search warrant they threatened. Better to keep this to herself for now.

Much to Amber's relief, the rest of the search proved fruitless. There was no sign of the Admiral's ring in the condo, no indication that her grandmother was anything but a carefree retiree living her best life under the Arizona sun. In fact, the whole place was kind of depressing, once she started thinking about it.

The only personalized piece of artwork hanging on the walls was the nude painting. There were no family photos, no toothless grandkids or great-grandkids littering the refrigerator door, no sign that Jade had any ties outside of the ones she attached to herself. What few books she owned were more for show than entertainment—had anyone ever actually read *A Brief History of Time*?—and even her refrigerator contained nothing but a collection of wilted lettuce and four different brands of green olives.

Amber made a valiant effort to get Tatiana to eat some of the lettuce, and even had a go at a few of the olives, but he had about as much interest in the pathetic offering as Amber did.

"Well, at least I tried," she said as she put the lettuce in a bowl of water to perk it up. She also took the time to transfer the pilfered items from her pocket to her backpack. What she planned to do with them, she had no idea, but she felt better knowing they were protected by several layers of canvas and the growing pile of her dirty underwear.

"Well, Tatiana. We'd better go in search of sustenance. If you don't start eating soon, I'm going to have to do something drastic like take you to a reptile vet. That won't be fun for either of us."

After taking a moment to secure the knots of the tortoise's sling, she headed out the door. The day was full of promise, as bright and sunny as always, and she intended to make the most of it. Maybe she'd solve a murder. Maybe she'd find a missing ring.

Or maybe, just maybe, she'd lie by the pool and work on her tan. In a place like this, the opportunities were endless.

———————

In the end, she did exactly the same thing today as she'd done the day before.

Walking at a brisk pace around the pathway toward the main facility, she rounded the corner to almost collide with the stooped form of a youngish man with his teeth gritted and a walker clutched in his hands.

"Good morning!" she called with a cheerfulness that wasn't wholly faked. There was something about Ethan looking so sour and miserable that made her feel like *some* things were right with the world. "Where's your companion this morning? She was so delightful to me yesterday, I was hoping for a repeat appearance."

"Ugh. Not you again." He tried to shift the walker a few inches to the right, but the action only seemed to increase the pressure with which his teeth ground together. "Are you always this chipper in the morning?"

"To be honest, I have no idea. Until I came here, I rarely emerged from bed before noon."

He snorted in a way that signaled contempt for such a slovenly lifestyle.

"In my defense, I worked nights," she explained. "Sometimes for twenty-four or even forty-eight hours at a time. Stakeouts, you know."

"Right. Because you're a *private investigator*." The way he emphasized the words signaled just as much contempt as before. But then he noticed the tortoise strapped to her chest with a blanket and relaxed. As he did, some of his features seemed to come into clearer focus.

Hazel. His eyes were hazel. And his shoulders were wider than she first suspected, a latent strength radiating from the perfect ninety-degree angles of them.

"I see you took my advice about the sling," he said with a nod that direction. "How's the little guy getting on?"

Amber was tempted to keep up the cheerful façade, but the thought of the untouched lettuce made her smile fall. Some things were more important than annoying a judgmental grouch just for the fun of it.

"He's not eating," she said. "I think he might be depressed."

Ethan shifted his weight to the one hand that gripped the walker. "May I?" he asked. Without waiting for an answer, he lifted his free hand to the tortoise and tickled him gently on the chin. Tatiana basked in it with what Amber could have sworn was a bona fide smile.

"Hmm. He feels dry. The Arizona air can be tough on tortoises, especially since we don't know what he was up to these past few weeks. Give him a good soak and see what happens."

"A soak?" Amber echoed. Unthinking, she moved a protective hand around the tortoise. "You mean like a bath?"

"Yeah. Just put some lukewarm water in a tub and cover him up to here." Ethan pointed at the part of Tatiana's body where the upper and lower portions of his shell met. "Give him half an hour or so, and he should perk right up."

"That's...weirdly helpful, thanks." In fact, it was not only helpful, but downright *nice*. Maybe Ethan wasn't as bad as her initial instinct had suggested. "Why do you know so much about tortoises?"

He shrugged by way of response—and then immediately regretted the action. With another sharp wince, he returned his grip to the walker. "*Dammit.* I really wish I'd waited until Nancy was free to do this. I have no idea how I'm going to make it back to my room."

Amber paused as she watched him start to slowly turn around. "Is that your roundabout way of asking me for help?"

"No."

That seemed like an awfully surly response from someone who clearly needed a bed that was soft and a painkiller that was the exact opposite. "I don't mind," Amber said. "I don't have anywhere else to be."

"I'm fine."

He wasn't, but Amber knew enough about stubborn, wide-shouldered men not to push her luck. "Do you mind if I ask you a question?" she said instead.

He turned a wary eye on her. "A little, yeah."

"It's about the Admiral."

That seemed to startle him into another feature-identifying state of relaxation. This time, she noted that he had laugh lines that crinkled around the edges of his eyes. *Huh.* Strange to imagine this man *ever* laughing, let alone often enough to develop the physical signs of it.

"What about him?" he asked.

Amber let her gaze wander over to the low, flat building in the distance. Even though she'd been scanning for the cameras that were supposed to cover the grounds, she had yet to see any sign of them. "I talked to Giles, the security guy, last night. He said this place is wired tighter than a cryptocurrency mine."

"Yeah, so? What does that have to do with anything?"

"Well, you've heard about the missing ring, right? The one the Admiral's daughter is raising a big fuss over?"

He shook his head. "Look, if you want gossip, you're better off asking Peggy Lee. I never even met this Admiral guy everyone is talking about. I don't have much to do with the residents around here."

Given his bad personality and general lack of charm, Amber found this easy to believe. Ethan seemed like the sort of man who would bring store-bought cookies to a bake sale and then stand frowning at the table when no one wanted to buy them. Still, she pushed. As far as she could tell, Ethan was one of the only people living in this place who wasn't enmeshed in the fiber of it. That he was also her own age and seemed inclined to consider her a nuisance of the highest order didn't hurt matters.

If there was one thing Amber enjoyed, it was getting the better of men who underestimated her.

"I was just wondering if you've heard anything about the police checking the security tapes to see if there was a break-in at the Admiral's house sometime in the past few weeks. I already know they took the footage from the night he died, and since you seem to be staying at the nursing home facility where the security office is housed…"

Much to her dismay, Ethan proved as unsusceptible to bait as he was to flattery.

"Are you asking me to spend my free time spying on the security offices at a nursing home? In search of a ring that's probably wedged in a couch cushion somewhere? When I can barely make it to the end of this walkway and back without losing my balance?"

"Actually, I was hoping you'd slip up and tell me something about what the police suspect happened to the Admiral and why they're still here poking their noses around, but yeah." She cast him a hopeful glance. "*Do* you know what the police suspect happened to the Admiral?"

In that moment, Ethan became a man transformed. All of his features came into clarity as he opened his mouth, rolled his eyes heavenward, and laughed.

After the moment had passed, Amber would have trouble remembering the exact details of his expression. Even if someone gave her a million dollars to recall his features and offered her a million hours with which to do it, she wouldn't have been able to do much more than state the obvious: forehead and ears and mouth and nose. For a few seconds, however, it was like looking at one of those Magic Eye pictures, all those neatly patterned dots and swirls exposing a hidden image.

And, she noted, an *attractive* image.

"I can't believe it. You really are that shameless." He wiped his eyes as his laughter died away. "Thanks for that. I needed it." As if revived, he turned his walker around and resumed his shuffling walk back toward the main facility.

"Wait," Amber couldn't help calling to his retreating back. "Does that mean you *have* heard something?"

"Remember what I said about soaking your tortoise," he said by way of answer. "And if that doesn't work to bring back his appetite, you know where to find me."

Amber directed her next steps toward the garden plots, which seemed the most likely place to find tubs, water, and enough space to adequately hydrate a tortoise. Like the rest of the retirement community, the gardens were a hive of activity at this time of morning—and she didn't just mean the fat, happy bees swooping between the flowers.

"Hey, Peggy Lee," she said as soon as she espied the now-familiar red wig. The receptionist crouched next to a flourishing plot of leafy greens surrounded by a series of handwritten warning signs.

This Arugula is MINE

Trespassers will be reported

Nor thieves, nor covetous, nor drunkards, nor revilers, nor PEGGY LEE, shall inherit the kingdom of God

Since Peggy Lee was plucking the scruffy leaves and shoving them surreptitiously into her pockets, Amber felt fairly certain the older woman had seen that third sign.

"Get down, you fool," Peggy Lee hissed as soon as she spotted Amber. She grabbed the hem of her shirt and tugged. "They'll see you."

"Who will see me?" Amber fell easily into a crouch next to her. "If it's the stolen arugula you're worried about, I promise to keep my mouth shut. I'm no snitch."

Peggy Lee glared at her. "I'm not *stealing* it. I'm teaching Hannah a lesson in manners. And I'm only here because the Admiral's son got in this morning, and I didn't want to miss his arrival. Look."

Amber glanced in the direction Peggy Lee pointed. Sure enough, the Admiral's condo had several cars parked out front—all of which looked expensive enough to house Amber in style for at least a year. As amused as she was at Peggy Lee's clandestine attempts to spy, she wasn't sure what the woman found so interesting. The condo would obviously have to be cleared out now that the Admiral was dead, and his kids would just as obviously be the ones to do it.

"Are he and his sister staying here?" Amber asked.

Peggy Lee snorted. "They never stay anywhere that doesn't have at least five stars. Last Christmas, they were too late to get a room at the Hilton, so they just didn't come. Left the Admiral all alone for the whole holiday." A pinched expression contorted the features of Peggy Lee's face, turning her Utah mole into something more closely resembling Rhode Island. "Something's going down today, and I intend to be here when it does."

"In that case, we're much better off looking like we belong here." Amber rose to her full height. She held out a hand to help Peggy Lee to her feet, an action that involved much creaking and groaning. "Take it from me—spying is a lot easier when you can come up with a legitimate excuse for lingering. One of my favorite stakeouts was the time I had to watch an apartment across the street from a dog park. I got to borrow my neighbor's adorable Shiba Inu for the whole week."

Peggy Lee brightened. "That's right. You're our resident crime expert. What else do you suggest?"

The thought of Peggy Lee taking some of Amber's less traditional investigative advice and running with it caused a shudder to move down her spine. The less the woman knew about things like paying off informants, faking DNA results, and sweeping for cell phone bugs, the better.

"That's enough to get us started," Amber said firmly. "But what I really need right now is a shallow tub and a garden hose."

Both of these things were easy enough to procure, along with an explanation of why Amber was giving the tortoise an impromptu bath.

"If all it takes to spark an appetite is a few inches of lukewarm water, then Nasty Nancy is in for an unpleasant surprise," Peggy Lee mused as she watched Amber untie Tatiana and lower him gently into the tub. "One of her favorite cures for anything related to the digestive tract is a suppository. And let me tell you—she's none too gentle about the insertion. If you think her ability to find a vein is bad…"

Amber wasn't sure whether to laugh or cry. "What's the deal with her, anyway? I ran into her outside the main facility yesterday. She yelled at me for running over her patient—which, to be fair, I almost did." She paused before adding, "I don't really understand what his deal is either. You've probably seen him around. Youngish guy? Hobbles around with a walker?"

A look of genuine pleasure folded the lines of Peggy Lee's face. "Ethan Adler, you mean?"

"You know him?"

"Of course I know him. His room is across from the reception desk— and even if it wasn't, he wouldn't have escaped notice for long. In case you can't tell, we don't get a lot of young residents around here."

"What's wrong with him?" As soon as the words left Amber's mouth, she winced. The guy irritated her, obviously, but that didn't mean she could lose all sense of tact. "What I mean is, why does he need a nursing home? He's not, like…terminal, is he?"

Peggy Lee splashed some water over the top of Tatiana. Although Amber couldn't detect any discernible signs of vitality in the tortoise, he didn't seem to dislike the bath, so she figured there was no harm in it. "Bless you, no. He's here to recover from a hip replacement."

"*A hip replacement?*" Amber barely repressed a shudder. "That sounds awful."

Peggy Lee ran a finger down the line of Tatiana's back, unimpressed by Amber's show of sympathy. "Bah. You'd be surprised how many of us are ambling around on titanium hips and knees and doing just fine with it." She glanced up with a sudden glare. "But the recovery is no walk in the park, young lady, so don't you go thinking that everyone can hack it."

Amber felt a sudden and profound urge to salute. Not for the first time, she realized how little she knew about her grandmother and all her podcast friends. She'd always assumed that the elderly loved talking about the past—their lives and loves and losses—but this group was very much the kind who lived in the moment.

"Are any of your parts bionic?" she asked, curious.

Peggy Lee sniffed. "That's an impertinent question, and I don't have to answer it."

On a hunch, Amber tried again. "What about the Admiral? Did he have any preexisting medical conditions?" She thought, but didn't add, *Ones that might have caused him to throw furniture around the podcast studio before dying a completely harmless and natural death?*

This time, Peggy Lee didn't sniff so much as huff. "I don't see what business that is of yours. George had his own personal cross to bear, as do all of us." The lines of her face suddenly relaxed. "Poor George. *And* poor Ethan. If you don't have anywhere to go to recover from something big like hip surgery, you either have to hire a private nurse or book a stay in a nursing home like this one. I expect the kid doesn't have anyone to take care of him, so he ended up here. He and this tortoise have that in common."

Amber felt a pang as she glanced down at Tatiana, his legs moving back and forth as he attempted to free himself from his watery prison. Obviously, she had no idea what it meant to undergo something like a hip replacement, but she *did* know what it was like to be the one creature no one wanted to take care of. Witness her flight from Seattle to the grandmother she'd never met, the way not a single one of her parents or brothers had called to find out how she was doing, the fact that Bones's only emotion at her departure was one of irritation.

She was so unwanted that there wasn't even a Nextdoor thread to wonder what became of her.

"Nancy seems to like Ethan, so he does have that going for him," Amber pointed out.

Peggy Lee snorted. "You don't thank the devil for taking a personal interest in your affairs."

Amber smiled, but something about the situation didn't sit right with her. "She seems to be universally hated around here. Why do they keep her on staff if she's so unpleasant?"

Instead of answering, Peggy Lee turned her attention toward the Admiral's condo, where the sound of a door slamming resounded through the air. Since it was followed by the sound of angry voices, Amber instinctively dropped into a kneeling position, her body hidden behind a large tomato cage. Peggy Lee groaned and shook her head.

"If I go back down again, there's no way I'm coming up. They'll just have to arrest me."

"Sorry." Amber grinned. "Old habits die hard. I doubt anyone's going to arrest us for being nosy."

As if on cue, the whirring flash of blue and red lights entered the street in front of the Admiral's condo. The sirens weren't on, but Amber didn't like the speed with which the squad car came to a halt. When it came to the cops, going fast was never a good sign. The wheels of justice were ones that ground slowly…until they didn't.

Both she and Peggy Lee inched closer as a fiftysomething man in a too-tight golf shirt and pleated khakis stepped out onto the front porch. Even if his sour expression and the fact that he was standing on the Admiral's property hadn't given him away, that brindled hair was a sure sign that he was Michelle Vincent's brother.

"It's about damn time," he said in a booming voice that was obviously used to being heard. "Have you blocked all the exits? We don't want a runner on our hands."

Officer Peyton stepped out of the car, his mustache looking particularly wilted for such an early hour. As soon as Amber caught sight of those drooping handlebars, her own heart sank accordingly. "As I've said before, Mr. Vincent, the chances of the suspect attempting to flee the premises are very slim. At her time of life—"

"Don't talk to me about the suspect's 'time of life,'" came the angry retort. "If it weren't for her, my father would be enjoying his own 'time of life' right now. And when you find that ring—"

Michelle stepped out onto the porch and put a hand on her brother's shoulder. Both Amber and Peggy Lee strained to hear what she was saying, but her words were cut off by the arrival of another police car—this one outside the bowling alley and with full sirens blaring.

Amber and Peggy Lee shared a quick, worried glance. Neither of them needed to look in that direction to know who the police were arresting, and neither of them waited around to hear what else Michelle and her brother had to say.

Pausing just long enough to scoop Tatiana out of his bath and tuck him under her arm, Amber ran.

11

"Nothing brings families together like
weddings, births, funerals, and the
occasional cold-blooded murder."

—*DEATH COMES CALLING*, SEASON 4 EPISODE 9

"YES, MOM. I'M AT THE station now. No, Mom. They won't let me see
her. She's with her attorney."

Amber sat back against the uncomfortable plastic seat, her eyes closed
and her free hand pinching the bridge of her nose to keep the encroaching
headache at bay.

Her headache wasn't, as might be supposed, caused by the indefin-
able scent of police stations everywhere—a mixture of antiseptic cleaner,
unwashed bodies, and rusted metal. It also wasn't caused by the fact that her
seventy-six-year-old grandmother had just been fingerprinted and booked
for murder.

The cause came a few short seconds later.

"I told you about her, Amber. I warned you how it would be. But you
don't listen. You *never* listen."

Amber could practically feel her mom's sigh ruffling her hair over the
phone.

"It's just like that time you insisted on climbing up onto the roof to help
your father clean the gutters when you were eight. Or the time you threw
that tantrum about not being allowed to zip-line with your brothers and
their friends. We were paying off the bills for those hospital visits for years."

Amber didn't need the reminder. Her right thigh sometimes still ached from where the pins had been inserted to fix her bones in place after she'd fallen off the roof, and the scar from where she'd pinched her hand in the zip line showed a faint, silvery white under the fluorescent lights of the police station.

"I get it. I'm disobedient and a shame to the family." She continued before her mother could throw more of her childhood accidents in her face. "But don't you think you should come out? This is serious. They're talking murder charges."

Her mom snorted. "What good would it do? Your grandmother only cares about one person in this world, and that person is herself. Mark my words—she's going to milk this for every scrap of attention she can get. The best thing you can do is pack up your things and cut all ties. Otherwise, she'll get her hooks in you and never let go."

Not for the first time, Amber wondered what had driven her to pick up the phone and dial the familiar number for her childhood home. What had she expected? That her mom would come running to the rescue? That she'd set aside a lifetime of grievances at the prospect of her own mother spending the rest of her life behind bars?

That she'd wonder what had driven Amber to run to Arizona in the first place?

"Isn't that the whole point of family?" Amber asked, unable to keep the bitter note out of her voice. "That the hooks are in whether you like it or not? That they *stay* in even when things are hard?"

The silence on the other end of the phone spoke volumes. "I'm not sure what you want from me," her mom eventually said, her tone flat. "If it's bail money you're after, I can't help. Your father and I just put a down payment on that cruise to Iceland, and it's nonrefundable."

"What did she do to you?" Amber asked by way of response. Calling her mother had been a mistake. Coming to Arizona had been a mistake. In fact, every decision she'd made for the past few years had been a mistake of some kind. "I know you two don't get along, but she's your *mother*. She gave you life. Doesn't that make you feel a little bit beholden to her?"

"I don't know, Amber. You tell me. How many times have I told you not to reach out to her? Yet you did it anyway. Behind my back. In defiance of everything I've ever asked of you."

Amber hung up. It was a childish thing to do, and she'd have to call back later to apologize, but clicking that button felt good. *Too* good, if the way she sprang out of her chair and rushed to meet her grandmother's court-ordered attorney was any indication. No one should ever be that excited to speak to a public servant.

"Well?" Amber asked as the attorney came bustling out. "What are the charges?"

The attorney, a harassed, much-too-young woman in a poorly fitting pencil skirt, blinked at Amber. She seemed surprised to find that anyone would have waited the six hours that had passed since she'd watched her grandmother being handcuffed and lowered into the back seat of a police car, but what other choice was there? Lincoln had given her a ride to the precinct, but he'd only lasted about two hours on the hard plastic chair before giving up and going home.

"We're looking at murder in the first," the attorney said with a clipped tone that didn't bode well for the rest of the conversation. Amber had dealt with public defenders before—usually when Bones had been hired to help drum up evidence to support a defense claim—and had always found them to be some of the most difficult people on the planet. *Not* because they didn't want to be helpful, and not because they didn't care, but because they carried more burdens on their shoulders than Atlas himself.

"Oh." Amber's knees grew weak as she fell back into her chair. "That's not good."

A startled laugh escaped the woman. "No. It's not good." She nodded at the seat next to Amber. "May I?"

Amber nodded as the woman dropped a stack of files on one seat and fell to the opposite with a sigh. She was remarkably pretty, what with her cropped natural curls and a shade of lipstick that her mother would have called bordello red, but she looked as though she could use about a week of sleep. Possibly two.

"Uh oh. It must be *really* bad if you're willing to sit down and take the time talk to me about it." Amber reached into her pocket and pulled out a Ziploc bag of Lincoln's famous sugar-free oatmeal cookies. In true Lincoln fashion, he hadn't wanted to leave her without a snack. "Cookie? I'm afraid they have raisins in them, but they're still pretty good."

The woman eyed the bag warily before grabbing one. "Thanks. This is likely to be both my lunch and my dinner today." She ate one bite, squeaked with approval, and reached for another. "Oh, wow. You're a really good cook."

Since Amber needed this woman on her side—and her grandmother's—she took full, shameless credit. "Thanks. There's plenty more where these came from…if you can promise me at least *one* piece of good news in exchange."

The attorney took her time swallowing. First ten seconds, then ten more. The cookies *did* have a lot more unidentifiable grains and seeds than Amber would have put in, but this was taking things too far.

"I know this arrest has something to do with the missing ring that George Vincent's kids keep going on about," Amber said to get the ball rolling. "They think my grandmother stole it or is hiding it or something, but I can tell you myself—I checked the condo. There's no sign of it anywhere."

The attorney rolled a wary eye her direction.

"And if this is about the money my grandmother won in the death betting pool, I think we can both agree that eight thousand dollars is hardly a motive for murder when she could have just as easily married the guy and taken everything he owns—including that stupid ring."

Once again, the attorney kept her bordello red lips tightly closed. Amber recognized this tactic for what it was—nothing got people talking faster than sustained and willful silence—but she couldn't help herself. Her mind had been going over and over the facts of the case in an endless loop, and nothing added up. Her grandmother was an old lady. One with a murder podcast, an air of mystery, and a slight gambling addiction, yes, but also one who had no real reason to wish her friend harm.

Amber believed that with her whole heart. She *knew* it.

"The way I figure it, anything else the police have at this point is only circumstantial—unless, of course, that security tape from the night of the Admiral's death showed something." Amber's brow knit as she thought through her conversation with Giles and how unsurprised her grandmother had been to see him show up when he did. "But I'm pretty sure my grandma knows exactly where all the cameras in the retirement community are located and that they would have been watched that night, so—"

"Whoa, whoa, whoa." The lawyer held up her hands. "Slow down there. I got the case files for this less than an hour ago. The only things I've looked at so far are the arrest warrant and the autopsy report. The rest of this is news to me."

Amber bit down on her tongue before she made the mistake of saying more—and then focused on what really mattered: the case. Like the photograph of a crime scene placed in her hand, there were clues here to uncover. She just had to slow down and think like a private investigator.

"So you've seen the autopsy report?" Amber asked. "You know how the Admiral died?"

The attorney nodded and lowered her voice. "This is between you and me, but it looks like your grandmother's friend had enough drugs in his system to fell a horse. That in and of itself isn't suspicious enough for a murder charge, but…"

Amber swallowed heavily, her thoughts straying to the empty pill bottle currently hidden in her backpack. She pushed them aside almost as quickly. She was the only one who knew about those pills, and she intended to keep it that way.

"But that doesn't take into account the signs of struggle in the studio and the anonymous phone call to the police," Amber offered.

"Afraid so," the attorney said with a shrug. She sighed before adding, "The arresting officer also mentioned something about a key to the podcast studio, but I haven't had a chance to follow up on that yet. Check back in a couple days, and I might have made heads or tails of it by then."

Amber was unable to keep the disappointment out of her voice. "A couple of days? You're going to leave an innocent woman locked up that long?"

It was the wrong thing to say. "Look, I'm sorry if the wheels of justice don't turn fast enough for you, but I'm doing the best I can. You wouldn't believe how many cases they have me juggling right now—it was over a hundred at my last check. Though I will say that your grandmother is the only murder on my docket, so that's something."

The attorney shoved the file back in place and got to her feet, but not before pulling a business card out and handing it to Amber. She tapped the name, Jessica Baldwin, and the phone number underneath it. "That's me, and that's my office. I'm rarely in, but you can leave a message. I'm usually able to get back to you within one to two business days."

None of that did much to make Amber feel optimistic about her grandmother sitting alone in a jail cell, but she pocketed the card anyway. "Can I at least see her?"

"Afraid not. The bail hearing will be early next week, but that's the best I can offer. Until then, sit tight, try not to worry, and if you happen to find that missing ring lying around somewhere, let me know ASAP."

Amber nodded, but she already knew that there was no universe in which she'd hand over a prime piece of evidence to an attorney juggling a hundred different cases at once. At this point, she'd be better off selling the dratted ring and getting her grandma a flashy, expensive lawyer in Jessica's place.

As if sensing the trend of her thoughts, Jessica checked her smartwatch and sighed. "I gotta go. I'm late for a briefing, and this thing has my heart rate at twice what it should be. Don't lose hope, okay? Even if your grandmother is found guilty, they'll only give her ten to twenty years due to her age. I've seen a lot worse."

Amber watched as Jessica hoisted her files and staggered out the door. Her hope—what there was left of it—disappeared out the door with her. At seventy-six, ten to twenty years might as well be a death sentence. To lose this woman she'd only just met—to sever the one tie she had to a family member who flung open the doors of her home and hugged without question—was impossible.

Her grandma couldn't be a murderer. There was no way she had a malicious bone in her body. A mischievous bone, sure. A melodramatic one, decidedly.

But she loved her friends. She'd loved the Admiral.

And despite only knowing her for a week, Amber felt certain her grandmother loved her too.

Her throat felt thick and her eyes hot as she grabbed her cell phone to call Lincoln. She didn't enjoy having to beg her grandmother's friends for rides when they were probably in a worse state than she was, but she didn't know what else to do. Her finances didn't allow for the indulgence of a cab, and she felt pretty sure that the hundred-degree heat would prevent her from walking any further than the diner on the corner. And without her mom's support to get her through this, she was, quite literally, alone.

Again. *Always.*

Amber blamed the tears in her eyes for how long it took her to recognize the person who strode through the doors of the police station a few seconds later. That massive stride, the way the entire room seemed to shift to make way for him, the warm, pulsing scent that always carried a little too much Axe body spray for her taste…

"Bones!"

No sooner was his name out of her mouth than his arms were around her. Amber blamed that too. Just when she'd thought she'd no longer feel the enveloping embrace of someone who knew her—who saw her for all her faults and didn't immediately shut the door in her face—here was the one man in the world who'd always had that power.

"It's okay, babe," he murmured as he tucked her under his chin and held her. His voice ruffled the hair at her temple, his chest rumbling as he spoke the words she both dreaded and longed to hear. "I've got you now. Whatever this is, we'll get through it together."

12

"When in doubt, brazen it out."

—*DEATH COMES CALLING*, SEASON 2 EPISODE 6

BY THE TIME AMBER MADE it back to her grandmother's condo, she was almost grateful to see that Officers Peyton and Katz were on-site and tearing the place to pieces.

"Gimme five minutes with them," Bones said as he leapt out of the driver's seat of his twenty-year-old Lexus and started rolling up his shirt-sleeves. He turned to make sure she was watching before he finished.

In a fit of postcoital sentimentality, Amber had once told Bones that the act of exposing his forearms was one of the most attractive things a man could do—better, even, than benching whatever hundreds of pounds he was up to these days or splurging on the not-cheapest bottle of wine at dinner. At the time, he'd only laughed it off, but someone had clearly been reviewing his notes since then.

"I'll get the cops cleared out of here in no time," he added. "Those two look like they'd run away from a cat stuck in a tree."

"Don't." Amber slammed her door and bustled up to join him. In the fifteen minutes it had taken to drive to the retirement community, Bones had told her fifteen separate times that he didn't hold her accountable for running away in the dead of night or even for stealing his beloved Tatiana. He wasn't sorry for his choices leading up to that event—he was *never* sorry for those—but he was ready to let bygones be bygones.

Which, ugh. She'd always hated that expression. She was holding on to her bygones for good reason, and she planned to keep an eye on them until they could be trusted not to betray her into saying something she'd regret. Like, *I'm sorry.* Or, *Yes, Bones. I'd be happy to keep being your secretary if it means you'll take me away from this mess.*

"I can handle these two," she said as she brushed past Bones to where the two officers were standing in conference near the front door. "I've been working them for a few days already."

"Working them?" Bones echoed, laughing. "You mean your ol' I'm-just-a-poor-little-woman-what-can-I-do routine? By all means, go ahead. I love when you pull out the feminine wiles."

Until he laughed, Amber had been in the act of doing just that—an extra sway in her hips, a sultriness to her movements that didn't match the arid heat of her surroundings. But as she drew nearer to the two cops, she found herself adopting her normal gait instead. Maybe it was the perverseness of her nature that forced her to do the exact opposite of what was expected, or maybe it was because she'd had a long, tiring day that was likely to keep on being long and tiring, but she suddenly had no desire to play a role.

Unless, of course, that role was worried granddaughter, capable investigator, and general human being. In that order.

"Any luck finding the ring?" she asked as she approached. "I assume that's what's happening in here, yes? And that there's a search warrant to go along with the arrest one?"

Officer Peyton's mustache twitched at this sudden change in her demeanor, but he didn't comment other than to say, "We're not allowed to share that information at this time."

"So that's a no on finding the ring, then. Anything else that screams *murderous old lady* to you? Handcuffs in the bedside drawer? A single knife missing out of the block in the kitchen? I'd offer you a few more ideas, but I don't want to do *all* your work for you."

Officer Katz seemed to deflate with each passing word. "Doing our duty. Not pleasant for anyone."

Amber took pity on Officer Katz and managed a smile. Not a *flirtatious* one, but a friendly one. He looked as if he needed it. "Don't worry, Officer

Katz. I know this isn't your doing. I saw the name of the detective on the booking sheet—Detective Vega, I think? I'm guessing she's the one calling the shots."

"Yes. Yes, that's it." He stared at his shoes. "She's good. Very…thorough."

Uh oh. Amber didn't care for the sound of that. In her experience, *thorough* was the word you used when phrases like *hard-ass*, *by the book*," and *all the personality of a wet blanket* were off the table.

"That's nice," she lied. "I'm happy to hear it."

"You are?"

"Of course. If she's good at her job, then she'll be quick to realize that my grandmother is innocent and she's made a terrible mistake in arresting her." Amber tried peering between the two officers to see what was happening inside. "How much longer until you'll be cleared out? You've had hours in there. If it's not too much trouble, it's been a long day, and that bathtub is calling my name."

"Oh. Um. About that." Officer Peyton cleared his throat, but he was interrupted by a cool, clipped voice that Amber would have recognized anywhere.

"I'm afraid you're laboring under a misapprehension, Ms. Winslow." Geerta Blom parted the two officers like Moses approaching the Red Sea. "The rules regarding long-term guests are very strict around here. While your grandmother was in residence, you were allowed one month of visitation. However, if your host is absent, I'm afraid you'll have to make other arrangements."

Amber blinked. Either Geerta was a master of understatement, or she was passive aggressive to a degree that made her mother look like a WWE brawler.

"*If my host is absent*?" she echoed. "You mean, if my beloved grandmother is hauled up on false arrest charges? If she faces a lifetime in prison for a crime she didn't commit?"

"Yes, that's it." Geerta's thin lips parted in a smile. "I'm so glad you understand. It's one small step from this to having our residents turn their homes into Airbnbs."

This was said with such a blatant disregard for reality that Amber didn't bother trying to plead her case. Which was for the best, probably, because what could she say? That living here for a week gave her some kind of right to her grandmother's home? That Jade would even *want* Amber staying in the condo while she was facing a trial for her life?

"It's okay, babe." A heavy hand came crashing down on her shoulder and squeezed. She was so startled by it—and by how good it felt to have Bones's strong, solid presence at her back—that she only squeaked. "You can come stay at the hotel with me. But you'll need a few minutes to get your things together. Why don't you have this nice officer accompany you while I chat with…?"

His voice trailed off in an obvious way that would have made Amber laugh out loud, if not for how effectively it worked.

"Geerta. Geerta Blom." A shade of red diffused the woman's face, bright enough to break through her thick layer of foundation. "I'm the director here at Seven Ponds. And you are?"

Bones's chest swelled so full of hot air that Amber could feel him bumping her back. "My friends call me Bones. So do my enemies, but that's between you and me."

Amber wasn't looking at Bones while he spoke, so she couldn't say for sure that he winked, but the vibes were right.

"Oh, my." Geerta's color deepened. "Do I dare ask?"

Amber didn't wait to hear more before she brushed past the officers and into the condo. It was a strange twist for Bones to be the one flirting his way through a sticky situation, but she was wise enough not to interfere.

"That your boyfriend?" Officer Katz asked as he followed her into the house. Officer Peyton followed too, but Amber suspected that was mostly because he couldn't stomach the sight of Bones seducing Geerta any more than she could.

"My *ex*-boyfriend," she stressed as she made a quick scan of the living room. As expected, everything was in upheaval. Couch cushions were stacked at random, every drawer was pulled open and rifled through, and a few of the ceiling panels had been pulled loose and examined. She imagined things only got worse in the bedrooms and bathroom.

Grateful that her backpack and the empty pill bottle were both safely stowed in Bones's trunk, she made her way to the guest room. As soon as she saw that the mattress had been literally slit along the side, stuffing spilling out everywhere, she sighed. "Really? You couldn't have just opened it up at a seam?"

"Some of the guys got a little overzealous," Officer Peyton apologized. "They don't get to do a lot of searches like this."

Officer Katz was too busy trying not to stare at the naked painting of her grandmother, so his contribution was merely a grunt.

"I'm assuming they didn't find anything," Amber said as she grabbed a few toiletries from the bedside table and found the two pairs of underwear she'd left hanging to dry on the shower rod. Those, she noted, had been carefully avoided as though they might contain nuclear particles. "You two have been overseeing this case from the start. You know my grandmother didn't do this."

"Well, now." Officer Peyton shifted his gaze a few inches above her head. "She seems like a nice enough broad."

Officer Katz grunted again and hooked his thumb at the painting. "This her?"

"I was too scared to ask for sure, but yeah, I assume so." Since this was likely to be the last chance she'd have to openly question these officers while they were still abashed enough to be honest, she asked again. "It's just the three of us in here. You'd tell me if you found anything, right?"

There was a little more wobble in her voice than she cared for, but she couldn't regret the question when they both shook their heads.

"Nothing to find," Officer Katz said.

Officer Peyton amended this with, "Just a few prescriptions in the medicine cabinet and some legal documents worth taking a look at."

Since Amber had already seen the prescriptions for herself, she latched on to the latter. "What kind of legal documents? Like…a will?"

Please not a will listing her as the Admiral's beneficiary. Anything but that.

"I didn't get a good look before they were booked into evidence, but they seemed pretty straightforward. Power of attorney, life insurance, that sort of thing." Officer Peyton's gaze clicked down to meet Amber's. "You'll get them back before too long. Were you two discussing legal matters before she was taken in?"

Amber shook her head, a tight feeling in her chest cinching like a rubber band. Nothing good could come of documents like those. If they *were* related to George Vincent, and her grandmother had profited materially from his death, no judge would look kindly on her case. And if they *weren't*, and her grandmother had simply been getting her affairs in order…well, that wasn't much better.

Why would her affairs need attention? Because she knew she was about to be arrested? Because she was changing things over to include her long-lost granddaughter? Or simply because a dear friend had recently died and reminded her that these things needed to be taken care of?

"We never talked about anything like that," she managed. "But thank you for letting me know."

Amber felt deflated enough after that to leave the two officers to their search. Geerta and Bones were exactly where she'd left them, though the former had shed her cashmere sweater and was looking so flushed that there was an actual bead of sweat on her upper lip. Amber was glad to find that the woman *could* sweat, but she found herself wishing it had been a product of the heat rather than a one-man assault on her senses.

Yeah, okay. She got it. Bones looked like the model on a romance novel cover. He could reduce grown women to a melting puddle of hormones. But did he have to lay it on quite so thick?

As much as Amber hated to admit it, she was starting to see these flirtatious antics for what they really were—maybe even, God forbid, the way Ethan Adler saw them. As a cheap ploy, a parlor trick, a shortcut that undervalued everyone involved. She had a brain in her head and plenty of wits about her—there was no need to *always* resort to the lowest common denominator.

Fast on the heels of this realization came another, far more alarming one. *Oh, geez.* Was her mother right? Was setting a honey trap really worth the results it yielded? Amber's entire adult life had been predicated on the belief that her mother was wrong about everything. To upend that belief now—when her life was already spiraling out of control—was too much.

"Your, ah, Bones has been keeping me entertained with some of the stories of your cases back in Seattle," Geerta said as she fanned herself lightly with her hand. "I knew you were a private investigator, but I had no idea that kind of life was so…glamorous."

Amber took her lower lip between her teeth. She was guessing Bones hadn't told her the bit about peeing in a Gatorade bottle.

"It can be," she said. "But to be honest, it's mostly a lot of sitting around and waiting for people. Also paperwork."

Bones slung his arm around her shoulder. "Don't be so modest, babe. You know how much you love the thrill of the chase. This one time, she climbed up an ancient fire escape in a full-on ball gown just to sneak into a fundraiser. Heels like this." He held up his fingers to approximate the six perilous inches of those particular shoes. She'd needed the extra height to see over the crowd and find her mark, but her toes had been bruised so badly that she'd had to wear a pair of knockoff Uggs for a whole week afterward. "Caught the bastard too. Got great photos of him shaking hands with his political enemy in a back room."

Geerta turned to her with interest, but Amber refused to elaborate. As a matter of fact, that case *had* been glamorous, and she *had* been rather proud of being able to shed some light on the political wheeling and dealing that had been running rampant in government circles, but what was the point? Bones had still refused to see her as an equal—was, at this exact moment, still refusing to see it.

"Did you get everything you needed?" Geerta asked, her voice once again crisp as she eyed the way Bones slid a hand up to the back of Amber's neck and lightly clasped it. The gesture had always been a favorite of his, possessive and unthinking and deeply carnal because of it. "I won't be able to let you back into the condo after this. You have no idea what kind of bureaucratic nightmare I'm facing. The Vincents have the entire city calling for blood."

She frowned as she spoke. For the first time, Amber felt a pang of pity for the other woman. As much as she'd have liked to make Geerta the villain of this piece, the director was in the unenviable position of running a facility where one resident had been murdered and another arrested for it—and all while the Admiral's kids were raising as much of a fuss as they possibly could.

Clearing up her grandmother's name seemed almost easy in comparison.

"I have what I need," Amber said.

Geerta nodded and started making her way down the stairs. "Good. Then I hope very fervently that I never see you again." She stopped and looked back over her shoulder. "Though I get the feeling you won't go away easily, will you?"

This was said in a purely rhetorical spirit, so Amber didn't bother answering as she and Bones took their leave. Every step toward his car felt heavier than the last. Her entire being balked at the prospect of going with Bones to his hotel, where the mistakes of her past were just waiting to be repeated, but she needed to be close at hand to help her grandmother.

If that meant sharing living space with a man who'd once told her, without a hint of irony, that women were biologically predisposed to cheat because of their innate need to have a "backup protector" should their first choice be killed by a wayward mammoth, then so be it.

She'd suffer a lot worse if it meant getting to the bottom of this case.

Amber hadn't even opened the car door when a savior descended upon them like a fairy godmother in haute couture.

"*There* you are, love." As if by magic, Camille appeared behind her, her tall form swathed in a white ruffled sundress with feathers that fanned out like a peacock's tail. She took one look at Amber and clucked her tongue. "You poor thing. You look as though you've been lost at sea for weeks. Come on back to my place. Lincoln is making dinner, Raffi is attempting to teach your tortoise how to sit and stay, and Julio is, well. I'm sorry to say it, but he's already starting a betting pool about whether or not your grandmother is likely to go free."

Amber laughed. Nothing about this situation warranted it, but the idea of these sweet, irreverent, completely oblivious people placing odds on her grandmother's prison sentence allowed for nothing else.

"Then you'd better put me down for twenty bucks on her going free," Amber said. "Because I'm not resting until she does."

With a relief that was disproportionate for the time and place, she extended her hand to Bones in a gesture of dismissal. She couldn't recall a single time the two of them had ever done anything as formal as shaking hands, but it seemed the safest approach to send him on his way.

It didn't work. Instead of taking her proffered hand, he frowned down at it—and at her.

"What the hell, babe? Who is this? I thought we decided you were coming back to the hotel with me."

Amber sighed. She should have known that Bones wouldn't make this easy. What was it Peggy Lee had said before? *You don't thank the devil for taking a personal interest in your affairs.* She wouldn't go so far as to call Bones a *devil*, but there was a definite whiff of sulfur about him. If she was being honest, that flash of wickedness was half his charm.

"Her name is Camille, and she's a friend of my grandmother's," Amber said. "She does public relations for the *Death Comes Calling* podcast."

Her hand fell as she spoke the words aloud. She'd only uttered them as a means of introduction—a way for Bones to find an intersection between his interests and Camille's—but they sank like stones in the pit of her stomach. She'd been so grateful to see a friendly face back at the police station that she hadn't stopped to consider *how* Bones had found her—not just in Draycott, Arizona, but at the very building where her grandmother had been booked for murder.

The grandmother he didn't know she had. The grandmother who ran a podcast they both happened to enjoy.

"But you knew that already, didn't you?" she asked, eyes narrowed. "About this being where the podcast is recorded, I mean. And that this is where you'd find me."

To give credit where it was due, Bones didn't try to weasel his way out of being caught. With only a slight flush, he crossed his arms and said, "What else was I to think when you went running to Draycott, of all places? Other than the business license for *Death Comes Calling*, the only other things this town has to offer are a bunch of crystal stores, overpriced art galleries, and way more golf courses than a population this size needs. I figured you came here looking for a job on the podcast or something."

Amber could hear Camille suck in a sharp breath. Although she would've normally preferred to hold a conversation like this somewhere private, she appreciated the moral support.

And the witness.

"You used our phone guy to track the call," she said and immediately wrinkled her brow. "No. Wait. Issei's way more loyal to me than he is to you. I'm the one who found him, and I'm the one who always made sure he got paid. That means you must've tracked me directly."

She popped open the trunk of the car and grabbed her backpack. Without waiting for Bones to say a word, she started rifling through the contents, careful to keep the empty prescription bottle and locket out of sight.

Her clothes, her wallet, Tatiana the hula girl endlessly playing her ukulele, and a faded paperback copy of Dashiell Hammett's *The Thin Man* made up the bulk of her earthly possessions. Putting a tracker on a book was almost impossible, and there was no way Bones would have defiled his beloved good luck charm by sticking a piece of electronics under her grass skirt. That only left…

"My backpack? Seriously?" She started running her fingers along the inner seams, not stopping until she caught a small, lumpy piece of string. Sure enough, someone had done an inexpert job of sewing the spot where the lining had been sliced open.

Probably because covering our tracks had always been my job.

As soon as she pulled a loose thread and extracted the small tracker, she dropped it to the sidewalk and crunched it underfoot. The crack was satisfying, but not nearly as satisfying as Bones's expression, which was a cross between guilt and soul-deep fear.

He took a step back, but Camille placed herself behind him. The feathers of her dress fluttered as Bones bumped into her, trapped.

"It's not what you think," he pleaded, his hands up. "I only did it for your own protection."

"When?"

Bones swallowed heavily. "I don't remember. A few months ago."

Amber took a step toward him. The idea that she—all five feet two inches of her—and Camille—much taller but with a waiflike delicacy to her build—could do anything to harm Bones was laughable, but he seemed to interpret the threat as it was intended.

"Okay, a lot of months ago. Ten maybe. Or eleven. I don't know exactly when. But you were heading off on your own to serve court documents to that compound outside Lynden. I was worried about you, that's all. I wanted to be able to find you if things went south."

Amber halted. As far as excuses went, it was a solid one. That particular job had been one of the more terrifying of her career—not because of the people, who'd been unsettlingly welcoming for a registered hate group—but because the road up had been twenty miles of unpaved, winding wilderness.

Still. "Why didn't you say something at the time?" Amber asked. "Or at least take the tracker out after I got back safe and sound?"

Bones rubbed a hand on the back of his neck, his expression changing from one of guilt to sheepishness. "To be honest, I forgot. You know how bad I am at that kind of thing. I didn't remember until our phone call, when you said all that stuff about how I'd never be able to find you." He chuckled in the sudden, whole-body rumbling way that had always held the power to disarm her. "You know I can't resist a challenge. It's the one thing we've always had most in common."

Amber felt herself halting even more, and not just because of that chuckle. The truth was, that bullheaded tendency to pick up every gauntlet thrown their way, to keep pushing long when normal people would have given up, wasn't as common a trait as it seemed. Especially not in a tall, handsome package like Bones.

They'd had good times, the two of them. Before she got so determined to follow in his professional footsteps, back when tracking criminals had been more of a hobby than a potential career—

Amber caught Camille's hardened expression before she could finish the thought. She had no idea how a woman swathed in feathers could look so ferocious, but those sharp cheekbones looked as if they'd happily cut Bones to shreds.

"Amber, if you don't tell this young man of yours to clear out this instant, I'm going to shout for those officers and have them do it for you. I will inform them that he threatened bodily harm, and that he's carrying a gun in an ankle holster above his left boot. I will also inform them that I saw a man exactly matching his description skulking around the gates the night the Admiral was murdered." A smile touched her lips, but it didn't soften the severity of her expression. If anything, it only made her look *more* dangerous. "They won't believe me about that last one, but as soon as they verify the weapon, they'll have no choice but to follow up on the rest. They may even book him next to your grandmother. Wouldn't that be delightful?"

Amber choked. Bones did, in fact, carry a gun above his left boot whenever the weather was too hot to allow him his favorite shoulder holster. But how Camille could see it when his jeans were pulled down so low was beyond her.

Bones turned toward Amber with such a comical frown that she almost felt sorry for him. He wasn't used to being told off by women, especially when the woman in question was wearing high-end fashion and had been alive before the Cold War.

"You told her about my SIG?"

"Of course not. When would I have had the chance?" Amber shook her head before Bones could say anything that might derail her again. Drat the man. He'd always been exceptional at pushing her to the brink and then yanking her back as though he were the only one capable of saving her. "But she's right about it—and she's right about the rest too. You can't stalk me halfway across the country and expect me to fall into your arms. I appreciate the ride back from the police station, but you can go home now. I'm fine."

Bones did an admirable job of hiding his annoyance. She could detect signs of it in the way the square lines of his jaw tightened, and how the vein in the center of his forehead throbbed, but when he spoke, his voice was calm.

"You heard that Geerta woman, Amber. It sounds like she's answering to people way above her pay grade, so I doubt she'll fold easily. You can't keep living here while your grandma is in jail, so you might as well come stay at the hotel until we can figure something else out."

An impossibly cool hand touched her shoulder. "That Geerta woman may be able to kick Amber out of *one* condo, but she doesn't have the power to kick her out of all of them. She's my guest now. And when our month is up, I have no doubt that Lincoln or Raffi or Julio will be delighted to take her in. Even Peggy Lee might be convinced, though no one's seen the inside of her condo in years."

Amber wasn't sure why *this* was the thing to break the dam of tears that had been threatening her all day. She barely knew this woman, and they had zero ties of kinship to bind them, but that didn't seem to matter. Camille was opening the door to her home without question—offering Amber a safe way out of a dilemma she'd had no part in making.

"Thank you," she sniffled. "I shouldn't take you up on the offer, but—"

"That's enough of that." Camille slid her arm around Amber's shoulder and began directing her away from the car—and away from Bones, who was watching Amber's waterworks with something akin to horror. In the three years they'd been together, she'd never once cried in front of him.

"Amber, I'm sorry." He lifted a hand to reach out to her, but one glare from Camille had him dropping it like a brick. "I didn't think you'd be this upset to see me. We had a fight, that's all. I got angry and said things I shouldn't have, but we can work through this. I know we can. I only want to help."

Camille answered for her.

"The best thing you can do for her right now is go away," she said in a voice that left no room for misinterpretation. "I'm taking care of her for the foreseeable future, and that's all you need to know."

13

"Solving a murder is no fun unless there are at least as many suspects as a game of Clue."

—*DEATH COMES CALLING*, SEASON 5 EPISODE 5

AMBER AND CAMILLE WALKED INTO a scene of mass destruction.

Like her grandmother's condo, Camille's was small and much too chilly, the air conditioner humming in high gear as it struggled to offset the early evening heat. Unlike her grandmother's condo, it was much more exquisitely decorated. Everywhere Amber's gaze landed was on a piece of art that had obviously been selected, curated, and displayed to make it feel as though she was in a museum rather than a home. Even the furniture—all white and made of modeled plastic that looked about as comfortable as a cement bench—seemed as if it had no place in a living, breathing space.

She might have stopped on the threshold and refused to step through if not for the sounds of activity reverberating off the walls…and the fact that Tatiana was whirling around an exquisitely patterned white rug atop a Roomba vacuum.

"That's fifteen minutes! Who had fifteen minutes?"

"I have twenty, and you know it, Julio. Stop trying to nudge him off. That's cheating."

"I'm not nudging him. I'm checking to make sure he isn't going to be sick. Do tortoises get dizzy?"

Amber leapt into the room before either Julio or Raffi—both of whom were much too old to be placing bets on a tortoise who was even older than they were—could see their bet through to completion.

"Are you two serious?" She clicked the Roomba off and scooped Tatiana into her arms. After anxiously checking him for signs of illness—*could* tortoises get dizzy?—she decided the tortoise looked exactly the same as before. His skin was softer, courtesy of his bath, but he didn't appear to be otherwise affected. "I trusted you guys to take care of him while I was at the police station. He could have been hurt."

Of the two men, Raffi looked the guiltiest. He straightened the bow tie around his neck with a sigh. "I know it's monstrous, but Julio insisted. He's never met a wager he can turn down."

Julio straightened to his full five-foot-six height. "That's rich coming from you. Why, you were the one who—" He caught sight of Camille standing behind Amber and cut himself off. Amber could only assume that she'd brought out the same death glare that had worked so effectively on Bones. "Sorry, Amber. We were just having a little fun."

"Tatiana never seemed to be in any real distress," Raffi added. "I wouldn't have allowed the game to continue if he had."

Julio snorted. "*Game?* This was a serious wager. There was no way he was making it five more minutes on that thing unless you taped him down."

Camille glares or no Camille glares, Amber feared the argument would continue indefinitely if she didn't change the subject. She'd worked around her fair share of backroom poker games and shady bookkeepers, but she didn't think she'd met anyone as obsessed with their friendly wagers as Julio.

"Can you at least tell me if you guys got him to eat something?" she asked. "I'm starting to get really worried."

As if on cue, Lincoln walked around the kitchen counter with an apron tied about his waist and a plate in one hand. At first, Amber thought the beautiful arrangement of fruits and vegetables were meant for her, but as he laid down the star-patterned assortment of strawberries, lettuce leaves, carrot tops, and bell pepper slices, she realized he'd gone to all the trouble for Tatiana.

"If this doesn't whet his appetite, I don't know what will," Lincoln said.

"*Our* dinner will have a lot more butter and cheese than this, but it won't be ready for another hour or so."

Camille clapped her hands, bringing them all to order as efficiently as a kindergarten teacher corralling her herd. "Excellent timing, Lincoln, thank you. I was hoping we'd be able to sit down for a council of war before we eat. Has everyone had time to prepare their presentations?"

Raffi shook his head. "Without a copy of the toxicology report, there's not much I can do at present, but I'm happy to lend an ear. Or a hand. Or any other part of my anatomy that may come in handy."

Julio snagged one of the pieces of bell pepper and crunched it. The bite must have gone down the wrong tube, because he took a moment to clear the phlegm from his chest before continuing. "Ditto over here. I found an appraisal of the ring on an online auction site from a few years back, but it doesn't tell us anything we didn't already know—it was worth a cool three million then and is worth a hot three million now. Peggy Lee's still digging into the personal finances of both the Vincent kids, but it'll take her a few days to crack the servers."

Amber set Tatiana down in front of the plate of produce. She had the feeling she was going to need to give this group her full attention if she wanted to make any sense of what was happening.

"I'm sorry. Are you guys talking about the Admiral's toxicology report? And saying that Peggy Lee is hacking into his kids' bank accounts?"

She may as well not have spoken for all the attention the four elderly podcasters paid her.

"We haven't looked enough into that mysterious phone call yet either." Camille lowered herself onto one of the uncomfortable plastic chairs, her white feathers blending perfectly with the environment. With one elegant leg crossed over the other, she pulled a notebook out of her purse and started jotting down notes. "I hate to burden Peggy Lee more than we already have, but it would be helpful to know who was keeping such a close eye on the podcast studio the night the Admiral died…and why. Perhaps we could get our hands on that information another way. Say, a bright young PI with a morally questionable phone guy in her pocket."

She cocked her head at Amber. "What do you say, love? Is that doable?"

"Doable?" Amber asked as she glanced from face to face. Camille looked serene, Raffi guilty, Julio flushed, and Lincoln sympathetic. "Do you mean you're investigating to find the real murderer? Like you would for a podcast?"

"Not *like* we would for a podcast," Lincoln corrected her. He poured out a glass of white wine with a label that Amber didn't recognize and set it in front of her. "Literally for the podcast. Jade used her one phone call on me. She told me to make sure you were taken care of and under no circumstances to let this opportunity go to waste. She said nothing in the boxes of files comes even close."

All four heads around her nodded in unison. "We needed a new case, and behold!" Raffi pulled a red silk handkerchief from his pocket and waved it. "One was delivered directly into our hands. Now. *Think*, Amber. Did you learn anything interesting at the station? Anything that might add to the picture?"

She squeezed her eyes shut and did as he asked—not to think about any clues that might have fallen into her lap, but about how impossibly ludicrous this whole situation was. Not only had one of their dearest friends died in the very studio where they were purporting to record this new podcast, but another of their dearest friends had been arrested for it. In no way, shape, or form should this have been a cause for celebration.

Yet here they were. Pouring out buttery chardonnay and solving a murder. Working together to find the real culprit and free her grandmother.

Her eyes popped open again.

"I haven't seen the toxicology report, but my grandma's attorney said something about there being a lot of drugs in the Admiral's system," she said, the words slipping out before she could stop them. "She didn't use the word *poison*, but it was strongly implied. Considering the state of the podcast studio, I'm guessing he didn't go down easily. Either the poison was the kind that causes muscle spasms—strychnine comes to mind—or he fought off his killer until the bitter end."

No one said a word, so she kept going.

"I agree that the anonymous phone call is worth looking into, but a more important question is the key." She paused and tapped her teeth, unable to stop now that she was on a roll. "The attorney mentioned that too. I didn't think about it at the time, but when Raffi, my grandmother, and I broke into the studio to grab the case files, the lock had already been broken by the police. But my grandma said the door only locks from the outside."

Raffi nodded so vigorously that his toupee started to slip. "That's true on both counts. The lock's been broken for years."

Amber snapped her fingers. "That means the Admiral couldn't have locked the door behind him. And because we're talking about a converted garden shed with soundproofing on every wall, there aren't any windows that would allow someone to get in or out another way."

A conflicting rise of pride and dread assailed Amber as the implications of this statement settled in. The pride came from figuring out why the police had been so sure of foul play; the dread from realizing that there was no other interpretation.

Cold-blooded murder. Cold-blooded murder that her grandmother was currently taking the fall for.

"Someone else had to have been the one to lock the door," Amber said, clinching the matter. "And that someone is most likely the killer. After they finished administering the poison, they left him alone in there—either already dead or well on the way to getting there."

An uneasy glance passed around the room, growing exponentially as it flitted from face to face. Amber took her lower lip between her teeth and pushed through. This was the thing she excelled at—the background clues, her way of not looking directly at the picture, but at all the surrounding circumstances.

A man dead inside a locked room. A missing ring worth three million. A group of elderly friends who seemed to delight in nothing so much as drama, intrigue, and mystery.

Camille leaned back in her seat, one long leg crossed elegantly over the other. "What exactly are you saying, dear?"

Amber swallowed. She didn't love having to put the question in words, but there didn't seem any way around it. "I know my grandma has a copy, and Raffi said that he'd left his at home the evening of our break-in, but who else among you has a key?"

One by one, every hand in the room came up. A few of them

wavered, but they still rose and stayed that way until Amber had clocked every one.

"And Peggy Lee?" she asked.

Raffi nodded. His voice was quiet but assured. "We had one made for everyone in the podcast. Many of us don't sleep as well as we used to, so it made sense that we all had access to the studio whenever we wanted. To pass the time, you understand, when the rest of the world is asleep."

"We solved some of our best cases that way," Lincoln added. Even though Amber hadn't taken a sip, he topped up her wineglass. "Burning the midnight oil. Or, in my case, the three a.m. oil. That's when the sleeplessness always seems to come for me. The worry monsters, my wife calls them."

Amber didn't need to hear any more—and she needed to say even less. These people might be amateur crime-solvers, but they were sharp and determined amateur crime-solvers.

And unless she was very much mistaken, one of them was a sharp and determined crime-*doer*, as well.

Julio was the first to put her findings into words. He clapped his hands and began animatedly rubbing them together. "Oh, boy. This is gonna be the biggest, baddest betting pool we've had yet."

"Julio, you can't place bets on this," Amber said, but she didn't know why she bothered. If the untimely death of one of them couldn't break up their enjoyment, then she didn't know why one of them turning out to be a murderer would.

"You believe that one of us on the podcast team is the killer." Camille spoke slowly, as if each word carried its own weight. A strange smile touched her lips as she took a long, leisurely sip of her wine. "Oh, my. This is going to make for a *great* season."

14

"Poisoning is a woman's crime...so if you're a man and you want to get away with murder, you know what to do."

—*DEATH COMES CALLING*, SEASON 3 EPISODE 10

"DO YOU THINK THERE'S A chance Tatiana has been poisoned?"

The next morning, Amber strode into the rec room where Peggy Lee had directed her. Tatiana was once again bound to her chest with a makeshift sling, once again staring up at her with his dark, unreadable eyes. Eyes filled with hunger? Pain? She was getting so desperate to find out that she'd actually decided to take Ethan up on his offer to find him.

She stopped on the threshold as the sound of gunfire burst all around her.

Such had been the stress of the past twenty-four hours that she immediately ducked and took cover. She was in a full crouch, her arms clasped protectively around the tortoise, before she realized how ridiculous she must look.

"No fair! You only took us out because you have the M4. You'd have been lost without it."

"Don't be absurd. Bruce only has the Lockwood, and he's been picking you off one by one for the past half hour."

"It's all in the breathing, lads. Slow and steady gets your man every time."

Amber leaped to her feet before anyone—namely, Ethan—could notice that she was cowering behind a potted palm tree. Although her instincts had been sound, and one ought always to take cover when bullets flew through the air, she should have recognized the sounds of *Call of Duty* the moment she heard them. A girl didn't grow up with two brothers determined to prevent her from enjoying any and all of their video games without learning a thing or two.

"Personally, I've always preferred the rocket launcher, but that's just me," she said as she came the rest of the way into the room. "Can I have the next round, or is this one of those boys-only crowds?"

"Amber!" Ethan looked as though he would have leaped to his feet, but all he did was drop his controller. "What are you doing here?"

"I came to seek your advice about Tatiana," she said, enjoying herself more than the situation warranted. A better woman would have taken pity on a man who was literally trapped on the couch, unable to get up without the assistance from his nurse or the walker that sat nearby, but Amber had never been better at anything—especially when it came to taking the moral high ground. "But if you're busy playing video games with your little friends…"

The old man named Bruce—the one with the alarming affinity for picking off his foes one by one—chuckled and rose to his feet. His lilting Irish accent did much to imbue him with an air of authority. "We've just finished, love. But if you ask me, a rocket launcher should only be used in times of extreme duress. The damage those things do is unthinkable."

She eyed Bruce's upright posture and the way he spoke with a gravity that didn't match the setting—that of a nursing home rec room with an enormous television set to play violent video games—and came to a quick conclusion.

"Is that game advice or life advice?" she asked and then didn't wait for an answer. "Let me guess…the Troubles?"

A look of delight transformed him. With a kindly pat on her shoulder, he said, "Bang on, love. I heard you were a smart cookie. Consider me tickled to find the reports true. How's your grandmother holding up?"

This unexpected show of support for her grandmother's situation made the dratted tears well up in her eyes again, but she managed to subdue them. "Oh, you know her," she said flippantly. "It'll take more than one murder charge to bring her down."

Bruce nodded. "You let her know we're all pulling for her. We play *Call of Duty* every day at ten, so if you find yourself with some time on your hands and a penchant for shedding some blood, feel free to pop in."

The rest of the men filed out behind him, grumbling good-naturedly about weapons and terrain and how much time Wallace had spent camped out. By the time the rec room was emptied, Ethan had managed to get to his feet, but he still bore the pink, slightly abashed look of a grown man who'd been caught playing video games with other grown men in the full light of day.

"I didn't start the group," he said before Amber could open her mouth. "In fact, I'm the worst one of the whole lot. Between Bruce, who knows pretty much everything a man can about guerilla warfare, and the rest of them, who've been playing this game together for the past decade, I'm usually dead within two minutes. They only invite me out of pity."

Amber felt her lips twitch. "I didn't say anything."

"You can google it. It's a whole thing. Retirees make up a huge percentage of online gamers these days." Aware of how he must sound, Ethan flushed even pinker than before. "I've already read every book I brought with me, and if I have to spend another minute watching Fox News with my roommate, I might throw myself out a window just for the change of pace."

Amber was still smiling but she felt a stab of pity too. There was plenty to keep her active and occupied around the retirement community, but that was because she had full mobility and was currently solving a murder. Take those two things away, and what did she have? A tortoise who wouldn't eat? A condo that was so much like an art gallery that she was afraid to even use the glass that Camille set out on her bedside table?

Seriously. The thing had been a hand-blown showpiece with flecks of real gold in it. Amber had slaked her thirst the night before the good old-fashioned way by sticking her head under the faucet.

"Well, if you're desperate, maybe you can help me with Tatiana." She unhooked the tortoise from her sling and set him gently on a table. "I gave him the bath like you suggested, but he still hasn't touched his food. Lincoln made him a whole bougie salad last night and everything. Julio ended up eating most of it."

Ethan started to move behind his walker. She could tell that he was painfully aware of her eyes on him as he did.

"Go ahead and ask," he said as he hobbled toward the table. "I know you're dying to know what's wrong with me."

"I'm not, actually." She tickled Tatiana under his chin the way the tortoise liked. "I already got the full scoop from Peggy Lee. You're quite a point of interest around here, you know. A hot young thing like you? The olds can't get enough."

He glanced quickly over at her, but his expression was unreadable. "I'd say that makes two of us. Where'd you stay last night, by the way? I wasn't sure you'd be back. My nurse said something about you being booted from your grandmother's place now that she's...you know..." His voice trailed off in some confusion.

"A wanted criminal?" Amber suggested. "A murderess? The prime suspect in the grizzly murder of her dearest friend?"

He flushed. "I wasn't going to say that."

"It's fine." She tried shrugging, but the burden of worry lingered heavily on her shoulders. "Camille—that's the friend of my grandma's with the gorgeous wardrobe and killer fauxhawk—offered to let me stay with her. And when my time there is up, Raffi, Julio, and Lincoln have all extended similar invitations. I won't have to leave here for a very long time."

He released a soundless whistle. "Damn. I take it all back. That heavy-handed charm of yours must work."

"*Heavy-handed*?"

"C'mon, Winslow. Who do you think you're fooling? That whole shtick with the cops? The way you flit around here wheedling everything you want out of anyone and anything with a pulse?"

Even though Ethan spoke no more than the truth, she felt a surge of annoyance move through her. "What about you? Smiling and simpering at Nasty Nancy, making her yell at perfectly innocent women who are just trying to walk their tortoises in peace."

He choked. "*What* did you just call her?"

Too late, Amber remembered that Ethan actually liked Nancy, and that the nurse was responsible for providing him with the kind of intimate care that forged deep bonds. Perhaps calling her names wasn't the best approach.

"It's not important. Just a thing I overheard," she said. And, since offense was the best defense, she was quick to turn the tables. "And what's she doing gossiping about me, anyway? She doesn't know me. She doesn't know anything about me."

He tapped his chin as though in deep thought, but the fact that Amber could see his distinct features—the lightly carved laugh lines around his mouth, a small scar along his brow line—was a clear sign that he was amused.

At her? *With* her? It was too soon to say.

"I'll admit that she can be a bit…abrupt at times, but I wouldn't call her 'nasty,'" he eventually said. "Is that what your grandmother's friend group calls her? I swear, this place feels like the set of *Mean Girls* sometimes—or at the very least, a high school of vampires. From what I hear, that podcast group is the worst of the lot. A clique of bullies who only care about themselves."

Amber wasn't about to sit back and let this man insult the only people in the world who were keeping her afloat right now, even if those laugh lines were starting to prove *very* distracting.

"Nancy misses people's veins on purpose, and some of the things I've heard about her affinity for suppositories would give you nightmares." She laughed as he visibly balked. "Unless you've already experienced that for yourself? Don't worry. I won't ask. Better to keep some mystery between us, don't you think?"

"Very funny. Do you always antagonize the people you ask for favors?"

"Only if they start it," she retorted. "But if I have to suck up to you and play nice in order for you to tell me if Tatiana has been poisoned, then I'm game. I'm sure Nancy is lovely and her nickname is unwarranted. Underneath that hostile exterior lies a heart of gold and a deeply misunderstood character. From now on, I'll only call her Nice Nancy. And you can be Empathetic Ethan. I'm sure it'll catch on in no time."

Ethan rolled his eyes. "I'm just saying. These old people can be pretty brutal to one another. If you don't believe me, join the Nextdoor app and take a look. Some of the stuff on the gardening threads will blow your mind."

Even though he spoke lightly, something inside Amber sat up and took notice. "You're on Nextdoor?"

He shrugged and started gently poking at the tortoise. "It helps pass the time. Nancy's the one who got me hooked. She and some of the admin use it to keep track of the residents—see what they're up to, what they're worried about, that sort of thing. It's a great way to keep an eye on the pulse of the place."

"What's your username?"

He stopped in the act of gently prying open Tatiana's mouth. "Why?"

"Because I want to be friends," she lied.

His eyes narrowed with suspicion, but he answered readily enough. "It's Hawkeye93."

Amber made a mental note to look him up later. If nothing else, it would be amusing to see what he thought of the whole Hannah/Peggy Lee arugula feud.

She stood with her hands clasped behind her back and a determined silence on her lips as he performed what looked to be an expert examination of the tortoise. He poked and prodded and murmured in a low voice that seemed to soothe Tatiana into a state of conciliation.

"Other than the not eating, what makes you think he's been poisoned?" Ethan asked as he brought the tortoise up to his ear and listened for a few seconds. "Have there been any signs of distress or pain? Swelling or discharge?"

"Not really, no. He's pretty chill most of the time." She paused as Ethan listened to the tortoise's breathing before setting him back down again. "How do you know so much about animals, anyway? Are you a vet or something?"

"Look at you, big-shot private investigator. You figured me out, and it only took you about a week to do it."

This time, it was Amber's turn to balk. "I'm not a private investigator. Not a real one, anyway."

"Well, I'm a real vet, and your tortoise seems fine. He's probably eating when you're not looking. Keep track of his fecal output for the next few days and let me know if you see or smell anything off."

Amber's nose wrinkled. "Ew. I'm not doing that."

Ethan shrugged. "Suit yourself. If you're really worried, you should take him to an actual veterinary clinic. There's not a lot I can do from here." A serious expression flashed across his face. For the longest moment, Amber was afraid that he was going to say something about Tatiana's state of health, but his words proved worse than that. "Why are you so worried about poison, anyway? This doesn't have anything to do with the way the Admiral died, does it? You think they both got into something they shouldn't have?"

Amber didn't know how to respond. On the one hand, it was preposterous to think that someone would have simultaneously poisoned both a man and a tortoise, especially when the tortoise in question had been missing for several weeks prior to the Admiral's death. On the other hand, how much did she really know about her grandmother's friends? Their names and addresses, sure. The fact that they were obsessed with murder, yeah.

But they were all strangers, when all was said and done. Strangers with a cavalier disregard for human life and a copy of the key that gave them the opportunity necessary to end a man's life. Strangers who were almost *giddy* at the prospect of discovering which one of them had stolen the Admiral's ring before doing away with him.

"That thing you said earlier," she began slowly, "about how my grandmother's podcast friends are like a *Mean Girls* clique?"

His gaze caught hers and held it. "What about it?"

"This might sound strange, but do you think—"

The sound of approaching footsteps prevented Amber from finishing her question. Her first feeling was one of relief, since to put such a thing in words would be to give it life—veracity, even. Better to keep this inside the podcast group for now, leave it in the realm of fantasy where it belonged.

This feeling was soon replaced by one of deep, unabated irritation. Mostly because she was quick to recognize that tread and the man it belonged to.

"Not much security at this place, is there?" Bones asked as he stepped into the rec room. He shoved his hands into his armpits and made a survey of his surroundings as though scanning for the most likely exits and immediate threats to his safety—which, Amber knew, carried a ring of truth. In the event of emergency or apocalypse, Bones was definitely the person you wanted by your side. "The guy at the security gate sounds as if he needs to be on oxygen, and the little old lady at the reception desk isn't much better. She sounds like she needs to be muzzled. And what's the deal with their big red buttons?"

As was usually the case whenever Bones entered a room, he filled it completely. What space his physical body didn't take up, his booming voice and huge personality did.

"Their names are Julio and Peggy Lee, thank you very much, and the buttons are just for show. The *real* security is run in a back room by a man named Giles who sees and hears everything, so you might want to be careful what you say." Amber regretted the words the moment they left her lips— not only because of the amused expression on Bones's face, but because of the startled one on Ethan's.

"That's my girl," Bones said with an approving grin. "What else do I need to know?"

She didn't want to answer him, especially considering how closely Ethan was watching, but to do so would be to admit that Bones had any power over her—to embarrass or impress, to influence or control.

Which he didn't. *Obviously.*

"I haven't been able to find the cameras installed anywhere on the grounds or in the buildings, so I'm guessing they're designed to blend in with the background. The police have already confiscated the tapes from the night of the Admiral's death, but I don't know what's on them, and the defense attorney assigned to my grandma's case is so overloaded that it could take her weeks to check for herself. I've been meaning to ask around to find out if there are backups of the tapes being stored somewhere, but *I've* been so overloaded that I haven't had the chance yet. It's on my to-do list though."

Bones rubbed a hand along his jaw. The rough scrape of it was loud enough to fill the air, as if his permanent five o'clock shadow demanded to be heard as well as seen. "Not a bad start. Can we make anything of the list that guy—Julio—keeps to log visitors? See if anyone of interest has been stopping by lately?"

Amber shook her head. "Not really, no. He told me himself that all you have to do is jot down the name of the person you're visiting, and you're in. And he's not exactly…reliable."

Bones arched one of his brows. So did Ethan, but only one of them made it look like he was both James Bond and the villain he was determined to track down.

"Damn. He a sus, then?" Bones asked.

Amber saw no reason to lie. She'd already said more than she should have to both these men, and to be honest, it was nice to have a sounding board. She wasn't used to solving cases with only a tortoise to talk to. Tatiana was a good listener, but his feedback could use some work.

"He's not *not* one," she admitted. "Not only did he have a key to the podcast studio, which was locked behind the Admiral the night he was murdered, but he has a bit of a gambling habit. There isn't a contest, challenge, or conversation around here that he can't find a way to turn into a financial opportunity."

"Uh, excuse me?" Ethan raised his hand. "Am I going to be found stuffed in a trunk somewhere if I keep overhearing this? Because I can head to my room, but you need to give me about five minutes to make my escape first. It's not very nice to force murder confessions on a man who can't fight back."

Bones turned toward Ethan as though seeing him for the first time. Since Amber knew he'd clocked the other man the moment he entered the room, intimidation was his most likely intention. In all the time she'd known him, Bones had never met a man he didn't feel the need to assess, classify, and dominate—in that order.

"What's wrong with you?" Bones asked with all the blunt insensitivity Amber had been striving to avoid. "Aren't you kinda young to be withering away in a place like this?"

A grimace of displeasure crossed Ethan's face before he turned into the bland mask that erased all his features. For some reason, that made her own displeasure mount. Just when she was starting to make headway with the guy…

"Didn't your mother teach you any manners?" Amber rolled her eyes. "Sorry about him, Ethan. He's not the most subtle of men, but he's harmless."

"Like hell I am. I'm the most dangerous man either of you have ever met. I could kill you both in under sixty seconds flat." Despite the harsh words, Bones offered Ethan his hand. "The name is Bones. I'm Amber's boyfriend."

"*Ex*-boyfriend," she said with enough stress on the first syllable to render most men speechless.

Bones, alas, was not most men.

"We'll see about that, won't we?" He winked at Ethan, who had to shift and maneuver to free up a hand to take the ones Bones was holding out. From the way Ethan winced, Amber guessed Bones was proving his masculinity with a grip that would make a Vulcan proud. "You'll have to forgive the shop talk. I'm a PI, so it comes naturally."

Ethan's gaze shifted from Bones to Amber, his expression inscrutable. "You're here to help get Amber's grandmother out of jail?"

"That's right." He slung a proprietary arm around Amber's shoulder. She tried to shrug it off, but there was no way to get rid of him without making a scene or at least jabbing him in the eye with her elbow, so she let his forearm dangle. "Amber and I have been big fans of the *Death Comes Calling* podcast for years. I can't wait to meet the woman behind it all."

This, at least, sounded sincere.

"And you think one of the old people here did it?" Ethan looked more at Amber than Bones while he asked the question, but that didn't stop Bones from doing the answering.

"That's what I'm here for." He tugged Amber closer, practically folding her under his massive bulk. "When Bones is on the case, satisfaction is guaranteed. Isn't that right, babe?"

Amber had no doubt what Bones was doing—and why—and the moment she caught Ethan's gaze, she realized he knew it too. That flash of understanding infuriated her in ways she'd never known were possible.

Yeah, okay, her ex was staking a claim in the most obvious way possible. And, yes, the idea that he had anything to fear in a slight, difficult-to-pinpoint veterinarian recovering from a hip replacement in an old person's home was laughable, but that was Bones in a nutshell. Did Ethan really have to look *that* amused about it?

"I don't know what I think yet," Amber said. She ducked and twisted out of Bones's grasp. Although she managed to escape the manacle of his arm, she'd been right about both looking and feeling ridiculous about it. To cover her embarrassment, she grabbed the tortoise and held him close. "All I know is that I can't stand back and do nothing while a living creature suffers. Not the Admiral, not my grandmother, and not poor Tatiana here."

Bones gave a start of surprise. "Tati-*what*?"

Too late, Amber remembered that she'd given the tortoise the same name as the hula girl. Bones had never had much of a sense of humor, particularly where things like good luck and superstition were involved. Fighting a giggle, she turned her attention to Ethan.

"Thank you for your help with Tatiana," she said with the polite, bland tone of a hostess bidding a guest goodbye. "I really appreciate it, and I'll let you know about his, uh, bowel movements."

"What a treat for us both," Ethan agreed blandly. With more dignity than most men could muster under the same circumstances, he gripped the edges of his walker and started heading for the door. "See you around, Winslow. Don't forget to look me up on Nextdoor. I promise not to block your friend request."

Bones could hardly wait the amount of time necessary for Ethan to leave the room before he pounced. "What the hell kind of animal is that in your arms, and why did you name her Tatiana?"

There was only one way to save herself after that, so Amber handed the tortoise over to her ex. He would roar and puff and blow like the big bad wolf from fairy tales, but he wouldn't hurt an innocent animal.

"*He's* a tortoise, and I call him Tatiana because he likes it. He's ninety-eight years old and recently lost the only person in the world who cared about what became of him." She paused a beat before continuing. "No one deserves to feel like that. Not even a reptile."

As expected, Bones accepted the tortoise warily but carefully, holding the animal at arm's length as he examined the beady eyes staring up into his. "You can't name a boy tortoise Tatiana. That's cruel and unusual punishment."

"Your protest is duly noted, but the name stays." She paused even longer this time. As displeased as she was to have her ex barreling into her life uninvited, she was forced to admit that he would come in handy if one of her grandmother's friends really *was* a murderer. She was already too emotionally close to this case due to her grandmother's arrest; add in the kindness with which she'd been treated by the podcast group, and all her biases were cemented in place.

The right thing to do—the *professional* thing to do—would be to excuse herself from the case entirely. Unfortunately, that wasn't an option. Mitigating her involvement by letting Bones assist was the best she could do.

"But since you came all this way and you don't seem to have anything else to do…" She let her voice trail off.

"I'm here for you. I mean it, Amber. Whatever you want, whatever you need, just say the word."

She didn't believe him, since she'd been telling him for *years* that all she wanted was to be treated like his professional equal, but she wasn't about to look a gift private investigator in the mouth.

She wasn't going to do anything else with his mouth either, but he didn't realize that part yet.

"Then I need you to get me a copy of those security tapes," she said as she untied the sling from around her torso and handed it to her ex. He eyed the throw blanket with the same disfavor he'd shown the tortoise, but she didn't care. If he wanted to stick around and grovel or redeem himself or whatever else he had planned, then he could start by wearing Tatiana. Her back was already starting to ache from the strain of his weight. "Lie, cheat, steal—I don't care how you do it, just so long as we get our hands on evidence of what happened that night."

To Bones's credit, his only response was to stand perfectly still and watch as she wound the sling around his chest. "Why? What are you going to do?"

She was standing behind him, so she didn't bother to hide her grimace. The truth was that if one of the six remaining members of the *Death Came Calling* podcast really *was* the murderer, then her grandmother wasn't in the clear. If anything, her position was only more precarious.

Like everyone else, Jade had a key to the podcast studio. That ticked off the opportunity box.

Motive was equally incriminatory, since a three-million-dollar ring could be used to point the finger at just about anyone.

And as for means, well…Amber's hand went instinctively to her pocket, where the empty prescription bottle sat. She had no idea how she was going to get the pharmacist on-site to tell her what she wanted to know without making her grandma's case worse, but she had to at least try. Theories of strychnine were all well and good when coming up with the sensationalist plot of a murder podcast, but if a person *really* wanted to do away with someone, few things beat an overdose of good old-fashioned painkillers.

"I have something I want to check," she said. "It's probably nothing, but I need to do it on my own."

Bones scanned her face as if searching for something, but he eventually gave up. With a sigh both for her and for the animal now nestled securely against his bosom, he said, "And this'll make us even, yeah? If I help you free your grandmother, you'll come back home to Seattle where you belong?"

For the longest moment, Amber toyed with the idea of lying to him. It would be so easy to string him along for a few weeks, relying on his skills and his strength to carry her through this, but that wasn't fair. Not to Bones and definitely not to herself.

"How about a compromise?" she asked. "You do this, and I'll give you Tatiana—*hula* Tatiana, not the tortoise?"

He didn't look pleased at this meager offering, but he was either too stupid or too smart to take her at her word. With a nod, he accepted the olive branch.

"Sure thing, babe. If this is what it takes to get my good luck charm back, you can count me in."

15

*"Just once, wouldn't it be nice if the murderer
was a truly despicable human being?"*

—*DEATH COMES CALLING*, SEASON 4 EPISODE 8

SINCE THE LAST THING AMBER wanted was for Peggy Lee to see what she
was up to—and ask her inevitable barrage of questions—she took a scenic
route through the nursing home.

Once she got past the reception desk and rec rooms, the white marble
tiles gave way to more functional linoleum, the spacious ceilings and trickling fountains replaced with linen closets and nursing stations. The smell
of antiseptic also got much stronger. The potted plants remained, though,
and so did the quiet, cheerful efficiency of the staff, who helpfully pointed
her in the direction of the pharmacy where she falsely purported to "go fill a
prescription for my great-nan." Everyone was so busy and focused on their
own tasks that they barely gave her a second glance.

The pharmacy was little more than a booth set into a far wall. It was presided over by a man who looked like Santa Claus, assuming Santa Claus had
recently discovered CrossFit and decided to give the paleo lifestyle a try. His
snowy beard was trimmed to perfection, his lean cheeks and curled mustache
like something out of a nineteenth-century Chippendale's calendar.

"Hello, little lady," he said with a smile and a wink that reaffirmed her
belief that he'd once cavorted among a team of snowy reindeer. "You look
lost. Anything I can help with?"

"Actually, yes." Amber's first instinct was to lean over the counter to give

Ripped Santa a glimpse of her cleavage, but she stopped herself and adjusted the neckline of her shirt to a more decorous height. If she couldn't do this the way real investigators did—with intelligence and determination, guile that had little to do with sex appeal—then Ethan was right, and she wasn't worthy of the PI title.

She pulled out the pill bottle and set it on the counter instead. "I was hoping you could tell me whether or not you were the one to fill this prescription."

Ripped Santa blinked for a moment before taking the bottle. He pulled a pair of readers out of his pocket and examined the label for all of twenty seconds before nodding. "Of course. Almost all the residents have their prescriptions filled here. It saves them a lot of time and trouble to bring them to me." He glanced at her over the top of his readers, his blue eyes kind. "You must be the granddaughter."

"I am," Amber said. Her chest felt tight, but she didn't fight the sensation. If anything, she leaned into that overwhelming feeling of drowning. She was going to need all the sincerity she could get if she wanted answers. "And since you know that much, I'm guessing you also know that Jade's been arrested. Since we have no idea how long they're going to keep her locked up, my grandma asked me to gather up her medications and a few belongings. Most of the bottles were full, but I was shaking so badly that I accidentally spilled these ones down the sink. I wanted to make sure she didn't need them before I headed over to the police station."

The kind blue eyes turned toward her with a shrewdness that couldn't be denied. "Spilled them down the sink, eh?"

"It's not what you think," she said, since she knew very well how this looked. Painkillers of this strength found their way down a lot of sinks. "I'm not an opioid addict, and I'm not trying to cheat the system. You can send the prescription directly to the jail if you don't believe me. I only want to make sure my grandma isn't suffering because of me."

The eyes softened as he returned the bottle to her. "In that case, you can relax. I filled this for her—oh, six, seven months ago? She had a nasty spill down her front steps. She and her friend Camille both." He touched the side of his nose and winked, thus solidifying himself forever in her heart as the jolliest of elves. "A little too much to drink, if you ask me. Those two are always getting up to something like that."

Amber's feet felt suddenly rooted to the spot. "She and Camille fell down the stairs?"

"Nothing was broken," he was quick to reassure her. "Just a few bumps and bruises. I didn't think it was serious at the time, and since it sounds as if there were plenty of pills left over, they probably didn't need them for more than a day or two."

Amber said all the right things in the five minutes that followed this interview. She thanked Ripped Santa for his help, complimented his mustache, and discussed such inanities that occurred—yes, her grandma was doing okay; no, she didn't think her case was desperate; sure, she'd let him know if there was anything else he could do to help—but everything was done on autopilot. First and foremost in her thoughts was the fact that not only her grandmother but *Camille* may have been sitting on a wealth of painkillers.

Then again, for all she knew, everyone around here was hoarding hydrocodone like it was candy. If death by overdose ever had a likely springboard, this place held the starting gun.

Amber's steps were mechanical and her thoughts deeply internalized as she wound her way back through the maze of hallways. It wasn't until she stepped through a mechanized door that whirred and clicked behind her that she realized she'd taken a wrong turn somewhere.

"Um…" She turned and tried the handle behind her, but the whirring had stopped and the door was securely locked. She glanced around to find that she was in a quiet, cheerful waiting room painted in a calming shade of green. Several overstuffed chairs and comfortable couches lounged at perfect angles, homemade quilts and hand-stitched afghans spread over every available surface.

She peeked around the nearest corner to find herself looking into a room that contained a bed, a rocking chair, and a woman sitting next to the window, her long white hair in a braid over one shoulder.

"Excuse me?" she called softly to the woman. "Could you point me in the direction of—"

"Is that you, Laura?" the woman replied. As soon as she turned to catch sight of Amber, her lips parted in a smile. Wisps of her downy hair had escaped from the braid, framing her face in a way that softened the deep lines carved there. "How nice of you to visit. I hope you didn't bring Samuel with you. Last time he ate all my favorite almond cookies."

Amber's eyes widened as she beat a hasty retreat. It was the cowardly way out, she knew, but she was starting to put the pieces together. The locked door, the hushed and calming atmosphere, the slightly vacant look in the woman's eyes…

"Oopsy daisy." A pair of hands fell to Amber's shoulders to steady her as she almost ran over a short Hispanic woman in floral dress, bright white sneakers, and a stethoscope draped around her neck. "You look as if you're in the wrong place. Don't tell me—you turned left at the water fountain, didn't you?"

"I, um." Amber struggled to subdue both her embarrassment and her guilt before the woman could clock either sentiment. Considering how much the woman's eyes twinkled as she watched these internal struggles, Amber guessed she wasn't doing a very good job. "Yeah, actually. I did. Is that woman in there—"

"Hazel has been with us a long time," the woman said without once losing her smile, "but I doubt she'll see us through the end of the year."

"Oh." The word contained, at once, everything and nothing. Amber didn't know much about late-stage dementia, but she doubted it was a pleasant experience for anyone involved—particularly the woman sitting by the window, waiting for a person who would likely never come.

"You seem harmless enough, but I'm afraid I'm going to have to ask you to leave," the woman continued. "The residents in this ward are easily agitated, so we only allow family and staff back here. It's for your own safety as well as theirs. I'm sure you understand."

Amber *did* understand and was quick to realize her error. "Of course. I'm so sorry. I didn't mean to intrude."

The woman—a doctor, Amber belatedly realized—smiled with quick and ready understanding, but that didn't stop her from propelling Amber toward the locked door. "If you come with me, I'll let you out," she said.

Amber did as she asked, but the sound of a beeper stopped them both before they made it more than a few steps.

"Drat." The doctor frowned down at the pager clipped to her belt. "That's me. I need to get this. Check in with Nancy—I believe I saw her in room 202—and she'll get you where you need to go. And don't look so worried, honey. Hazel is being well taken care of. And she's luckier than most—her grandson works here, so he pops in almost every day to chat. It's the ones who don't get any visitors at all you should feel sorry for."

Without another word, the doctor turned on her heel and squeaked efficiently down the hall. Amber was left to head toward room 202 on her own.

The door was slightly ajar, but the last thing Amber wanted was to intrude any more than she already had—especially if Nasty Nancy was busy with a patient. On tiptoe, she peered through the open slit to see a room similar to the one in which Hazel had sat. The furnishings were less ornate, and the patient was lying supine on the bed, attached to a machine that assisted with breathing, but it was otherwise identical.

Except, of course, for the kitten-scrubs-covered woman hunched over a desk muttering to herself.

Instinct had Amber automatically regulating her breathing. Forcing her heartbeat to slow and her steps to remain light, she inched closer, her every sense on alert as she tried to figure out what Nancy was doing.

At first, it looked as though the nurse was rifling through the drawers of the desk, her movements hurried as she looked for something: Medical supplies? Notepaper? *Jewelry?*

Amber's breath slowed even more as she considered the implication of what she was witnessing. The Admiral's kids had been so caught up in accusing her grandmother of stealing the three-million-dollar ring that they hadn't stopped to consider who else might have had easy access to his home. As far as Amber could tell, the nurses here didn't make house calls, but who would have thought twice to see Nancy wandering the grounds?

As Amber leaned closer, she saw the nurse swipe an electronic tablet from the desk and tuck it into her pocket. She then bustled to the patient's bedside and checked his vitals as though nothing unusual had just happened.

Amber toyed with the idea of calling the nurse out, but as she cleared her throat and Nancy whirled around, she rapidly changed tack. The surprise on the nurse's face—which just as quickly turned to a sour smile that made Amber physically recoil—was enough to send even a man like Bones running.

"What are *you* doing here?" Nancy demanded. "You aren't allowed in this ward. No one is. Besides, I thought Geerta kicked you out of the facility."

"She did, but then Camille kicked me right back in." Amber hooked her thumb over her shoulder. "I was visiting with Ethan and took a wrong turn somewhere. A nice doctor said to find you so you could let me out."

Nancy's sour expression didn't change. "You were visiting Ethan? *My* Ethan?"

"Yep. He's been helping me get Tatiana back on his feet." She flashed her most dazzling smile. "Just like how you've been helping Ethan. Isn't that fun? Next thing we know, you'll be turning to me for help to complete the circle. Well, I guess the real circle would be if you asked the tortoise for help, but you know what I mean. Although he *is* good company if you ever feel yourself in need of a companion."

The way Nancy's nostrils flared did little to affirm Amber in this belief, but the distraction worked. The nurse gave one loud *harrumph* before heading for the door. "Fine. It's this way. But if you know what's good for you, you won't come poking around this wing again."

Amber couldn't help herself. "Why? What happens back here?"

Nancy cast a glare over her shoulder as she typed in numbers on a keypad—hidden behind her hand, no less. Instead of answering Amber's question, she practically spat her next words. "I know what your grandmother is. I know what she did."

It was on the tip of Amber's tongue to retort in kind—especially since she could see the outline of the tablet bulging in Nancy's front pocket—but she decided it would be better to wait until Nancy didn't hold the literal key to her escape.

"In that case, you should know better than to say things like that to me," Amber said as the door swung open and she made good her escape. "You might not know *me* very well yet, but my grandmother and I are a lot more alike than you think."

16

"The motivation for every criminal activity can
be boiled down to one of three things: sex,
power, or money. And since money can easily
buy the other two, I think we have our answer."

—*DEATH COMES CALLING*, SEASON 1 EPISODE 12

CAMILLE WASN'T IN THE CONDO when Amber returned.

If Amber were a less suspicious-minded person, she might have thought
nothing of her hostess's absence. According to the excursion board set up
behind Peggy Lee's reception desk, there were plenty of activities designed to
keep everyone's minds off the recent murder and arrest. A hired bus to visit
the desert blooms, a historical tour and outdoor tea, and a trip to the local
Costco were just a few of the exciting options available to the residents of
Seven Ponds Retirement Community for the day.

Somehow, however, Amber didn't think a woman whose home boasted
the exact same Chanel hand towels as Derek's—only ones she was actually
allowed to use—had gone to Costco.

"I might as well use this time to get some work done," she said as she
rolled up her figurative sleeves. She didn't feel *good* about searching the home
of the woman who'd generously opened her doors to her, but she didn't see
what other choice she had. If Ripped Santa was to be believed, Camille had
just as much access to death-inducing pain pills as her grandmother.

She also had a key to the podcast studio, a sharp-eyed intelligence
undimmed by time, and a veritable fortune on her back.

As far as Amber was concerned, that made her suspect number one. Or,
at the very least, *accomplice* number one.

"Okay, Camille. Let's see what's happening behind closed doors."

After a brief search of the bathroom—no pain pills—and the kitchen—no rat poison—she tiptoed to the primary bedroom and stepped into the walk-in closet, her fingers practically itching as she started to rifle through the rows of neatly hanging clothes. It had been her intention to search the closet for a safe—the most likely hiding spot for any and all things related to crime—but she soon became distracted by holding several exquisitely tailored gowns up to her person and imagining a world where she might actually have a reason to wear one.

Which, okay, was hardly helpful in this particular situation, but it had been a rough few weeks.

One dress in particular called out to her. It was a masterpiece of green silk cut on the bias, short enough in the hem that it might actually fit her. She'd already kicked off her shoes and was about to shimmy out of her shorts when her fingernail snagged on a loose thread.

This, in and of itself, wasn't extraordinary. Like the rest of her, Amber's fingernails were neglected and fraying, belonging more to an anxious teenager than a grown woman who had any right to wear green silk. But once the thread started pulling, it didn't stop. Her initial feeling of dread—how on earth would she explain this to Camille?—quickly gave way to one of suspicion.

"Since when do thousand-dollar couture gowns fall apart at the slightest touch?"

Amber's brow furrowed as she flipped the dress inside out and began to examine the seams. Sure enough, the stitching was shoddy, with several bits of string hanging loose and the label slightly askew. Hanging the dress back up and hoping its frayed state wouldn't be noticed, she started examining the rest of the clothes.

Upon first glance, everything Camille owned looked as gorgeous and expensive as the woman herself. But like so many things around this retirement community, the glamor only went surface-deep. Some of the clothes were genuinely good fabrications, but others—like a dress labelled Ferianii with one too many *i*s or a pair of heels cheekily named Jimmy Shooes—weren't even pretending to be anything but what they were.

Cheap knockoffs. A false front. *Lies.*

"It's not possible," Amber breathed. "Camille is a woman of taste. Of *class.*"

On a hunch, Amber put the closet back into a semblance of order and dashed out to the living room. She chose the first piece of artwork at random—a colorful pop-art piece that looked like either a mountain or a city street, depending on which way you looked at it—and lifted it off the wall. Running her fingers over the frame, she popped it out only to find she wasn't holding the solid canvas of an actual painting but a flimsy reproduction, similar to the kind found in museum gift shops.

In fact, as she peered closer at it, she realized it *was* from a museum gift shop—and she would know. For most of her life, her own walls had been adorned with cheaply framed cutouts from calendars, a hack she'd learned in her late teens and had found so helpful that she'd stuck with the habit.

But that didn't make any sense. That was what *broke* people did.

Broke people who are trying desperately to give the illusion that they're anything but. Broke people who might even be so desperate that they'll steal a three-million-dollar ring to avoid owning the truth.

With shaking hands, Amber started checking the rest of the artwork only to find more of the same.

Cheap poster.

Printed reproduction.

A vase that still bore the unmistakable "Made in Bangladesh" sticker on the inside.

The implication of her findings was so overwhelming that Amber dug into her pocket and pulled out her phone. And then she called the last person on the face of the planet she'd ever thought she'd turn to for help.

"Look, Amber. If this is about Grandma Judith, I should warn you that Mom already told us we're forbidden from giving you any bail money," Derek said as soon as he picked up the phone. "Not that I have any to give you, anyway. Both of the twins are in select sports leagues this year. Do you have any idea how much hockey gear costs?"

"No, and I don't care." Amber's voice was curt, but that was pretty much *always* the case whenever she talked to one of her brothers. "And stop pretending like you're some impoverished baron about to lose the family lands. You're a state employee, which means your salary is part of the public record. I've known exactly how much you and Chrissy make every year since you graduated from college."

"What? That can't be right. You're making it up."

She sighed and pinched the bridge of her nose. She had neither the time nor the energy to explain to her brother how government transparency worked. Camille could return any minute to find her home in tatters. "Do you still have those Chanel hand towels in your guest bathroom?"

Derek gave a grunt of dissatisfaction. "For the last time, Amber, it's not that hard to understand. We've explained it countless times. The top drawer has plenty of nice—"

"That's not what I'm calling about," she said. Derek, whose well-paid governmental job consisted of, as far as she could tell, endless meetings over which he presided without interruption, would go on forever if she gave him a chance. "I need you to grab one for me and describe it. In explicit detail."

"Um…are you okay? Have you been getting enough fluids down there in Arizona?"

She snorted. "If by *fluids*, you mean vodka and gin, then yes. I'm doing fine. Just do this, okay? I need to check something."

"Mom's really worried about you, you know," he said, but with a distant air that made her think he was making his way to the bathroom in question. "Dad too. They're talking about staging an intervention."

"An intervention for what? Caring too much about my grandmother? Trying to clear the family name when no one else will?"

"What family name? Mom says she doesn't even go by Judith Webb anymore. Hasn't she been married like eleventy billion times?"

"You're missing the point entirely," Amber returned. The sound of a door opening was the only thing keeping her on the line.

"Okay," he said. "I have a towel. What about it?"

Amber hurried to the bathroom and grabbed one of Camille's white and gold embroidered towels. "Describe it to me."

"It's a towel, Amber. You've seen it—*you used it*. It's white. It has gold letters with the forward and backward Cs."

"Okay, but what about the stitching? What color is the thread? What would you say about the texture?"

"Are you sure you wouldn't rather talk to Chrissy about this? She knows more about laundry than I do."

Amber rolled her eyes. Her brothers subscribed so wholly to the division of household gender roles that Derek probably thought he'd be tainted by association. "I trust you to satisfy my curiosity," she said dryly. "Go for it."

"Fine, but you owe me." Derek released a series of muttered grunts before following it up with a curt recitation of facts. "The stitching is like stitching. It's straight. And white."

Amber examined Camille's towel more closely, her finger running up and down a seam that had a few zigzagged sections and a decided yellowing to the thread. "Go on," she urged.

"And I don't know what else! It's soft. And puffy. That's why Chrissy buys them. She says they're the only brand that doesn't get worn down when you wash them."

A final sense of unease flooded through Amber as she turned the towel over and rubbed it on her forearm. She was no textile expert, but that didn't feel like the luxurious nap of a fifty-dollar hand towel. "Could you send me a quick pic of the embroidery?" she asked. "I doubt I'll be able to see much detail, but it's better than nothing."

"What does this have to do with anything?" her brother asked as he followed her instructions.

Sure enough, a photo pinged on her phone. Amber had been right about not being able to see the details, but what she could glimpse was enough— the edges crisp and precise, the gold threads as bright as the day they'd been purchased. These weren't the same hand towels. They weren't even in the same *league* of hand towels.

"It's a clue I'm following up on," Amber said with a frown. "For once, I think I might be in over my head. People have to be pretty desperate to fake fancy hand towels, don't you think?"

Derek offered no reply to this, which was just as well, since Amber had no idea what she was actually asking. Part of her suspected that what she really wanted was a partner she trusted—someone who could discuss the case without being obliquely mysterious or pompously condescending—but she feared the real reason went deeper than that.

I think I mostly just want a friend.

"I gotta go," she said quickly. "Thanks for the help."

"Wait, Amber," he cried before she could hang up the phone. She paused, but it took him a good twenty seconds to speak. "What's she like? Our grandmother, I mean? Is she as bad as Mom always made her out to be?"

Amber wasn't sure why, but Derek's question caused her knees to grow weak. She sank to the toilet seat, the fake towel still clutched in her hand.

"She's beautiful," Amber said, unwilling and unable to lie on this particular subject. "And nice and generous and always hugging me—you have no idea how much. Like she doesn't even have to think about it first."

"Oh," Derek said. Just that—just *oh*. He might have been one of their mother's favored children, but that didn't mean he'd been hugged as a kid any more than the rest of them. "And did she…you know…?"

"Commit an act of murder? Kill one of her closest friends in the whole world?" Amber shot off the questions rapid-fire, but her answer was subdued. "I don't know, Derek. That's what I'm trying to find out."

"Oh. Okay." He cleared his throat. This marked the first time in the entirety of their lives that he seemed to *want* to keep her on the line. "Keep me updated on your progress, okay? And, uh, if there's anything else Mikey and I can do…"

Amber was tempted to ask him for a loan, if only to witness how quickly this whole concerned façade disappeared, but she held her tongue. She was tired of always fighting with her brothers, of setting herself at odds with the people who were supposed to know and love her best. Somewhere in there was an analogy for how humans weren't like tortoises, carrying their homes on their backs with the kind of self-sufficiency that leant itself to centuries of loneliness, but she wasn't about to look too hard for it.

Tatiana deserved better. *Amber* deserved better.

"I'm okay for now, but I'll let you know," she said. Almost as an after-thought, she added, "I'm good at this, Derek. I know you and the family think I'm a waste of space who hasn't earned the right to call herself a

Winslow, but investigation is kind of my thing. And I've got a lot of people down here willing to pitch in and help."

"I know," he said simply. "People always seem to like you. Grandma Judith too, apparently. That's the one thing Mikey and I have never been able to get people to do."

That was when he fulfilled his role and hung up the phone—always the first, and always with an abruptness that made her head spin. For once, however, she wasn't tempted to throw the phone at the nearest wall.

Had she and her brother just had a moment? Had he actually *complimented* her?

She barely had time to digest these revelations when a more unsettled feeling took over. Derek may have just ranged himself on her side, shifting her whole worldview while he did it, but more pressing questions were rapidly taking front and center.

Namely, just how much financial trouble was Camille in…and what the devil was Amber going to do about it?

———

Amber found Julio exactly where she expected him: hard at work manning his security station.

"Well, hello!" he called cheerfully as she strode up to the outer gates, her hands deep in her pockets and her mind just as deep in thought. "To what do I owe the pleasure of a visit? It's not—"

His sudden spike of alarm wasn't lost on Amber, who was quick to reassure him. "No, it's not Grandma. I tried calling the station a few minutes ago, but they had to keep putting me on hold. Not that I think they'd let me talk to her anyway. They won't even let me know how she's doing."

"There, there. I'm sure she's fine." He reached out and awkwardly patted her shoulder. His hand shook slightly, and she noticed that instead of swaggering around with his usual bow-legged stance, he had a stool propped behind him. "Jade isn't the type to let her spirits get dragged down by one little murder charge."

Amber managed a smile, but she doubted that even her bold, sunny grandmother could be comfortable behind bars for longer than a night or two. "Are you sure you should be out here at this time of day?" she asked as she took note of the sheen of sweat covering Julio's brow. "No offense, but you look tired."

"I was going to say the same of you, but I thought it would be rude." Grinning to show he meant no harm, he patted the stool behind him. Amber wished he'd have the sense to rest on it himself, but she didn't want to hurt his feelings, so she sat down.

Besides—she wanted information out of him. As much as she hated to use her tactics on a man who wasn't in the peak of health, she knew that there was no better environment for interrogation than extreme heat and discomfort. She wasn't saying she was willing to resort to *torture*, but she wasn't the one who controlled the climate in Arizona.

"To what do I owe the pleasure of this visit? Don't tell me—you're here to interrogate me. Of all the podcast members, you think *I'm* the one who killed the Admiral." He practically cackled with delight, a sound that disintegrated into his signature wheeze. "Tell me, my dear. How did I do it? And what was my motive? I can hardly wait to hear what you come up with."

"It's a bit early for the big reveal, don't you think? I'm just doing what Horace Horatio would want me to do—following the money trail."

Julio's eyes lit up. "Yes! Excellent! What else?"

She refused to let herself be swayed by his enthusiasm. "Well, you're the podcast accountant, so you tell me. I looked it up online and found that you get about fifty thousand downloads a month. Collectively, what did you earn last year?"

"Hmm. That's hard to say." He tapped his teeth in concentration. "Fifty thousand downloads a month *sounds* like a lot, but between the extra fees the retirement community charges us to use the studio, all the work we put in, and the bribes we have to pay to get our hands on the best cases, those numbers don't stretch as far as you'd think."

Despite his apparent focus, Julio's gaze never quite met her own.

"Ballpark it," she suggested. "As a favor to me."

"Then on the grounds of Fenway Park, I'd say we lost about five grand. *Maybe* closer to four. We're still owed an advertisement check from Dinner

Done Easy, but they've been hard to pin down. They weren't happy with the quality of some of our ads."

Amber blinked. "You're telling me the podcast *loses* money?"

"We did almost turn a profit in year two," he said, a touch of defensiveness to his tone. "But that was when we upgraded our recording equipment, so we ended up having to pool our resources. Lucky for us, I had a good run at the casino right before the bill was due."

Amber opened her mouth and closed it again, at a loss to find the right words. She'd heard several people remark on the high cost of living in the retirement community, but she'd assumed that was the usual kind of elderly grumbling—*Back in my day, gas was a dollar a gallon. The economy would improve if kids these days would stop wasting all their money on iPhones. It's one banana, Michael; how much could it cost?*—not that anyone was in genuinely dire circumstances. But if Camille was struggling, and now Julio was too…

"Julio," she said slowly, trying not to sound as alarmed as she felt, "is that why you're always betting on everything? Because you need the money?"

He shook his head, his raspy chuckle filling the air. "Bless you, honey, that's not for *me*. I'm just the bookie. I don't even take a cut."

"Yeah, but—" She wrinkled her brow in concentration. "If you're not gambling for your own sake, then who are you doing it for? My grandma? Or…Camille?"

He straightened to his full five-foot-five height. "A gentleman never tells. But if you're thinking there's anything havey-cavey about what we're doing, you can think again. Our little wagers are no different than Bingo Night up at the main residence. We just like our stakes a little more interesting, that's all."

Amber would have liked to ask a few follow-up questions, but Julio reached out and patted her on the shoulder in a way that was both condescending and dismissive. "Keeping an eye on the money is a good start, Amber. It's what we always do when we crack open a new *Death Comes Calling* case. You let me know if there's anything else I can do to help."

With that, he offered her a mock salute before carefully sliding the door to the security stand shut. Amber thought about demanding more out of the old man, but he was so nonchalant about the way he opened the book he'd been reading—a worn John Grisham paperback—that she felt sure further questioning wouldn't be worth the effort. For whatever reason, he didn't seem particularly concerned that there might be a financial motive to the Admiral's death.

Her steps were slow as she turned back toward Camille's condo. No matter how hard she tried, she couldn't shake the feeling that Julio, like the rest of the podcast group, was hiding something from her.

"I swear, it's almost like they *want* me to find them guilty," she said as her feet scuffed against the now-familiar retirement community pathway.

"*There* you are, babe. Finally."

Bones leaped up from the bottom step of Camille's condo, his expression one of mingled relief and annoyance. The relief she attributed to herself; the annoyance likely belonged to the tortoise still strapped to his chest.

"Where've you been all day? I tried calling you like eight times."

"Sorry. I got caught up following a lead and then turned off my phone in case Derek tried to call me back. I'm not sure I can handle a second conversation with him today."

"Your *brother*? Why would you talk to him? He doesn't give a rat's ass what happens to you or your grandmother."

She sighed and turned her attention to Tatiana. She was tempted to tell Bones about the way Derek had been almost human on the phone, how his curiosity about their grandmother was as lively as her own, but there was no point. Bones had never understood why she tried so hard to maintain a relationship with her family. He'd left his own behind the day he'd turned eighteen and enlisted with the Navy, and as far as she could tell, he'd never once regretted their loss.

"I needed his help," she said. Then, with that furrow still pinched on her brow, she added, "Bones, I don't think Camille is as rich as she lets on. I'm starting to think none of the podcast members are."

"Is this based on evidence or conjecture?"

She tamped down her annoyance at this elementary question—she'd stopped relying on conjecture *years* ago, thank you very much—and focused on the facts. "Julio all but admitted it just now, but there's more to it than that. I searched her walk-in closet earlier today, and it turns out all her clothes are knockoffs."

He snorted. "So she shops the fell-off-a-truck specials. What's the big deal? Lots of people do that."

"So," she repeated with careful emphasis, "that got me looking at the rest of her artwork and décor. Her house is like a museum, but when I—"

"I'm assuming there was no safe in the closet then?" He didn't even wait for her to finish her sentence before unhooking Tatiana from the sling and handing him back to Amber. "Or is this like the time you didn't see the teddy bear nanny cam that was literally right in front of your face at the Ernesto house?"

"Bones, are you listening to a word I'm saying? I had Derek check the hand towels and everything. They're just as fake as the rest."

"Right. Because hand towels are what's going to solve this case." He shook his head the same way her mother did when she was questioning the likelihood of the hospital handing her the wrong baby at birth. "You didn't even look for a safe, did you, babe?"

"I did!" She clutched the tortoise to her chest, drawing comfort from the calm, uninterested stare of the animal. Tatiana would never judge her. Tatiana would never call her *babe* in that condescending way. "Or…I guess it would be more accurate to say that I started to look for one. Only it seemed to me that the more important thing to do was—"

Bones clucked his tongue and stopped himself just short of giving her a pat on the head. "Do you want me to head in there and see if I can find it? I'm still waiting to hear back from that Giles guy at security, so I have some time on my hands." He leaped up and started to head into the condo. "This is what I mean about the two of us making a good team, Amber. You need me to keep your head on straight."

She knew she shouldn't ask. She didn't even want to.

But "And what do you need me for?" escaped her lips anyway.

His grin dawned smug and wide. "Easy. You can keep lookout in case any of those old biddies comes back."

17

"When one door closes, you have no choice
but to open a window...or pick the lock."

—*DEATH COMES CALLING*, SEASON 2 EPISODE 2

AMBER DIDN'T INVITE BONES TO help with the next step of her investigation.

And by *didn't invite*, she meant she slammed the door in his face.

"Can you believe the nerve of him?" she asked the tortoise as she stepped into Camille's living room. She'd been careful to put all the artwork back exactly as it had been before, so the condo looked as pristine as it had when she'd arrived. "Thinking I can't find and open a safe without him there to oversee me. What, like he's a master safecracker? Like there's some major heist operation out there just salivating to get him on their team?"

Tatiana blinked his understanding. The action may have been caused by a wayward speck of dust, but Amber chose to believe that the tortoise was on her side.

"I don't care what he says. The fact that everything in this condo is a fake means something. And I'm not resting until I find out what."

Without pausing too long to consider her actions, Amber dug into her backpack and extracted the hula girl. Driven partly by her lingering irritation with Bones and partly by an innate need to add something real to the space, she set the plastic Tatiana on the mantelpiece next to a miniature female torso sculpture.

The two women looked good next to each other—one lightly swaying as she settled into place and the other eternally raising her marble breasts to the sky—but even more satisfying than the look of the hula girl was Amber's ironclad belief that Bones would never notice her sitting there.

"He thinks *I'm* the one who doesn't notice the clues that are right in front of me?" she asked the tortoise with a huff. "We'll just see about that. I'm tired of him always underestimating me."

The tortoise blinked again, but there was something different about it this time. Something *knowing*.

"You and I have a lot in common, huh?" she asked as she lightly tickled the tortoise's chin in the way he was growing to like. "We might not look like much, and we might get lost for months at a time, but we'll be around long after the rest of the world falls away."

Tatiana yawned in reply, which seemed about right for the way Amber's day was going. Even the animal completely dependent on her for survival wasn't interested in what she had to say.

Since she had no idea when Camille would return and make her search impossible, she set the tortoise on the ground and left him free to roam the condo while she made a beeline for the walk-in closet.

If there *was* a safe inside that room, it was hidden in such a way that Amber couldn't find it. The same was true of the rest of the condo. No matter how many paintings she peeked behind or how many floorboards she tested with her feet to look for a loose panel, there was no sign of anything out of the ordinary.

Granted, Camille could easily have a safe deposit box somewhere, or even be carrying the Admiral's ring on her person, but—

"Hello? Is anyone home?" The front door slammed shut, startling Amber out of her ruminations. "Amber, are you here?"

There was nothing in Camille's voice to suggest that she was the least bit worried about Amber having free rein over her home, so she pushed aside as many of her suspicions as she could and went to join the older woman in the living room. She also stopped short when she saw what Camille was holding.

"I hope you don't mind, but I did a touch of shopping today. I hate for you to have keep running around in your grandmother's castoffs—Lord knows I love the woman, but she dresses like a teenager who stole her daddy's credit card for the first time." A gold-edged shopping bag bearing the name "Coral Boutique" was thrust unceremoniously at her. "Go ahead. Try it all on. The receipt's in the bag if you need to exchange sizes or if it's not quite your style. But I do have an eye for these things, so I think you'll like what I chose."

Amber didn't doubt it when she peeked inside the bag to find a sage-green romper in her exact size, as well as several tank tops to go under it. A new swimsuit, a few breezy button-downs, some linen shorts, and a lace-tiered skirt completed the summer wardrobe of her dreams.

"You got all this for me?" Amber asked. She surreptitiously peeked at the receipt to find a total well over the four-hundred-dollar mark. "Camille, I can't possibly accept—"

"Oh, go on then. I don't have any grandchildren of my own to spoil." Camille clucked and shooed Amber in the direction of the guest room. To look at her, with her pleased smile and crisp white palazzo pants, you'd think she was just a wealthy older woman doing a good deed for the day. But Amber knew better.

She can't afford this, but she's doing it anyway. For my grandmother. For me.

"Have you had any dinner?" Camille called as Amber slipped into her room and started to change. "I was thinking we could grab some salads at the café and eat them poolside with a nice bottle of prosecco. The sun should be setting in half an hour or so."

That sounded exactly like what Amber wanted to do, and the romper she slipped on felt exactly like what she wanted to wear. To be seen so thoroughly—and so generously—made her feel like the worst traitor known to mankind.

Tatiana must have shared her sentiments, because the tortoise crawled out from under the bed and looked up at her with a fixed, disapproving stare.

"I know," Amber said as she dropped to the floor and put herself eye to eye with the animal, her chin propped on her hands. "I should take this all back tomorrow. I should move out of this condo and stay in the hotel with Bones. I should—"

The tortoise turned around, as uninterested in Amber's thoughts as Bones had been. The insult of being rejected by a reptile might have been the straw that broke her back, but as the tortoise meandered out of her view, she was left looking at a shoebox in the dead center of the floor underneath the bed.

"Wait a minute…" Before reaching for it, Amber turned her gaze on the tortoise. Tatiana did nothing more than look back at her before continuing on his way, but Amber could have sworn there was a flash of wisdom in that ancient, grizzled gaze of his. She was reminded forcibly of his random appearance outside the steak house.

"Don't tell me you really *are* good luck," she said and snagged the box before giving the tortoise a chance to answer.

Not that she needed the animal to tell her what she was looking at. As she lifted the lid and peered inside, it was to have all her suspicions come slamming into her at once.

There, nestled in crinkled fleur-de-lis tissue paper, sat the most enormous tangle of jewelry that Amber had ever seen. Only instead of the sentimental locket and costume jewelry of her own grandmother's collection, this stuff looked incredibly expensive.

And incredibly real.

If there was one nice thing about investigating a murder in a retirement community where everyone was a suspect, it was the opportunity to research while Amber worked on her tan.

She felt guilty about putting on the white cutout swimsuit that Camille had bought yesterday, and even guiltier when she saw how fantastic it looked on her, but she assuaged her conscience with the promise that she'd only turn her grandmother's friend in if she found concrete evidence of her guilt.

"It's not like the Admiral's ring was in the box," she told Tatiana as she carried the tortoise to a lounge chair shaded by one of the oversized red and white umbrellas. "Those jewels could be family heirlooms for all I know. Or gifts from Camille's past lovers. I bet she's had her fair share of those."

Even as she spoke, she knew she didn't believe her own words. People didn't store heirlooms in cardboard boxes under their beds, and they didn't hide expensive gifts from past lovers and then walk around wearing head-to-toe designer knockoffs.

Not *innocent* people, anyway.

"Okay. Let's do this." She made sure Tatiana was comfortably situated in the shade before pulling out her phone. She hadn't much time to investigate the jewelry hoard last night, but she had taken a quick picture of the box's contents. It would have to be enough. "You click at me if you suspect anything's up, okay, Tatiana? I'm counting on you to be my eyes and ears."

Tatiana didn't click, but he did turn and stare balefully at her.

"Don't worry." She reached over and tickled the tortoise's chin. "I'll sign any training paperwork you want me to afterwards. Unlike *some* people, I'm fully aware that I couldn't do this without you."

She glanced quickly around the pool to make sure she was alone before pulling up the Admiral's Facebook page. She doubted she'd find an inventory of all the jewelry he'd owned in his lifetime on there, but it seemed as good a place to start as any.

At first glance, his social media bore all the usual hallmarks of a man who'd come into his prime in the 1970s. Boomer jokes about how hard it was to get out of bed, holiday well-wishes, and several dozen photos of Tatiana made up the bulk of his content. She lost a good fifteen minutes oohing and aahing over pictures of the tortoise in various costumes—how on earth had the Admiral gotten that cowboy hat to stay on Tatiana's head?—before it dawned on her that she'd seen nothing of his children.

According to his social media, the Admiral was a man who liked tortoise rescues and pastrami sandwiches. He always rooted for the Navy in the annual Army versus Navy football game, was endlessly planning a trip to Hawaii that never seemed to materialize, and had yet to meet a spy thriller he didn't love.

But there was nothing about his kids. No pictures. No messages. No pokes.

"That's either very weird or very sad," Amber said as she moved on to the next phase of her research. "But it doesn't look like he was much of a diamonds-and-emeralds man. I doubt Camille took any of that jewelry from him."

The question now became whether or not she'd gotten the jewelry from anyone *else* at the retirement community. And there was only one place where that information was sure to be found.

The Nextdoor app took a few seconds to load, but any reservations Amber might have had about it being a hotbed of activity disappeared the moment she saw how many updates there'd been since the last time she checked it.

> Has anyone else noticed how nice it is around here now that Jade McCallan is gone?

Even though that *wasn't* the rabbit hole she was looking for, she jumped in anyway. Especially when she noticed the name of the person responsible for that and several follow-up posts: ConcernedCitizen1443.

> I heard that granddaughter of hers is poking her nose around where she doesn't belong. Watch out. She's probably trying to pin the murder on someone else. You could be next.

"Well, that's rude," Amber said. "I'm a professional. I'd never do anything like that."

> That whole group has been nothing but trouble since the podcast started.

> What do you want to bet they killed the Admiral on purpose for ratings?

> They probably already sold the miniseries rights to some big hotshot TV producer.

> Oooh, they should get Angelica Houston to play Jade. I've always thought they looked alike.

NOT HELPING, BOOBOOGMA87.

One by one, cruel messages continued to fill the feed. It wasn't until one member—Hawkeye93, to be exact—stepped in to support BooBooGma87 that Amber started to realize she wasn't *entirely* alone.

I think we can all agree that we'd want an Amber of our own if we found ourselves being charged with murder. Cut her a little slack.

Amber was so surprised by this unexpected championship from Ethan that she didn't notice the looming shadow overhead until it was too late.

"If you were planning on hanging out by the pool all day, you could have at least called to invite me." The looming shadow materialized into an equally looming Bones. With the sun directly behind him, it was impossible to make out the expression on his face, but Amber could hear the annoyance from here. "I take this to mean you didn't find the safe last night?"

Amber's own annoyance surged, but she was too desperate for a sounding board to tell him off the way she longed to.

"Stop being such a baby and sit down," she hissed. "But be careful of Tatiana. He's not feeling well this morning."

"It's probably all the chlorine that's upsetting him," Bones grumbled, but he did as she asked, even pausing to give the tortoise a light pat as he went. He also paused to give Amber's reposing form a thorough once-over, his gaze lingering on the cutout portions of the swimsuit. "Damn, Amber. Are you setting a honey trap? Should I come back later?"

"I don't *just* show skin for the sake of the job, you know," she snapped, though not without a slight flush of pleasure. Murderess, jewel thief, or not, Camille definitely knew her swimwear. "And before you ask, it isn't for you either. Here. Take a look at this and tell me what you think."

She pulled up the photo of the jewelry on her phone and shoved it at him.

"I didn't find a safe, but I found the next best thing. Does this stuff look as real to you as it does to me?"

Bones pursed his lips and blew out a long whistle. "I'd have to get my hands on it to say for sure, but even a fake stone of that size would be worth something. You're telling me this was sitting in the old broad's condo?"

"Her name is Camille, and yes. I was just looking on the Nextdoor app to see if anyone has reported any missing jewelry."

"And?"

"And I hadn't gotten that far when you interrupted me."

She snatched her phone back before Bones could "accidentally" close out the app and start snooping around the rest of her content. Then she said the one thing that had been bothering her most since she discovered the box of jewelry.

"Bones, what if Camille stole all this stuff? What if it's, like, a compulsion or something? Would she really have killed one of her closest friends just to get her hands on more?"

She took her lower lip between her teeth as she waited for the reply. As much as she hated to admit it, she needed his reassurance right now—the detached, almost careless way he treated crime and criminals as just part of the world they all inhabited. She didn't *want* Camille to be guilty. She didn't want any of her grandmother's friends to be guilty.

They'd given her a home when she didn't have one, furnished her with clothes when her own supply ran out, and made sure she remembered to eat. They were stand-in parents and grandparents to someone who'd never known much of either, friends just when she needed them most.

"Please," she practically begged. "Give me a rational explanation for all this."

Bones must have sensed the desperation in her voice because he relaxed into the lounge chair. As this also included him propping his massive arms behind his head and stretching all six feet four inches of his body until his every muscle popped, she sensed a double motive.

"I already told you that you're reading too much into this whole financial motive," he said. "Unless your grandmother's friends were hired to take a hit out on the old guy or got themselves listed as the beneficiaries on his life insurance policy, I don't see why they'd have resorted to murder. There are a lot easier ways to get your hands on a man's fortune."

Amber sat up and pulled her sunglasses down from her eyes. "Say that again?"

"I dunno, babe. You keep going on about this missing ring like it's a reason to kill someone, but if he was part of their friend group, wouldn't they have just asked him for a loan instead? Besides, didn't you say your grandma could have married the guy at any point?" He shrugged. "I think we need to consider a different motive. Unless this Admiral of yours knew who took the ring and was about to turn them in, why would anyone have gone to the trouble of killing him over it?"

"Bones!" Amber gasped.

"What?" He made a big show of glancing around them as if looking for a bad guy hiding in the shrubbery. "What's got you so worked up all of a sudden?"

"That's it. That's the motive. You figured it out." Amber was so delighted with Bones—and with herself—that she threw her arms around him. She might have kissed him too, but there was *far* too much of her skin showing to make that a wise choice.

Amber forced herself to take a deep breath and lean back.

"I can't believe I didn't think of it before," she said. "Especially since I caught Nasty Nancy stealing a tablet from a patient's desk yesterday."

"Nasty Nancy?" he echoed. "That's not a very nice thing to call someone."

"Yeah, well. She's not a very nice person." Amber leaped to her feet and began pacing the length of the pool. "It makes perfect sense. For all we know, she's been stealing from the residents for *years*. She wouldn't want to give up a cash cow like that without a fight. If the Admiral caught her in the act and threatened to go to Geerta, she may have decided to do away with him. She'd know about the late hours they kept at the podcast studio, so it would be easy for her to wait until he was alone in there to pounce. And—oh!" Her steps picked up. "She's a nurse, so she'd know exactly which cocktail of drugs would kill him. *Enough to fell a horse*, the lawyer said. Only he fought back, and someone overheard them."

She came to a sudden halt in front of Bones.

"Please tell me you were able to get your hands on those security tapes," she said. "If we could place her near the studio that night, even if she was just walking by or scoping it out…"

"Oh, I got the tapes, all right. That's why I'm here so early. I came to see Giles."

"And?" Amber practically vibrated with excitement.

"They were wiped clean."

The vibrations stopped. So did her frantic pacing. "What do you mean, *wiped clean*? As in, someone erased the copy they have here at the facility? Or the one they turned over to the police?"

He looked almost pleased to be the bearer of such bad tidings. He splayed his hands helplessly, the span of his reach like that of a predatory bird. "I mean *all* of them."

Each word felt like the nail in a coffin closing around her theory.

"Giles told me the same thing he told the police. From the hours of seven p.m. to seven a.m., there's not a single, solitary thing to see. Your Nasty Nancy must have gotten to the tapes first."

18

"What's a little light larceny between friends?"

—*DEATH COMES CALLING*, SEASON 5 EPISODE 3

IT TOOK SOME DOING TO convince Bones to let her stalk Nancy on her own, but Amber managed it by promising to meet him for dinner at a restaurant of his choosing later that night.

The last thing Amber wanted to do was watch Bones work his way through an enormous rib eye while her grandmother sat in a jail cell eating whatever bland, beige meal she was served, but she was equally loath to have him skulking at her back while she spied on the nurse.

If she wanted to confront, Nancy, yes. Bones would be a sure asset. Ditto if she wanted to take the woman down a notch or two.

But this was a moment for finesse. For *intrigue*.

"Should I ask why you're lying on a hospital bed with a fake IV attached to your arm, or is this one of those situations where it's better if I don't know?"

At the sound of Ethan's voice, Amber let out a squeak. Her hand dashed out from under the sheet she'd pulled up to her nose and gripped him tightly around the wrist. "If you blow my cover, Ethan, so help me…" Realizing that it was bad form to physically assault a man who was recovering from a hip replacement, she loosened her grip just as quickly. "Sorry. I keep forgetting."

"You know, that might be the nicest thing you've said to me yet." He angled his body closer to the head of the bed to shield her from view. "There.

Much better. That hair of yours is recognizable from across the room. If you didn't want anyone to notice you, you should have put on a wig. Or at the very least, one of Raffi's toupees."

Amber choked on a laugh. She didn't love that Ethan had managed to see through her cover so quickly—she'd really thought no one would think twice to look at one of the many beds lining the hallway—but her sense of humor won out over dismay.

"I would never insult Raffi by letting him know that we can tell his hair is fake," she said. "But while you're here, could you scoot me closer to the nurses' station? I'm waiting for Nancy to get back from break."

"You want me to assist in a crime? In the place where I'm supposed to be resting and recovering? To help you spy on a woman who's been nothing but good to me?"

"Um, yes?"

"Sure. I'm not busy with anything else." With a playful whistle, he transferred his hold from the walker to the railing at the foot of the bed. Gripping it with both hands, he began slowly nudging her down the hall. "Don't tell me Nancy is the latest suspect in your quest for vengeance. I can tell you right now that it won't end well for you."

It took all of Amber's self-control not to sit bolt upright in the bed. "How do you know about that?"

From her angle on the pillow, she thought she could detect a wry twist to Ethan's lips, but it might have been her imagination. "Nancy told me all about finding you skulking around the memory ward. That makes your suspect either her, Dr. Lopez, or one of the residents currently being kept under lock and key. I might not be as sharp an investigator as your, ah, Bones, but I can pick the best candidate out of that lineup."

She didn't miss the way his voice wavered over the phrase *your, ah, Bones* and suddenly felt all the shame of her current predicament—lying in a hospital bed so she could spy on a nurse, dragging around an ex-boyfriend who was as subtle as a battering ram, befriending a contrary veterinarian and forcing him to participate in her schemes.

"Bones isn't *my* anything. I broke up with him weeks ago."

"I'm sure you did."

"I'm serious. He followed me here."

"He seems like the type."

"It's true! And I'd be just as happy never to see him again, only he does have a lot of experience with this sort of thing. And with my grandma behind bars..."

The bed came to a sudden halt. "There's no need to explain yourself to me, Winslow. I'm here as nothing more than a spectator with too much time on his hands. What's the endgame, by the way? Are we hoping to catch Nancy in the act of confessing her murder to one of the other nurses? Or is this merely an information-gathering escapade?"

"You don't have to make it sound like a dime novel," Amber muttered, but she realized Ethan had a point. "I was hoping to witness her in her natural environment, that's all. Get a feel for her routines and habits."

"Like Dian Fossey and her gorillas," Ethan agreed blandly. "Very wise."

Amber felt that choking laughter start to bubble up again, but she forced it back down where it belonged. "If you're only going to make sarcastic comments the whole time, you might as well—"

But the suggestions she had for Ethan, most of which weren't polite in nature, would forever remain unspoken. With a quick yank of the sheet over Amber's head, Ethan hissed, "Quick. She's coming. Look dead."

Amber had to physically bite down on her lip to keep from ruining her cover, especially when she heard Ethan call out in a friendly voice he'd never once used with her, "Ah, Nancy. There you are. I've been looking for you everywhere."

"Ethan! What are you doing out of bed? You know how exhausted you get after physical therapy. I thought we agreed you'd stick to juice boxes and *The Price Is Right* until the doctor's happy with your bone ingrowth."

Amber thought she could detect a note of annoyance in Ethan's voice as he replied, but he proved himself equal to the task of investigative wingman. "You've done such a good job taking care of me that I figured a few extra laps around the halls couldn't hurt," he said. "Are you just getting back from your lunch break?"

"Yes, and I—"

"Excuse me? You there? Are you the nurse I'm supposed to talk to about clearing out my father's condo? Because I've called three times already, and no one has even been in there to take away his dirty laundry."

Amber stiffened as the sound of Michelle Vincent's overly loud, overly demanding voice flooded the hallway.

"Honestly, it makes me wonder why we even bothered to pay so much for my father to live here. Geerta assured me that someone on staff would box everything up for us. My brother and I are *grieving*. We can't possibly do it ourselves."

"I've been meaning to get to it, but it's not my usual job," Nancy said, and in such a placating, wheedling sort of voice that Amber almost felt sorry for her. "Most families prefer to go through their loved one's belongings by themselves."

"Yes, well. Are most of those families dealing with the death of their loved one at the hands of another resident? Because I feel like that makes this case a little more pressing than most." There was a brief, uncomfortable pause. "Well? And who are you supposed to be?"

"The name is Ethan," came the dry response. "Ethan Adler. You must be the Admiral's daughter."

Michelle snorted. "*The Admiral.* I don't know why he was allowed to give himself that ridiculous name—or why anyone who works here was fool enough to play along with it. He only saw the ocean once in his whole life. Surely, given his condition, you should've known better than to—"

"Now, now." Nancy gave a cluck of her tongue, stopping the other woman short. "There's no need to get upset. We do whatever we can to make the residents feel at home here. Isn't that right, Ethan?"

"It's been like a tropical vacation from the start," he agreed. Even though Amber couldn't see him, she knew he was probably wearing his most mysterious, difficult-to-pin-down expression. "But if all you're looking for is someone to go through your father's house and box everything up, I might be able to help."

"You?" Michelle's disbelief practically made its own sound waves. "But you're…crippled."

"You noticed that, did you?" Ethan replied in a tone so dry that Amber could practically feel the static electricity starting to build up under the sheet. "Don't worry. The guy I have in mind is a lot more robust than me. He makes John Cena look like a wishbone."

"Is that supposed to be a joke? Because in case you haven't heard, my father was recently *murdered*. Forgive me for not finding it in me to laugh."

"It's not a joke. He's a…friend. He's visiting for a few weeks, and I'm sure he wouldn't mind putting a few of his muscles to good use. Believe me—he has more than any one person needs." Ethan hesitated. "Unless you'd rather wait until Nancy or one of the orderlies can get to it? Like she said, it's not their usual job. It could take a while before they can go through everything."

Amber held her breath as she realized what was happening—and what it would mean if Ethan could actually get Michelle Vincent to agree. Unfettered access to the Admiral's condo, a chance to go through his things at their own leisure. It was almost too good to be true.

"I'm not paying you," Michelle snapped.

"We wouldn't ask you to. Not considering everything you're dealing with."

Her voice started to sound more mollified. "And we'd like you to inventory everything. We've already gone through and taken anything of value—at least the things that weren't stolen by that horrible woman who killed him—but we still need a precise record. For the estate lawyers, you understand."

"I think we can find it in us to manage that."

"And if you see so much as a hint of that ring, we'd like to be notified *immediately*."

As if aware that any mention of the missing ring would cause a spasmodic reaction, Ethan's hand fell to Amber's lower leg and pressed down on it. "That's fine by me," he said slowly, "but forgive me for asking… I thought the lady who went to jail is the one stole it. Isn't that the whole reason she was arrested?"

"Oh, well. You know how these things are. The police haven't technically found it in her possession yet."

Nancy interjected, a sneer discernible in her voice. "Don't you worry, Ms. Vincent. They'll find it, all right. If there's one thing I know in this world, it's that Jade McCallan isn't worth the spit on a camel's back. She's got it hidden somewhere."

It was a good thing Ethan was still holding on to her leg because Amber almost gave everything away in that moment. Her grandmother was worth a dozen Nasty Nancys, and she'd have been delighted to inform the kleptomaniacal nurse of that to her face.

"So you think the ring might still be around Seven Ponds somewhere?" Ethan asked as though his fingers weren't digging five deep impressions into Amber's calf. "You haven't given up hope of finding it?"

"Dad wouldn't have sold it without telling us," Michelle firmly. "That was his mother's ring—and her mother's before her. She brought it over to America in the hem of the only dress she owned. It meant everything to him."

Ethan wasn't ready to let the subject drop. "So if we find it, does that mean Jade McCallan *isn't* a murderer? That this whole thing has been a terrible misunderstanding?"

Nancy sniffed loudly. "I think you're forgetting the drugs used to poison that poor man—and the fact that it was *her* podcast studio that was torn apart and *her* house where they found the forged power of attorney forms with his name on them."

Amber didn't hear the rest of the conversation. That it continued, she knew from the voices that carried on over her head. That it involved her grandmother, she knew from the way Ethan didn't let up his grip on her by so much as an inch. But her thoughts were too preoccupied with the mention of the legal forms for her to focus on anything else.

The day he'd searched the condo, Officer Peyton had mentioned those exact same forms: *Just a few prescriptions in the medicine cabinet and some legal documents worth taking a look at.* At the time, she'd been afraid it had been the Admiral's will he was talking about, but a power of attorney was just as bad.

Especially if it was in any way forged.

"Thanks again for taking care of this for me," Michelle said, eventually drawing Amber back to a sense of her surroundings. "And your strapping young friend will get started as soon as possible? My brother and I are putting up at the Hilton, but he has to fly back to New York next week. I'm sure you understand."

"My strapping young friend will be delighted," Ethan promised. He finally let go of Amber's leg. "Nancy, will you take me back to my room? I think you were right about overexerting myself. *The Price Is Right* and juice boxes sound like heaven right about now."

Since Amber felt fairly certain that no grown man had ever used the words *juice boxes* and *heaven* in a sentence before, she suspected Ethan was giving her a chance to escape from the bed without anyone seeing her. She waited until she could no longer hear the squeak of Nancy's shoes before poking her head out from under the sheet, ensuring the coast was clear, and hightailing it out of there.

She would have joined Ethan in his room, too, only when she cruised by, he was sitting upright in his bed, patiently sipping apple juice while Nancy bustled around the room putting everything in order around him.

Pausing just long enough to catch Ethan's eye and make a face at him— one he returned in kind—she headed out of the facility and toward Camille's condo. She could hardly hold a postmortem of the conversation with Ethan while his protector hovered nearby.

Besides, one of them was going to have to break it to Bones that he was officially charged with the task of sorting through the Admiral's condo— and since Bones enjoyed tedious grunt work about as much as he did paperwork—she was guessing that someone would have to be her.

19

"The first time I ever set foot inside a prison cell, I realized the goal wasn't to contain, but to control."

—*DEATH COMES CALLING*, SEASON 2 EPISODE 2

AT DINNER LATER THAT NIGHT, Amber was surprised to find Bones not only willing to search the Admiral's house for signs of the ring or any other clues that might help free her grandmother, but downright *eager*.

"Finally. A chance to get my hands dirty," he said as he rubbed said appendages over the fourteen-ounce rib eye she'd known he'd order. Since it was late in the evening and they'd chosen to eat at the retirement community steak house, they had the whole place to themselves. "I'll get started first thing tomorrow. Your little friend will help?"

"Ethan and I will *both* help," she replied firmly. Her much more normal-portion-sized halibut sat untouched in front of her, and even though she kept dangling bits of decorative parsley and kale under the table, Tatiana remained equally uninterested in all things culinary.

Only Bones, it seemed, could sit in a steak house and chew loudly while a woman's life hung in the balance.

"We wouldn't have gotten the key and a full-access pass without Ethan," Amber added as Bones stabbed his steak, sawed off a piece, and started chewing. "But I'm afraid you two will have to get started without me. They're finally letting me in to the jail to see my grandma tomorrow morning. I'll have to join you as soon as I'm done."

Which was why, at the bright and early hour of nine o'clock the next morning, she found herself sitting in the police station. Bones hadn't been pleased at the prospect of spending a few hours of quality time with a man he'd called, in no particular order, Ewan, Egan, Easton, *and* Evan, but since she'd threatened to take Tatiana with her on today's visit, he'd eventually relented.

"You can't take a tortoise to jail!" he'd exclaimed as he'd curled a protective hand around the animal. "They'll probably think you're smuggling something inside his shell and tear him apart looking for it."

Now that Amber was here, however, she wished she hadn't used Tatiana as a bribe. She'd been inside several county jails before, but only in the professional sense. Sitting under the flickering fluorescent lights and waiting for her turn to be led into the back was a lot more emotionally draining than she'd expected. She could have used the tortoise's comforting presence.

And when Officer Katz led her through to the small room where her grandmother was waiting, she felt the lack of an emotional support tortoise even more. All of a sudden, she had no idea what she was supposed to do with her hands.

"Amber! How nice and tan you're looking. I hope you've been enjoying your time in the sun." Her grandmother rose to her feet at Amber's entrance, her own hands spread wide in invitation. Amber looked quickly at Officer Katz, who colored and nodded once. Nothing more was needed for Amber to cross the room and fall into her grandmother's arms.

"They told me very sternly that I wasn't allowed to hug you or whisper secrets in your ear, but I couldn't resist," her grandmother said—*whispered*, even. "They're quite accommodating once you get to know them." Louder, and above Amber's head, she added, "Officer Katz, in particular, has been very good at making sure I have everything I need. Did you know that he was almost the arresting officer for the Sleepwalking Killer? How fascinating that must have been."

"Nasty business," Officer Katz agreed. "Very gruesome."

Amber felt an overwhelming urge to cry as her grandmother let her go and they both took their seats on opposite sides of a long wood-grain table. Although Jade *looked* wan, her hair hanging in dank locks around her face and bags under her eyes the size of suitcases, her spirits seemed to be fully intact.

"Why, child. What's the matter with you?" her grandmother asked as Amber struggled to contain herself. "Never say they kicked you out of Seven Ponds. I made sure Camille would take you in."

"She did. She has." Amber sniffled and wiped at her eyes with the back of her hand. She was even wearing one of Camille's outfits, her stomach full of Camille's breakfast and Camille's borrowed car outside. If her hostess was trying to divert suspicion by being the kindest and most generous person in existence, then it was working. "It's not that. You just look so…tired."

What she meant to say—and what her grandmother read between the lines—was that she looked *old*. Instead of the bright, bouncing woman who defied the laws of nature with her smile, Jade very much appeared to be what she was: a woman in her seventies who was sleeping in the same room as her toilet.

"I'm afraid that's because I'm not wearing my lipstick," her grandmother said apologetically. "You must have noticed by now that I'm never without it. Nothing shows one's age as much as the lips. They're always the first to fade."

Amber heard the sound of shuffling footsteps and a discreet cough as Office Katz left them to their visit. "Just going to grab a soda," he said in a loud, overly enunciated voice that had clearly been rehearsed ahead of time. "No breaking laws while I'm gone."

"Bless you, Officer Katz." Her grandmother blew him a kiss before turning a wink on Amber. "You see? I've learned a thing or two from you. I'm old enough to be that man's grandmother, but he still eats up flattery like it's a Hostess cupcake."

Amber dashed her arms across the table and clasped her grandmother's hand. "Grandma, don't. You don't have to pretend with me."

Her grandmother blinked at her. "Judging by the expression on your face, you'd think I was sitting on death row. Don't worry so much, child. Women my age don't get sentenced to death. We remind the judges too much of their own mothers."

"That's not funny." Amber sniffled. "How can you sit there being so blasé? This is a *murder* charge we're talking about. If they convict you, it could mean prison for the rest of your life."

Not even this could cause her grandmother to quail. She rubbed her thumbs soothingly over the backs of Amber's hands—yet another of those unthinking, loving gestures that seemed to come so easily to the woman. "Why are you in such a pucker? Aren't you and the group making headway with the case? I felt sure you'd have come up with a list of likely suspects by now."

It hadn't been Amber's intention to tell her grandmother about any of the discoveries they'd made thus far, but she should have known better. Jade McCallan wasn't a woman to shy away from the truth, however unpleasant it might be.

That was yet another trait they had in common. Her mother might hide her true self behind a veil of respectability, but Amber was and always would be exactly what she appeared.

"We have, but you aren't going to like it," she said.

"Try me."

"Fine. Then name the people in your podcast group."

Her grandmother's hands twitched, but she did as Amber asked. "Me, Raffi, Lincoln, Julio, Camille, and Peggy Lee."

"Then there's your list."

Her grandmother gave a short laugh. "Surely not *all* of them. Raffi and Peggy Lee weigh less than a sack of potatoes each, and Julio can't even make it to the end of the block without an oxygen tank."

"All of them," Amber repeated. She took her hands back and shoved them under the table. "We sat down and had a whole discussion about it. They're the only ones with keys to the podcast studio, and as you'll recall, the door had been locked behind the Admiral the night of his death."

"And no one has ever made a copy of those keys, I'm sure," her grandmother said in a tone of voice that sounded so much like Amber's mother that she almost gasped.

She *didn't* gasp, but her voice was strongly on the defensive as she added, "I'm also following a few promising leads on Nasty Nancy. I don't have anything concrete to tie her to the murder yet, but I'm working on it."

A crack of her grandmother's sudden laughter filled the air. "I like that much better! Tell me more. How did Nancy do it? And why? I can't wait to hear what story you come up with."

This sounded so much like what the podcast group had said—that one of them being the murderer made for great writing, that their ratings were sure to shoot through the roof—that Amber felt herself bristling even more.

"I'm not writing a *story*, Grandma. I'm solving a crime. You do realize those are two different things, right? And that your life hangs in the balance?"

Her grandmother waved her off as though she'd mentioned something as mundane as the Roman Empire. "Let's keep the focus on Nancy for now. That whole Nurse Ratched vibe is all the rage. Can't you just see her mug shot? That perm of hers wouldn't hold up three days in a place like this. The shampoo is straight lye."

Amber briefly wondered if this was what it was like to have a toddler: the attention span of a gnat, no concern for their own well-being, and a tendency to miss the thing that was sitting right in front of them.

"Grandma, I need you to take this seriously—to take *me* seriously. I can only help you if you're honest with me. All of this lying and intentionally being mysterious has to stop."

Her grandmother sat back in her seat with a blink. "Well, really. When have I ever lied to you?"

Since Amber was unable to pinpoint an *exact* lie, she didn't answer. She did, however, double down on her effort to get some actual answers.

"Fine. Then let's start by looking at the podcast group. More specifically, what's the deal with Camille's finances? Her condo is basically an art gallery showroom, but once I started looking around, I noticed that everything in it is a knockoff—the painting and the vases, even the towels in her bathroom. Her wardrobe is the same. Nothing in there is real."

She thought, but didn't add, *Except for the box of jewelry under the bed.*

Amber could immediately tell that she took her grandmother by surprise. A flicker of something that looked like annoyance crossed the older woman's face before settling into a pursing of her lips. "So you picked up on that already, did you?"

"That's not an answer, Grandma."

"Yes, because it's not my story to tell. And, if I'm being frank, it's also none of your business."

Amber fought the urge to drop her head to the table. If she didn't know better, she'd almost think her grandmother *wanted* to go to prison.

To protect someone else? Because she was bored? Or, worst of all, to boost the ratings of a murder podcast that hadn't earned her a dime in all the years she'd been running it?

"Fine." Jade must have sensed Amber's mounting frustration, because she gave in with a sigh. "If you must know, Camille's husband ran off with his much, *much* younger mistress—oh, five or six years ago now. His lawyer had a field day with her, the wretch. Left her with nothing more than the clothes on her back and a pension that barely covers her bills."

"Are you serious?"

"That would be a rather cruel thing to make up, don't you think? It's taken Camille a long time to pull herself together again, though between you and me, she misses the money more than that cad. She buys reproductions to hold on to what she lost, and we pretend not to notice. It works out well for us all that way."

Amber felt the air leaving her lungs. All of a sudden, Camille's immediate and vociferous reaction to Bones made a lot more sense. As someone who'd experienced heartbreak firsthand, she'd been the first to demand answers about what he'd done to cause Amber to flee Seattle, and she'd been equally proactive in making sure Amber was in no way dependent on him for a place to live.

Which was nice, yes, but didn't make her any less of a suspect. Money was a strong motivator, especially when one was used to having plenty of it to spare—and if she was making up the deficit by stealing jewelry, her guilt was even easier to believe.

Amber fingered the lace edges of the skirt Camille had bought for her with a growing sense of unease. "So she's broke?" she persisted.

"We're retirees in an economy that is constantly inflating itself beyond our means. Don't ask silly questions."

"Then what about Julio's gambling addiction?" Amber asked next. "Is he also hurting for money? I asked him about it directly, and all he would say is that he doesn't place the bets for himself. But I don't see who else stands to benefit from—"

"That would be Raffi, alas." Her grandmother heaved a sigh. Although Amber didn't quite trust the older woman's mournful expression, she didn't *not* trust it either. "The two of them used to hit the casino six days out of seven, and it almost ruined the poor man. We keep the gambling between us now—with a few others to sweeten the pot—to make sure he never outruns the grocer."

"*Raffi* is the one with a gambling problem?"

"It's not a problem so much as an itch, and we have it under control," her grandmother said tartly. "And before you ask, Lincoln and his wife are comfortably situated, we suspect Peggy Lee is sitting on top of a secret crypto mine somewhere, and Julio…well. With that heart of his, money is the least of his worries. He had what the doctors call a 'cardiac event' last year, and he's never been the same since."

Amber could hardly believe what she was hearing—only, wait. She *did* believe it. Since the moment she'd arrived at Seven Ponds Retirement Community, she'd sensed something special about her grandmother's pod-cast group. Not just the irreverence of them, but the *heart*. The kind of solidarity they shared, of friends coming together to support one another during their trials, was something that most people only dreamed of.

Amber certainly did. To have found it, and at their age, must have been something wonderful.

"Am I missing anyone?" her grandmother asked, a somewhat sarcastic tilt to her lips. "Any other deep, dark secrets you'd like me to expose?"

Amber had no idea where the next question came from, but it popped out before she could stop it. "What about Mom? What happened between the two of you to make her hate you so much?"

It would have been difficult to say which of them was more surprised to hear the question uttered aloud, but from the way Jade visibly blanched, Amber guessed her grandmother took the honors. Especially when she fol-lowed it up with a brittle laugh.

"Why, child. Whatever do you mean?"

"You know what I mean. When I called to tell her about your arrest, she refused to listen to my explanation. All she would say is that she wouldn't bail you out, and that she warned me how it would be." She paused, the corners of her mouth heavy. "But who says that about their own family? I've never gotten along with Mom, but if she were in trouble—*real* trouble—I'd be there to help her in a hot second. Same with my brothers, even though they've done nothing to deserve it."

Instead of answering her, her grandmother smiled. Actually smiled—a full spread of the lips and genuine pleasure in the pink of her cheeks. "You and your mom are talking again? That's wonderful."

"It. Is. Not. Wonderful." Amber spoke through her teeth. "She's aggravating. You're both aggravating."

"A child's relationship to a parent is such an important thing. Probably *the* most important thing. Witness this whole terrible situation with the Admiral and that silly little ring—as if any amount of money is worth the way those kids treated him. When you talk to your mom again, please send her my love." A light laugh escaped her grandmother. "She'll throw it right back at you, of course, but that won't bother me. I haven't let Effie bother me in a very long time."

With those words, Amber realized their foray into truth was over. Her grandmother may have never lied to her, but she certainly enjoyed being evasive.

Officer Katz returned to the room with a soda in his hand and the throat-clearing sounds of a bird in its death throes. Amber took the hint and got to her feet. Still, she couldn't resist one more attempt to make her grandmother see reason.

"Grandma, who do you think killed the Admiral? You were closer to him than anyone. Surely you must have a theory or two worth investigating."

"I think you're asking the wrong question, child." Her grandmother flashed a winning smile up at her. "Figure out the *why* first. The rest will sort itself out."

Amber could have screamed with frustration as Officer Katz led her out of the room, his plodding steps propelling her forward.

The *why* was that ring. The *why* was money. Nothing else made sense. By all accounts, the Admiral had never hurt anyone a day in his life. He was kind and generous, beloved by many, and so attached to the memory of his maternal ancestors that he valued the ring they'd passed on above all else.

If someone hadn't bumped him off to get their hands on that three million dollars, then what else was there?

"Now, now. S'all right." Officer Katz's hand came crashing down on her shoulder. She could feel the sweat of his palm through the thin fabric of her T-shirt. "Not many old broads can stand up in a place like this, but Jade's made friends of 'em all. Nothing to worry about there."

Amber didn't know why this gave her any relief, but it did. "You'll make sure that she eats? And gets plenty of rest?"

Officer Katz nodded, but not before a ghost of a grimace crossed his face. "Do my best," he promised. "But if I were you, I'd find that missing ring soon. Everyone in here cracks eventually. Hate to see it happen to such a sweet old lady as that."

20

"Oftentimes, it's the clues you don't
see that tell you the most."
—*DEATH COMES CALLING*, SEASON 4 EPISODE 11

AMBER ENTERED THE ADMIRAL'S HOUSE through the back door.

Even though she wasn't *technically* trespassing, she didn't want to risk being seen sneaking in by Geerta or, worse, Nancy Nasty. One of the most important adages of her childhood was that it was better to ask for forgiveness than permission, especially when said permission was almost unilaterally denied.

"Knock knock!" she called as she opened the sliding glass door on the back deck and slipped inside. "Please tell me you've found that ring. Or at the very least, a clue that will lead us to it."

"So I said to the guy, 'If you think this is bad, you should see what happens when I'm *really* angry.'" The sound of Bones's robust voice and even more robust laugh filled the air. "He couldn't get out of the room fast enough after that. At one point, I swear he was actually crabwalking his way out the door."

Amber bit back a groan as she stepped through the living room–kitchen combo—the exact same one in her grandmother's condo—and headed for the bedrooms. Even though Bones and Ethan had been here for literal hours, she doubted they'd filled a single box. When Bones was feeling bombastic, it was almost impossible to get him to focus on his task.

"Have you ever seen a grown man crabwalk before?" Bones continued as Amber approached. "I haven't laughed that hard in years."

"I can't say that I have," Ethan answered dryly. "I guess the world still holds some allure for me."

To Amber's surprise, the two men had made considerable headway on the Admiral's bedroom. A tower of tidy boxes stood against the far wall, each one neatly labeled in a hand that Amber *knew* didn't belong to Bones. They'd even managed to break down the bed, leaving it little more than a mattress and a stack of wood beams that had been wrapped with plastic to protect it.

"Babe! You're back!" As soon as Bones caught sight of her, he strode across the floor and made as if to hug her before remembering—she hoped—that they were very much broken up. His arms fell heavily to his sides, but he didn't lose his bombast by so much as a decibel. "We've got the bathroom, guest bedroom, and the Admiral's bedroom all packed up and ready to go. Looks good, eh?"

Amber peered around Bones's massive bulk to where Ethan sat in a plastic shower chair. Considering that the veterinarian's expression didn't contain a single distinguishing feature, she was guessing he'd found his morning as much of a trial as she had.

"I thought you were supposed to be snooping, not acting like a pair of hired hands," she said.

"Why not both? My man Ethan here kept the inventory while I did the heavy lifting. Turns out we make a great team." Bones dug an elbow into her side. "Almost as great as you and I used to be. Before…you know."

"You mean before you stripped me of three years of training and hard work? Before you decided it was okay to put a woman's life in danger because her greedy, cradle-robbing husband didn't want to have to pay alimony?"

Bones's face fell. Amber *almost* felt a twinge of guilt at having deflated the hot air out of him, but it passed as he put on a big show of innocence. "C'mon, babe," he wheedled. "You know that's not fair. A job's a job, even when we don't like the outcome."

Amber flung up a hand to stop him. Not only was she not in the mood to have this conversation right now, but she definitely wasn't having it while Ethan was sitting in the room with them. The man already considered her a hack. There was no need to hand over supporting evidence.

"At least tell me you found something more than just a bunch of IKEA furniture and old-man sweaters," Amber said. "And where is Tatiana? I thought you were going to keep an eye on him while you worked."

Ethan cleared his throat. "I had Bones put him in an enclosure out front so he could get some fresh air and exercise. I thought it might stimulate his appetite."

Amber was grateful for the intervention and was about to say as much when Bones said, "I wish you'd told me Ethan's a veterinarian. There's no excuse to let Tatiana starve to death with a literal expert on our doorstep."

Ethan cleared his throat. "Actually, tortoises can go quite a long time without food, sometimes up to three months if they're in hibernation. That's especially true of ones who have undergone trauma."

"Trauma?" Bones asked. "What the hell did you do to the poor guy, Amber?"

"Ethan means the trauma of being lost," Amber explained with a level of patience she felt deserved a gold star. Possibly two. "Before I found him, he'd been roaming around this place for something like a month. Plus, he just lost the man who'd been taking care of him for the past few decades. He's probably in mourning."

"That true?" Bones turned toward Ethan. "They can mourn?"

"I don't see why not. Elephants grieve their dead so deeply that they sometimes bury the remains and return to visit the grave. Who are we to say that tortoises can't feel the same?"

Amber knew Bones well enough to realize that he could spend hours debating this fact—especially in this mood—so she turned the subject before the conversation devolved further. "What's the word on the inventory? Find anything interesting?"

Ethan lifted the clipboard from his lap and handed it to her. "See for yourself. We left no coaster unturned."

Amber scanned the list, her eyes moving over the neat handwriting and detailed descriptions of every belonging the Admiral had ever owned.

royal blue socks, four pairs
signed copy of John Grisham's *Camino Island*
expired fish oil pills, two Costco-sized bottles

glutamine prescription signed by Dr. Lopez

192-piece Dewalt mechanics tool set, missing half-inch pear head ratchet

"Wow." Amber flipped the top page to find about a dozen more just like it. "This is…thorough."

"Yeah, well." Ethan shrugged. "I didn't have much else to do. Even in the peak of health, I doubt I'd have been much help. Your, ah, Bones didn't so much as break a sweat the whole time."

Bones stretched his arms out in front of him, flexing and cracking his joints in a way that Amber felt sure would come back to haunt him when he was the age of the Seven Ponds residents. "All in a day's work. You should see what I can do with an axe and a couple cords of wood."

Amber rolled her eyes but refused to engage. "So, what? Do we think the Vincent kids cleared out anything that might have been of use? Or is this whole thing just a wild goose chase?"

"Wild goose chase," Bones promptly said.

"Actually, I wouldn't be so sure about that."

Both Amber and Bones turned to stare as Ethan struggled to his feet. It spoke highly of Bones's understanding that he didn't try to help the other man, opting instead to cross his arms and lean against the doorjamb in a way that—like the exposed forearms—Amber had also once told him did much to improve his already impressive physique.

"Okay, so most of the stuff on that list is pretty typical of an old guy living on his own, right? Tortoise pellets, tweed suit jackets, more vitamins than one person could ever consume in a lifetime—you get the idea."

"Sure," Amber agreed, her optimism sinking as she scanned the other medications on the list—all of which looked ordinary and showed no signs of having been plundered in the days leading up to the Admiral's death. "So what are you seeing that we're not?"

"It's weird. There's nothing personal anywhere in the house. I've been living here for, what, three weeks? I couldn't tell you how many pictures of grandchildren I've had to ooh and aah over. Not a day passes that someone doesn't have a piece of macaroni art to show me or a newspaper clipping of their kid's newest business venture."

"Macaroni art?" Amber echoed, nodding. "You're right. I remember when my niece Muriel had that phase. She used to make those pictures by the dozen. I was always tempted to cook the pictures to see what would happen."

Ethan grinned appreciatively. "My nephew's the same. Only we *did* cook one once."

"No way. What happened? Did you eat it?"

Bones grunted before Ethan could respond. "What the hell does a bunch of kindergarten arts and crafts have to do with anything?"

"Nothing, maybe. But I don't see anything like that in this house. No photos, no mementos, nothing to make it feel like the Admiral was a *person*, you know?"

Amber couldn't help thinking about her grandmother's condo, which was lacking much of the same kitschy décor. With the exception of the oversized nude, which could hardly be attributed to the talents of a relative, very few items on display were of a personal nature. If you didn't count the locket containing her mom's photo, nothing in that house signaled that Jade McCallan was the least bit loved.

"Maybe the Admiral's kids took them?" she suggested. "As keepsakes?"

Even as she spoke the words aloud, she realized how silly they were. The only thing Michelle and her brother cared about was finding the family ring—and even that probably had less to do with sentiment than the three million dollars.

"It's possible," Ethan said dubiously. "But it almost feels like this place was halfway packed up already. Everything of *real* value is already gone."

"We could always ask Michelle when we hand over the inventory," Bones pointed out. "Depending on how she reacts, it could tell us more."

This was such a rational idea that Amber immediately relaxed—and then tensed right back up to catch herself slipping under his spell. That was the problem with Bones. Just when she felt as if she'd never met a more egotistical, aggravating lump of a man, he turned around and did something so logical that she found herself questioning everything.

And the worst part was, he knew it.

He pushed himself off the doorjamb and plunged his hands deep in his pockets, his grin wide. "We still have the living room and kitchen to go, so we'd best get cracking. Who knows? Maybe we'll find a pot of gold under the couch that'll get your grandma out by tonight."

"Don't tease," she grumbled, but she allowed herself to be led out of the bedroom toward the front. "Knowing our luck, all we'll find is dust bunnies and something ordinary like a fishing lure."

By the time they finished packing up the Admiral's house, Amber was sweating, dirty, and so irritated that she was tempted to leave her grandmother languishing in prison for the rest of her days rather than spend another afternoon like that one.

"So. *Bones*, huh?" Ethan leaned his arms on the kitchen counter, looking at her over the top of the coffee maker she was struggling to put into its original box. Bones had escaped out the front to check on Tatiana, leaving her alone with the veterinarian just when her foul mood had reached its peak. "How does one earn a nickname like that? Or is it better if I don't know?"

"Don't start with me," she muttered as she finally managed to get the appliance in and tape the box shut. "You enjoyed this, didn't you?"

"What? Watching you snip and snarl at a man who was impervious to your every barb?" He laughed and filled in the final inventory line. "A little bit, yeah. It was like watching a nature documentary. One of the really good ones where the female ends up eating her mate at the end."

She held back a snort. "Don't make me laugh. I'm too annoyed."

"Really? You hide it remarkably well."

This time, her snort managed to escape. "If you'd spent the morning at the station interviewing my grandmother, you wouldn't exactly be a barrel of sunshine either." She added the box to the stack along the kitchen all and stretched. She was going to feel the pain of this day's work tomorrow, for sure. "Thanks for doing this, by the way. I can't imagine your day was much better than mine."

"Yeah, I did have big plans to write letters to my loved ones and send them via carrier pigeon, but I can always do that tomorrow instead. The sky's the limit."

She smiled at his joke, but the mention of his loved ones got her thinking. "Wait. If you have a nephew, that means you have a brother or sister, right?"

"A sister, yes."

"Then why aren't you staying with her? Wouldn't it be a lot nicer to rest and recover surrounded by your family instead of in a nursing home?"

He heaved a sigh that she could tell, from the overblown sound of it, was about to precede a sarcastic remark. "The thing I liked best about you, Winslow, was that you didn't ask invasive questions. Now look what you did."

"She's that bad, huh?"

"Are you trying to private investigator me? It'll never work. Until I get back on my own two feet again, being mysterious is all I have."

"Oh, then she must be *really* bad. Don't tell me—she has an entire guest bathroom full of towels you aren't allowed to use."

He eyed her askance. "That's a weirdly specific guess."

Amber leaped up onto the empty kitchen counter and sat cross-legged on top of it. She knew that there were several different investigative threads she needed to pull on until she found the source, but the exhaustion of the past few days was finally starting to settle. With the exception of that first night, when she'd enjoyed the best sleep she'd had in her entire adult life, she'd been doing more tossing and turning than counting sheep.

"My brother Derek and his wife, Chrissy, are like that," she admitted. "Mikey's not as bad about material things, but he's a perennial complainer, which is worse. No matter how hard I try to tiptoe through his house like I don't exist, he'll find a random scuff mark on the baseboard or a lump in the pillow that somehow costs a hundred dollars to repair."

"Are you trying to charm me into spilling all my secrets again? Because I thought we already decided that wasn't going to work."

She gave a small start of surprise. "Do you find it charming for me to complain about my relatives? Because if that's the case, then, boy are you in for a treat. Want to know what my grandmother told me this morning?"

"Is it a confession of murder? Because as much fun as I'm having with this whole helping-you-catch-a-killer thing, I don't actually want to get involved." He stopped and tilted his head, studying her. Something about the defeated sag of her shoulders must have gotten to him because he sighed and added, "Okay, you win. Tell me about her crimes. But if the police start questioning me, I'm denying we ever had this conversation."

"It's not about the case. I mean, we *did* discuss the case, obviously, but that's not what's bothering me."

He didn't say anything, but his gaze remained unwavering, so she took it as a cue to continue.

"Before I came to Arizona, I'd never met my grandmother before—never even spoke to her on the phone. She and my mom had a falling-out before any of us kids were born, one that was so bad that my mom refused to let her have any part in our lives. Other than a handful of stories—usually ones with terrible endings—I didn't know anything about her."

"That's rough, Winslow. I'm sorry. You two seem so close."

Something about the frank simplicity in his response loosened the constriction around her lungs.

"That's just it. It took me *forever* to locate her whereabouts, and I had no idea what to expect once I arrived. But for her, seeing me was just a regular Tuesday afternoon. Then her friend died that same night and... I don't know." She cast a fleeting glance at Ethan, but he was wearing his bland listening face. If he'd shown any other sentiment—pity or horror or even mild interest—she might have stopped, but that calm façade put her at ease. "It's like she has no heart. It's not *normal*. She should be sad about her friend's death. Worried about prison. Curious about what drove me here and what my family's been up to all these years. I sometimes think..." She stopped and swallowed before putting into words the one thing that had been bothering her most ever since she arrived here. "What if my mom was right? My grandma is so warm and full of life, but what if that joie de vivre is all she has? What if, underneath it all, she's just as much of a soulless monster as my mom has always painted her out to be?"

Amber might have made the mistake of saying more—of admitting that what she really feared was her mother seeing those same qualities in *her*—but

Bones returned to the house with Tatiana once again strapped to his chest. He should have looked ridiculous, but something about his assured swagger made him even more hypermasculine than usual.

"We finally done in here?" he asked. Without waiting for an answer, he plucked the inventory list from Ethan's hand and glanced at it. "You've got great handwriting, mate. Like an old-timey scribe or something."

"I do my best," Ethan said dryly. "Did you want me to take that to Michelle Vincent and assess her reaction, or is that official PI duty?"

Bones yanked the piece of paper far enough out of Ethan's reach to make his meaning clear. "No need to trouble yourself any more than you already have. Amber and I can take it from here. Shakedowns are our specialty, aren't they, babe?"

Amber rolled her eyes in an exaggerated apology to Ethan, but he'd already turned away and was taking halting steps toward the door. She was tempted to call out to him, to assure him that she and Bones shared no specialties except for professional ones, but she didn't.

For one, she doubted he'd believe her. For another...well, it hardly mattered, did it? Ethan was a random veterinarian keeping himself entertained while recovering from hip surgery. She owed him nothing, and he owed her even less.

As soon as the front door clicked shut behind Ethan, Bones pounced. "Well?" he demanded. "Did you see it?"

She cast an anxious glance around the kitchen. "See what? A clue? For crying out loud, why didn't you say something before?"

"So you *didn't* see it," he said, scraping a slow hand across his jaw. "Interesting. I wonder if that's been the plan all along."

"What are you talking about? Bones, if you don't stop being purposefully mysterious and tell me what you found, I'll—" She cut herself off, annoyed for being unable to call a fitting punishment to mind. Unless she took to sword fighting, she'd never best him in hand-to-hand combat, and he was the one with things like a car, an apartment, and an actual job. Noticing how his hand moved to curl around Tatiana's lower limbs, she settled on, "I'll take your emotional support tortoise away from you."

He grinned. "Nice try. Emotional support animals are a protected class. You can't touch him."

"Only if you get a licensed mental health professional to back you up," Amber retorted hotly.

He seemed momentarily taken aback before deciding to hand her the win. "Touché, babe. I guess you *were* listening to some of my lectures—only not the one about criminals returning to the scene of the crime."

Amber was too distracted by the latter half of this statement to take umbrage at the former. "Criminals returning to the scene of the crime? What criminals? You mean my grandma? The Vincent kids? *Ethan?*"

She caught Bones's meaning the second Ethan's name crossed her lips.

"You can't possibly be serious," she said. "He's just a random patient here. You heard him—he's only been at Seven Ponds for three weeks, and most of that has been spent in a bed. Or playing video games. Bones, did you know that old men are obsessed with *Call of Duty*? I had no idea, but apparently it's a real thing. I googled it."

He waved this off with a scoff. "I taught you better than this, Amber. You should know not to fall for some random guy's sob story about his hip. What better cover for infiltrating a nursing home full of rich retirees?"

"Um, I don't think a lot of criminal masterminds are going around scheduling major orthopedic surgery in order to rob a few old people of their family heirlooms. Try again." She made the sound of a buzzer, but Bones only stood staring down at her, a look of condescending amusement curling his lips.

"Okay, maybe his close relationship with Nasty Nancy is a little odd, but not enough to count him as a suspect," Amber said, but no sooner had she said the words than more occurred to her. "And, yeah, it *is* strange that he has a sister and her whole family hidden away somewhere, and he still chose to recover here, but they probably live far away. Or they're like Mikey and Derek and he'd rather gnaw off his own arm than spend time with them."

She jumped down from the counter and started crossing the tile floor. Even in her flip flops, the new emptiness of the room caused her steps to echo. "I mean, *maybe* if he had to have the surgery anyway and figured he could kill two birds with one stone. Or if he discovered what Nancy was up to and demanded a cut. Only that seems like an awfully extreme reaction to a nurse who—"

She stopped as suddenly as she started. "Bones, you bastard. You're just saying all this because you don't like the idea of another man helping me with this investigation. Stop trying to make a perfectly innocent bystander out to be a murderer."

He tossed her the clipboard. The last thing she wanted to do was play his games and catch it, but instinct won out over pique.

"We just spent eight hours packing up a dead man's house," Bones said. "Look at that list, Amber. He didn't leave a single thing out. I know *my* motivations, but what's driving him? No one is so bored that they do that kind of thing for fun. And no offense, but he's definitely not looking to get in your pants. I know the signs, and that man ain't showing them."

"Don't be gross."

"I'm just saying." He nodded down at the list. "Seems like a good way to make sure your tracks are covered, that's all. Or to pick up a few more baubles on the side."

Since Ethan had once again been wearing his uniform of gray joggers and a faded T-shirt, this made her scoff. "Right. And where would he have put them?"

Bones shrugged. "Hell if I know. Maybe he stashed them somewhere. Or he swallowed them."

"*He swallowed them?* Like a circus geek biting off chicken heads?"

"Worth thinking about, anyway," Bones said, unmoved. His hand once again came up to cradle Tatiana. "We don't know anything about the guy, when everything's said and done. For all we know, he's in cahoots with the Vincents. This whole thing might be an elaborate setup to speed along an old man's death and get probate started."

There was so much reason in this—and it was such a welcome departure from making Camille or her grandmother the prime suspect—that Amber clamped her lips shut.

"I'll go pay that Michelle Vincent lady a visit and see if I can get anything out of her when I hand over the inventory, but I'm not holding out much hope," Bones added. "Broads like that are serious pros. They've been lying about everything from their dress sizes to their annual taxable income for years."

Amber didn't bother to counter Bones's claim. For one thing, she kind of agreed with him. For another, she needed to be alone so she could think.

It was preposterous to assume that Ethan was guilty of killing anything but time, but something about what Bones had said nagged at the back of her mind. With a quiet room to herself and some space to spread out, she should be able to figure out what that something was.

21

"The day cell phones were invented was a
sad one for serial killers everywhere."

—*DEATH COMES CALLING*, SEASON 1 EPISODE 8

NO AMOUNT OF QUIET AND contemplation could unravel the tangle
of the Admiral's murder. Amber *tried*—she really did. She went for a long,
sweaty walk. She took an equally long cold shower afterwards. She did laps
in the pool and painted her toenails and picked through the box of jewelry
under the guest bed as though it contained the answers to the universe.

It was no use. No matter which path Amber's thoughts trod, they always
ended up in the same spot: nowhere. Just like her life.

"Ah, you're finally awake, darling." Camille pounced early the next
morning, full of energy despite Amber's sleepless night. "Get up and tell me
if you think any of these capture your fancy. I've been meaning to clean out
my closet for ages, but I hate to think of my favorite gowns and coats lying
unloved in a warehouse somewhere. I'd much rather they go to someone
who can appreciate them."

Amber walked in to find what looked like Camille's entire wardrobe
spread out over the living room furniture. Pausing just long enough to check
on Tatiana, who was sitting and staring at a wall, she ran a hand over a mink
stole draped over the back of one of the white plastic couches.

"Is this real fur?" she asked.

Camille blinked at her. "Bless you, no. Do you have any idea what that
sort of thing costs? Not to mention the price of storing them long-term? I

remember my mother used to rent a cold storage facility for hers. Whenever we'd visit, I felt like I was walking into a room full of hibernating bears."

Amber stopped. "You mean they're fakes?"

Camille gave a low, throaty laugh. "Of course. Most of my clothes are, but you won't let my dirty little secret out. One must keep up appearances, after all." She handed Amber the slinky green dress. "Here. Try this one. You have the body for it."

Amber's fingers itched to take the dress in hand, but she resisted temptation. This time, she was ready to see Camille's generosity for what it was. Not a shopping spree for an honorary granddaughter, and not a favor to her grandmother, but something much more sinister.

It's a trap. A way to diffuse suspicion.

"You talked to my grandmother, didn't you?" she asked, suddenly exhausted by all the games being played around her. "About my visit to the jail?"

Only by a flicker of her eyelashes did Camille betray her surprise. Recovering quickly, she reached for a T-shirt dress in a downy shade of heather gray. "Perhaps this is more your style? I usually wear it with a turquoise belt, but you might—"

"Camille. Stop." Amber moved toward the other side of the room to avoid having any more bribes thrust at her. This wasn't the moment she'd have chosen for disclosure, and she could have cursed her grandmother for forcing her hand like this, but if she wanted to make any headway on this case, she was going to have to stop skulking around and start attacking at the source.

"I know all the artwork in your house is fake, and that your clothes are too," she said, her relief at admitting the truth so palpable that she could almost *feel* the stress leaving her body. "I know about the husband who ran away with your money and that you recently had a prescription for painkillers filled at the pharmacy at the main facility. I haven't found a safe yet, but if I do, will I find the pills there, or did you and my grandma use them all when you killed the Admiral?"

Instead of showing further signs of surprise, Camille let out a laugh. "So *I'm* to be the villain now, am I? How delicious. Tell me, was money my sole motivation, or was there more at play? A love affair between George and me, perhaps? Or a fit of madness caused by the full moon?"

Amber paused. She couldn't say for *sure* that the moon had been full the night of the Admiral's death, but she rather thought it had. "You didn't answer my question about the pills."

"If we're keeping track, then *you* didn't answer the third question the night we had our lovely dinner at the steak house," Camille countered. "I was promised three, if you'll recall."

Amber did recall. She also realized that this might be her only opportunity to get a straight answer out of the woman. "Sure. If you tell me why you're hiding a box of stolen jewelry underneath the guest bed, then I'll answer any question you want."

The attack was clearly an unexpected one.

"Oh." Camille lifted a shaking hand to her chest, her color draining away. "You found that, did you?"

Amber nodded, feeling so much like a traitor that the next words caused her physical pain. "The only reason you're not sitting next to my grandma in jail right now is because I didn't see the Admiral's ring inside the box. But I took pictures of the rest, so it won't do you any good to toss it into the nearest pond and pretend it was never there."

Camille's hand continued to shake as she thrust it out and clutched the back of her white couch. "Was the group right? Are you going to tell him?"

"The group?" Amber echoed, her mind working quickly. She'd assumed that Camille was working alone, but that had been a mistake. From the very start, the podcast group had seemed to operate as a single entity. "Do you mean they were in on it too? Are you guys running some kind of theft ring together? Is that why you killed the Admiral?"

Now it was Camille's turn to look confused, her color starting to return in large splotchy patches. "Theft ring? Darling, I think you might need some coffee. Or something a little stronger, perhaps? I've never stolen anything a day in my life. Or, while we're on the subject, killed a man."

"But…" Amber's brows drew tightly in the center of her forehead. She *did* need coffee, and probably something a little stronger to go with it, but she wasn't about to lose this opportunity. Not when they finally seemed to be getting somewhere. "Camille, that jewelry is real. I'm sure of it."

"Well, of course it is. Marius always bought the best. It's one of the only good things I can say about him."

"Marius?" Amber echoed.

"Whatever he said he'll pay you—whatever he promised in exchange for your services—it's not enough. You don't want to get mixed up with a man like that. Take it from someone who was married to him for twenty-five years. What he says and what he means are two different things."

No coffee was necessary to wake Amber up after that. She looked down at Tatiana, her maybe possibly lucky tortoise, and then back at Camille, her generous hostess with a taste for luxury and an ex-husband who'd done his best to strip her of it.

"Omigod." Amber's words came out as a rushed breath. "That's *your* jewelry, isn't it? From before? From when you were married?"

Camille nodded and toyed with the gold bracelet around her wrist—one Amber felt fairly sure was just cheap plating. "I know I ought to sell it, but your grandmother suspects Marius put it on a watch list with the local pawn shops. He would too. Not because he wants any of it back, and not because he needs the money, but because he won't be happy until he's taken literally everything." She paused, as if considering her next words carefully. "That's why he sent you, isn't it? To investigate me? It would be just like him, hiring the *one* PI he knew I'd open my doors to without question. Your grandmother feared it from the start."

Amber moved to the couch and sank down on it, her legs no longer able to support her full weight. Half of her was thrilled—Camille considered her a real PI?—while the other half felt the sinking realization that nothing around here was what it seemed.

Including herself.

"My grandmother thinks I'm a mole. A plant. A *spy*." Amber glanced up to find Camille watching her with an unreadable expression. "You all think that."

"We didn't want to think it," Camille protested gently. "But your grand-mother said—well, she made it sound like—Amber, you appeared out of *nowhere*. Jade was delighted to see you, obviously—we all were—but this wouldn't be the first time Marius has done something like this. When we were getting divorced, he conflicted out every decent attorney in a two-hundred-mile radius. Hiring an out-of-state private investigator who just so happens to be Jade's long-lost granddaughter would have been right in his wheelhouse."

Amber reached for Tatiana and pulled the tortoise into her lap, drawing comfort from the way he immediately settled into place.

"So *that* explains why you've all been so cagey with me," she breathed, more stunned than stung. "And why you've been so careful to keep me close."

"No," Camille said with an abruptness that made Amber feel glad she had Tatiana to anchor her. She was starting to feel like a ship being tossed across the seven seas. "That's not it at all."

"But—"

Camille cut her off with a *tsk*. "Listen to me, Amber. You asked your question, so now you have to answer one."

"I'm not done yet—" She tried again, but the effort was a futile one. *She* might have follow-up questions, but Camille wasn't a woman to be taken lightly.

"For my third and final question, I'd like to know what it is you're doing. If my ex-husband didn't send you to Draycott to spy on me, why are you really here?"

Amber shook her head as if to clear it. The answer to that should have been patently obvious, even to a group as wily as this one: "To meet my grandmother. To build a relationship with her."

"A woman you've gone thirty-one years without knowing? A woman you've never once made an effort to reach out to before?"

Amber opened her mouth and closed it again, at a loss for words. For most of those years, she'd been a child, a *dependent*. It wasn't her job to reach out to her grandmother. It had been her grandmother's job to reach out to her.

Yet she never had. She'd never even tried.

"It's not that complicated a question, Amber." Even though Camille spoke gently, there was an edge to her voice that cut deep. "You had a falling-out with that Bones character and ran to a stranger instead of your parents or the countless friends I feel sure you must have back home. Why? Why did you fly to a woman you'd never met and had no guarantee would even let you through the front door? What are you hoping to get out of her?"

Amber thought about lying—or about pointing out that Camille was in no position to make demands—but she suspected that Camille was just protecting her grandmother the same way her grandmother had been protecting Camille. The way the *entire* podcast group had been protecting Camille.

Which was why she shoved her hand in her pocket and pulled out the locket that she'd been carrying all week. Camille took it from her without surprise and let it dangle from her fingertips.

"Your grandmother gave you this?"

"No. I stole it along with the prescription bottle I mentioned before. I took the bottle because I was afraid the police would find it. The locket, well…I don't know. I think I took it for the same reason I came here. To see her. To *know* her." Amber paused and forced a deep breath. If she was going to get this out, then she needed to do it right. "Actually, that's a lie. I didn't want to know her nearly as much as I wanted her to know me. No one in my family ever has—not when I was kid with more energy than they knew what to do with, and not now that I'm adult who can't even pretend to have her life in order. I hoped that Grandma Judith might be the one person on this planet who was different."

Amber felt rather than saw Camille take a seat next to her. She also felt rather than saw the locket being placed back in her hand. Her fist closed around it, the silver warm to the touch.

"The worst part of this whole thing is that I was right," Amber said, her throat tight. "She *is* different. From the moment I walked into Seven Ponds, she's never once made me feel like I'm a disappointment." The full meaning of Camille's confession hit her like a sucker punch. "Not even when she thought I might have been hired by your ex-husband to find the jewelry you hid from him. Who does that? Who's *that* nice?"

"I wish you'd take the dresses," Camille said by way of reply. "The ones I put out are much more suited to a woman your age. Honestly, you'd be doing me—and the rest of this place—a favor."

"But I just accused you of murder," Amber protested.

"It's all right. Everyone makes mistakes."

Amber choked on a laugh. She also dropped her head so that it rested on Camille's strong, comfortable shoulder. "I don't really think you're capable of killing someone, you know."

"I imagine you wouldn't be sleeping in my guest bed if that were the case." A hand came up and started running soothing strokes through the strands of Amber's hair. The light touch felt so good that she closed her eyes and let herself fall into it.

"The problem is that I don't want *any* of you to have done it," Amber continued in a sleepy, faraway voice. "I like you all too much."

"And we like you too, darling."

"I don't know why. I haven't done anything to deserve it."

"Does someone have to deserve kindness to receive it?" Camille tutted gently. "What a terrible way to live. I had no idea your generation was so callous. Remind me not to cross any of you on a dark street."

Something about Camille's words nagged at her. Amber's eyes popped open again, all her sudden relaxation at an end. "Wait. That's it."

"It sure is." Camille continued speaking in her soothing voice, but the moment for comfort had passed. Amber bolted upright in her seat.

"No, you don't understand. My generation isn't callous. Not the way yours is."

Camille chuckled. "Is this about to become one of those Millennial versus Boomer memes? Should I make us some avocado toast to set the proper tone?"

Amber refused to let herself be sidetracked, even though a slice of avocado toast sounded delicious right about now. If Camille's jewelry wasn't a lead and there was nothing worth following up on inside the Admiral's house, then she needed to follow one of the only threads she had left.

"I'm serious, Camille. You're on Nextdoor. You've seen the posts about my grandma. Some of the people on there have been really mean to her—ConcernedCitizen1443 in particular."

Camille finally started to take her seriously. Her lips pulled together in a frown. "You think that's a clue?"

"It's as close to one as we're going to get. Concerned Citizen obviously has it in for you guys. Ethan said something similar about it before—that you guys are like a *Mean Girls* clique, and not everyone enjoys having you around."

"If you want a piece of life advice, Amber, here's one free of charge: not everyone in this world will enjoy having you around. And if you spend your whole life trying to make them—"

Amber cut Camille off before she could launch into a speech about the importance of being true to oneself. It was a speech she could probably benefit from, and it would be interesting to hear some of Camille's life stories, but there was a more important lesson to take away.

"Does Peggy Lee know how to track an IP address?" Amber asked. "To see where Concerned Citizen's posts are coming from?"

"I believe so, yes. If the messages are being sent from the Wi-Fi here at the retirement community, she should be able to find them easily enough." The frown lines around Camille's mouth smoothed away. "Amber, are you saying that your grandmother's internet troll is the killer? You think it's that easy?"

"I think it's a start." Amber sprang to her feet. "Enemies are enemies, no matter what platform they prefer—and anyone willing to hide behind a firewall is the type to skulk in the shadows, ready to attack the moment opportunity presents itself."

––––––––––––

"The call is coming from inside the house."

Peggy Lee's crackling laughter rang out, echoing off the marble fountains as she pressed one painstaking letter at a time on her keyboard. Amber had only ever watched hackers work on television, so she had no idea how it *actually* worked, but she was guessing most of them were at least able to type with two hands.

"Sorry. I always wanted to say that." Peggy swung the monitor around so it faced out. As she moved, her red wig started to slip down the side of her head to showcase a few wispy strands of white hair underneath. "I can't tell you the exact room, but those messages were sent from this facility."

"You mean from someone inside the nursing home?" Amber asked.

"Someone who lives in one of the long-term care rooms?"

"Looks like it." Peggy Lee reached up and straightened her wig. "Concerned Citizen only seems to post when they have something mean to say about Jade, and they always do it from the resident network router."

Amber studied the screen more intently, but the numbers and letters told her no more than a Latin textbook might. Curious, she asked, "What on earth did you do for a living before you moved here? Are you like a retired spy or something?"

"Bless your heart. Before my marriage, I was a switchboard operator."

"Really?" Amber tried not to let her surprise show, but the idea of a sixties-era landline job leading to skills like these seemed almost ludicrous. "So the hacking is a side hustle you just happened to stumble upon?"

Camille released an elegant snort. "Peggy Lee got fired from her switchboard job the moment they caught her recording private conversations between high-profile politicians. You can look it up at the library. There were at least a dozen articles written about it in the *New York Times*. It was quite a scandal at the time."

"Don't be silly. I was framed."

"From that moment on, she's been looking for literally every other way to snoop on the unsuspecting. I'm not saying she *definitely* worked for the U.S. government to help surveil Soviet assets during the Cold War, but…"

Amber turned her head toward the tiny woman. "So you *are* a spy."

"Camille is trying to be funny. I was a housewife. A mother. I was too busy hand-washing diapers to care about silly things like frequency-shift keying technology." Peggy Lee examined the screen and frowned. "Huh. That's odd."

Amber would have gladly peppered Peggy Lee with more questions, but she forced them aside and tried to make sense of the screen once again. "What is?"

One gnarled finger pointed at a series of numbers. "I said I can't tell you the room number, and that's true, but the memory ward runs on its own servers." Peggy Lee's nose wrinkled. "But how could anyone staying there be on Nextdoor? And why would they care what Jade was doing with her free time?"

Amber dashed a hand out and gripped the edge of the desk. "The memory ward?" she echoed.

"It's a euphemism for the dementia ward," Camille explained. "They call it that so the families don't feel as guilty for abandoning their relatives there to die."

Amber gave an internal wince at this harsh representation, but she had more pressing concerns to attend to right now—namely, that there was a very good way a certain someone could have accessed Nextdoor from that particular wing.

"She wasn't stealing a tablet from that patient," Amber breathed. "She was *borrowing* it. So she could post nasty things about Grandma without anyone tracing it back to her."

"Nasty things?" Camille echoed. She and Peggy Lee shared a quick look. "You don't mean—"

"Nancy is ConcernedCitizen1443," Amber finished for them. She started to dig out her phone, but Peggy Lee was one step ahead of her. The older woman was already entering the website for Nextdoor. "What do you want to bet she's the same one who made that anonymous call? She's had it out for Grandma this whole time."

All three of them turned toward the screen. Sure enough, Concerned Citizen's page was awash with commentary on Jade McCallan, the *Death Comes Calling* podcast, and the unfair distribution of parking spaces for staff and guests at Seven Ponds. Amber's first feeling at watching Peggy Lee scroll through the evidence was one of triumph. She'd *known* Nasty Nancy was up to no good, and she'd *known* she had it out for her grandma right from the start.

"But if she's only borrowing devices so she can post about the residents without getting fired, then she's probably not stealing jewelry," Amber said.

She might have continued in that vein, only the woman in question rounded the corner at a brisk pace. The moment Nancy caught sight of Amber leaning over the computer, her shoes squeaked to a halt.

"What are you doing?" the nurse snapped. "You can't be back there. It's for staff only."

Amber closed the Nextdoor window before Nancy could see it—and a good thing, too, because the woman lost no time in peering over their shoulders to see what they were looking at. Since all that was left was Peggy Lee's indecipherable series of numbers, the nurse was no more clued in than Amber had been.

"Sorry," Amber said, thinking fast. "Peggy Lee was just having a little tech trouble and asked if I could help out. Since I'm young and all. You know how it is with old people and technology."

"Now see here—" Peggy Lee began, but Camille ground her heel on her friend's foot before she could say more.

"Amber has been an absolute doll," Camille agreed. "I honestly don't know how any of us would be getting on without her. She's just like her grandmother sowing seeds of happiness everywhere she goes."

Nancy's snort of derision showed what she thought of that, but she said no more about the computer, so Amber counted it as a win. Unable to resist temptation, she tilted her head to examine the nurse. Nancy looked just as tightly wound and unpleasant as she had the day Amber had met her, but she noticed a pink barrette clipping her hair away from her face and the way a bright sparkle of eyeshadow was brushed awkwardly over her eyelids. When combined with the cheerful scrubs, she looked like a person who'd dressed in the dark—or who was simply desperate to be liked and had no idea how to go about it.

A pang of what felt like sympathy overtook Amber.

"I know you don't care for my grandmother, but she's not a murderer," Amber suddenly said. "Whatever she did to upset you, I'm sorry. I'm afraid she can come across as thoughtless sometimes. We both can. We have a way of getting so caught up in our own dramas that we forget everyone else is fighting battles of their own."

It would have been too much to say that Nancy *thawed* toward her, but she did relax.

"You're not nearly as bad as she is," Nancy said. Then, lest Amber get the wrong idea, she added, "But you can't come in here, swaying your hips and demanding your way just because you feel like it. That's not how health care works. People are trying to heal here. To *recover*."

Amber couldn't resist. "You mean people like Ethan?"

Nancy shook her head, looking so ferocious that Amber wondered if she'd been too hasty in that whole Nancy-is-an-actual-human-being thing.

"You leave Ethan Adler alone," she snapped. "After everything he's been through, the last thing he needs is for some hussy in booty shorts to throw all his progress out the window. I don't care if you *do* have a pet tortoise who just needs a good suppository to get things moving again."

With those parting words, Nancy took herself off again. Peggy Lee and Camille didn't wait until she was out of sight before dissolving into giggles.

"I *told* you that woman has an unhealthy obsession with anal cavities," Peggy Lee said between outbursts of laughter. "Freud would've had a field day with her."

Camille wiped the tears from her eyes. "How I wish Jade had been here to witness that. Life isn't the same without her around."

As much as that second comment gave Amber a pang, she didn't heed it. She was too busy recalling what Bones had said about Ethan swallowing the Vincent family jewels as a way to get them out of the house.

"Of course," she said, snapping her fingers. "Why did it take me so long to realize it?"

"Realize what?" Peggy Lee asked, but Amber was already darting around the desk toward the sliding entrance doors.

"Wait," Camille called after her. "Does this mean we no longer suspect Nasty Nancy as the murderer? I was looking forward to putting together the promotional materials for 'The Case of the Ratched Racket.'"

"Well, really, Camille. You can't call it the Ratched Racket or everyone will know who the murderer is before the first episode airs."

"So? Maybe we *should* do that. Play with the format a little. If we want to boost our ratings like Jade says—"

Amber left the two women to their squabble. As much as she agreed with Camille, and that it would bring nothing but satisfaction to cast Nancy as thief, villain, and murderer all in one, she felt almost certain at least one title—that of thief—no longer applied. And unless she was very much mistaken, she knew exactly how to prove it.

22

"A detective with a weak stomach will find
himself behind a desk before too long."

—*DEATH COMES CALLING*, SEASON 3 EPISODE 5

"SORRY, BABE, BUT THAT MICHELLE lady was a complete bust."

Bones was waiting for Amber inside Camille's living room, his booted feet up on the coffee table as he sat watching a football game. She would've been irritated at the sight of him—in fact, she *was* irritated at the sight of him—but he had Tatiana in his lap and was coaxing him to eat a frilly piece of green lettuce.

"He can't eat that," Amber said without preamble. She kicked Bones's feet off the furniture and reached for the tortoise. "My poor love. You can't eat anything, can you? You have a tummy ache."

Bones blinked up at her. "Did you hear a word I just said? That Michelle Vincent is as coldhearted a woman as I ever met. After all that free labor the vet and I did yesterday, she had the nerve to threaten to leave me a bad Yelp review. Can you believe it? *Me?*"

Amber cradled Tatiana in the crook of her arm and began gently prodding his stomach. She knew virtually nothing about the anatomy of tortoises, and even less about the diagnostics of lodged jewels in their digestive tracks, but she thought she detected a sign of discomfort in the way he squirmed.

"We'll have to ask Ethan for help again," she said. "Or maybe even call an emergency vet."

"Hello?" Bones waved a hand in front of her face. "Are you listening to a word I'm saying? That Michelle woman would peel the skin from your back and turn it into a coat if she thought she could make a buck off it. If anyone would kill her own father to get her hands on an heirloom ring, it's that broad. How we're going to get her to admit it, however…"

"I wonder if it would be better to call the police directly," Amber mused, ignoring him. "If we could get Tatiana under an X-ray, we might be able to prove it's there. That should be enough to get Grandma out."

"Police?" Bones echoed. "X-ray?"

"Actually, I'd hate to haul the officers in just to find that Tatiana is suffering from depression or the flu or something. Ethan is definitely the way to go."

"I thought we decided not to trust that guy," Bones said. "His being here is too convenient, remember?"

"Technically speaking, *you* being here is just as convenient," she countered. "Besides, I'm the one calling the shots. You're only here for moral and secretarial support. Otherwise, you're never seeing that hula girl or your good luck again."

Bones had to clamp his mouth closed to avoid reacting in his inevitable way—by blowing hot air all over her. Amber would have felt bad about cutting him off at the knees like that except for one tiny thing: the fact that Bones was sitting five feet away from his precious hula girl and had no idea how close he was.

Some private investigator. He was the literal definition of a man who couldn't see anything further than the end of his nose.

"Fine," he grumbled. "But if this blows back on me…"

"It won't," she promised. "Ethan will be able to tell me what I need to know."

Somewhere in the back of Amber's mind lay the thought that she was putting too much trust into a man she didn't know—not to mention a man who was protective of his personal life and past to a degree that practically screamed *criminal record*—but she consoled herself with the reflection that Bones would love nothing more than a chance to play hero if things went south.

"Just a little bit longer," she soothed the tortoise as she headed back outside. "I think I finally realized what's making you so uncomfortable."

Unable to resist a good mystery even now, Bones loped after her. "What is it? What did you discover?"

"I didn't," she threw over her shoulder at him. "You did. The only problem is, you decided on the wrong circus geek to worry about. Tatiana's the one we should've been looking at all along."

***

"I *could* give him a glycerin suppository, but it wouldn't be pleasant for any of us."

Dr. Ethan Adler was in full veterinarian mode, his sleeves rolled up to his elbows and a borrowed stethoscope around his neck. While it would have been a stretch to say that his forearms rivaled those of Bones, he made a decent showing of sinew and skin.

"Some mineral oil or pumpkin puree applied orally might also work, but only if we can get him to swallow it." Ethan looked up from where he was gently poking and prodding the tortoise. "How big is this ring supposed to be, anyway?"

Both Bones and Amber had been hovering a few feet back like anxious parents awaiting a diagnosis, but at this question, Amber pulled out the printed appraisal Julio had given her.

"Too big to pass comfortably," she said, frowning at the thought of that monstrosity of metal and diamonds sitting inside Tatiana's belly. The poor thing—no *wonder* why he'd been so hesitant to eat. She felt ashamed that it had taken her this long to figure it out. "I honestly don't know how he swallowed it in the first place."

Ethan fixed his gaze on Amber's, his hazel eyes sharp behind the pair of plastic-rimmed glasses he'd slipped on to examine the tortoise. Not for the first time, Amber wondered how she'd ever thought this man impossible to pick out of a lineup. He was still average in every respect—coloring, build, and height—but that was just on the surface. Like an untouched lake, all you had to do was plunk a few rocks into the water to set him in motion.

"Are you sure he did?" Ethan asked. "Swallow it, I mean?"

Bones released a sound that bordered on a grunt. "I thought you said you felt it in there."

"I did. I *do*." Ethan turned toward Bones without a trace of fear. Most people, when confronted with a six-foot-four heap of muscles grunting like a caveman, would have at least shown a qualm or two, but this was very much Ethan's domain. "But it's not really common for a tortoise to see a giant shiny object and think, *That looks tasty*. It'd be like you deciding to chomp down on a bowling trophy."

"I could eat a bowling trophy. I've eaten weirder things in my life."

This seemed like a strange—and hilarious—flex to Amber, but her response was cut short as a man entered the therapy room they'd requisitioned for the purpose of examining Tatiana.

"Well, well. And what do we have here? Did someone ring for a consult?" The lilting Irish accent that filled the room made Amber feel a disproportionate amount of relief. Ethan was proving himself to be a capable veterinarian, and they were closer than ever to finding the ring that would free her grandmother from jail, but there was something about Bruce's age and confidence that made her feel as if everything would be okay.

"Bruce, thanks." Ethan hobbled forward with his hand outstretched. The older man took it with a crinkly-eyed smile. "We suspect this tortoise here—a Hermann's, aged ninety-eight by all accounts—swallowed something he shouldn't have. He isn't taking food and has some lethargy. Amber has tried soaking to no avail, but we need to get our hands on that object. The sooner, the better."

"Hmm." The older man peered down at Tatiana through what looked to Amber like expert eyes. "Ninety-eight, you say? Surgery is obviously the quickest option, but the trauma of cutting off his shell and gluing it back on—"

Bones moved before any of them even realized it. "Not a chance!" He had Tatiana clutched in his arms, his stance poised as if to fend off an incoming horde of the undead. "You'll cut off this animal's shell over my dead body."

Instead of showing alarm, Bruce chuckled. "That could be arranged, son, but I'd prefer not to add to my body count this late in the game."

The derisive snort this elicited from Bones showed what he thought of Bruce's threat, but Amber was more than ready to believe the older man capable of following through.

"Cutting the shell isn't as bad as it sounds," Ethan said. "Tatiana's age is a drawback, obviously, but—"

"No." Bones set his jaw. "No surgery."

Amber felt a rising well of conflicting emotions. Like Bones, she'd become awfully attached to Tatiana in the past few weeks, and the thought of hurting him to free her grandmother wasn't something she relished.

But this was her grandmother's freedom they were talking about. Her *life*.

"Bones, I know it's not ideal, but we have no other choice. We have to do *something*."

To Amber's surprise, her plea actually reached him. "Then let's do the pumpkin thing," he said. "Or get an X-ray. There's no way in hell I'm letting any of you near this animal with a scalpel."

Ethan grinned. "Actually, to cut open the shell, we'd have to use a bone saw."

The roar this comment drew from Bones made it sound as though the gates of hell were being pried open with a rusted crowbar. Not unnaturally, it drew the attention of several people in the hall—only one of whom dared to enter.

"Oh, for pity's sake." With a squeak of her pink Crocs, Nancy entered both the room and the fray. "Give him to me. I'll get your blasted ring."

All four of them turned to stare as Nancy strode up to Bones, lifted the tortoise from his startled hands, and tucked him under her arm. Belatedly, Bones realized he'd been robbed of his pet. He pulled up to his full height, but not by so much as an inch did Nancy back down.

"Don't think you can stroll into *my* nursing home and start throwing your weight around," she said tartly. "And don't look at me like I'm going to do this silly animal a mite of harm. I've spent more time with this tortoise than all the rest of you combined. George never went anywhere without him. In fact, he—" She cut herself off, a frown pulling so hard at her lips that her glasses slipped down her nose. She shoved them back up again with a snap. "Let me do what I do best, is all I'm saying."

This sounded to Amber suspiciously like a trap. "Why? What are you going to do to him?"

"Exactly what you think, you fool. Do you or do you not want your grandmother back? If getting this tortoise to pass a piece of jewelry he never should've had access to in the first place is the only way to get it done, then you have no other choice."

Amber blinked—first at Nancy and then at the rest of the assembled crowd. No one did much more than blink back at her.

"Wait a sec," Amber said. "Does this mean you *don't* think my grandmother is a murderer? You believe she's innocent?"

"I'll need a few hours to get things moving," Nancy said by way of reply. "You can pick him up later this evening."

"But you were the one who sent all those mean messages," Amber persisted. Better to get this out now, while she had an ex–Navy SEAL, a retired Irish solider, and Ethan's exposed forearms to back her up. "You're Concerned Citizen. I saw you 'borrow' that tablet from the man in the memory ward. I know you've been the one harassing my grandmother." She hesitated for only a second before flinging her other theory into the fire. "*And* that you were the one who made that anonymous call the night of the Admiral's murder."

Not by so much as a flicker of her eyelashes did Nancy show signs of unease. "I didn't have any other choice. I tried calling security about the disturbance, but there wasn't anyone in the booth. You're a private investigator. You tell me—what else was I supposed to do?"

The question was a fair one. On the one hand, Nancy hadn't denied being her grandmother's internet troll. On the other, she was absolutely right. If security wasn't able to investigate the sounds of an altercation, then making that call to the police was the only other option left to her.

"Giles was at his kids' baseball game," Amber said, since it was the only thing she could think of. "That's why he wasn't there."

Nancy huffed. "Giles has never missed a shift in his entire life. And neither, for that matter, have I." She turned on one squeaky heel and stalked away, the tortoise clutched in her hands. Bones showed every disposition to follow her like a parent watching over a beloved child, but Ethan stopped him with a mild shake of his head.

"She won't hurt the tortoise," he said. "I know you guys don't think much of her, but she's a good nurse."

"She basically just admitted to bullying my grandma," Amber retorted. "How good of a nurse can she be if she spends half her shift on Nextdoor picking on the residents she doesn't like?"

Ethan looked at her so strangely that she suspected she might be growing a second head. "Don't be too hard on her," he eventually said. "I don't think you realize the effect that women like you and your grandmother have on ordinary mortals like us."

For the second time that day, Amber felt completely floored. She watched helplessly as Ethan cleared up his things and exited the room in Nancy's wake. She might have considered staring at the empty doorway too, only Bruce emitted a low chuckle.

"He's right, you know, m'dear." He patted a gentle hand on her shoulder. "If the two of you don't awe, then you terrify. Though when the object is packaged as nicely as you are, I suspect it's a little bit of both."

"Is that supposed to be a riddle?"

"Just an observation. Don't go breaking your shin on a stool that's not in your way."

Bruce chuckled again, this time following it up with a wink as he, too, took his leave. Since Bones was the only person left in the room, Amber had no choice but to whirl her confusion on him.

"Okay. That one really *was* a riddle, right?"

Instead of answering her or, at the very least, denigrating Nancy as someone who needed to be fired at the first opportunity, Bones scrubbed a hand along his jaw. "You think that cranky nurse was telling the truth about the security guard?" he asked.

"No. She's a liar and a fraud, and I don't think we should believe a single word out of her mouth." Amber shot the words out without considering them. Once she did, she was just as quick to take them back again. "Actually, yeah. She might be onto something. If the security booth was empty the night of the Admiral's death, then it would've been easy for the murderer to slip in and erase the tapes. Do you think Giles was paid to be absent?"

"Only one way to find out." Bones gestured for her to precede him out the door. "Lead the way. This is your case, babe. I'm only here at your command."

She bristled. "You know we're never getting back together, right?" In the back of Amber's mind, she knew that she was taking the wrong emotions out on the even wronger man, that her frustrations had little to do with Bones and more to do with the fact that he was the *one* person in the whole retirement community who wasn't trying to hide things from her. "All this being conciliatory and deferential, pretending that everything back in Seattle was just a blip—it's not going to work out the way you think. As soon as my grandmother is cleared, I'm giving you back that stupid hula girl and then I never want to see you again."

Instead of defending himself against her attack, Bones grinned. "Don't go breaking your shin on a stool that's not in your way."

Amber could have screamed with exasperation, but this was a nursing home, after all. She settled for a grunt. "You're as bad as the rest of them, you know that?"

"I'm exactly as bad as I need to be," he returned. "It's why we've always made such a great team."

23

**"If there's one person less trustworthy than a
criminal, it's a member of law enforcement."**

—DEATH COMES CALLING, SEASON 5 EPISODE 10

IF GILES WAS HIDING A deep, dark secret, he was excellent at it.

"Come in, come in." As soon as the security guard noticed Bones and
Amber appear in the doorway to the small, dark room lined with monitors,
he gestured them in. "The Diamondbacks game is about to start. I usually
pull it up on one of the main screens and crank the volume. Mr. Tanaka
across the hall is bedridden, but his family doesn't like him 'wasting what's
left of his life on sports.' What they don't know won't hurt them, eh?"

Without waiting for an answer, the large, cheerful man flipped a switch
to change the video feed to a baseball game. Winking, he turned the sound
up well past safety levels before ducking out of the booth. Unless Amber and
Bones wanted to lose their hearing, they had no choice but to follow him.

"First pitch is in five minutes, Mr. Tanaka," Giles called through the
doorway of a well-lit room practically overflowing with plants. "Saalfrank is
showing good form this year. We should sweep 'em."

Amber peeked inside to find that the Mr. Tanaka in question was little
more than a huddled and unresponsive lump of blankets. She shot a questioning look at Bones, but all he did was shrug and join Giles as he propped
open a nearby exit door and pulled out a pack of cigarettes.

"Sorry," Giles apologized as he lit one and pulled a long drag. "Filthy
habit, but it gives me an excuse to get out of the booth and stretch my legs.

Is this about those erased tapes again? Because I still don't have answers, and the police haven't been back to question me again. I think they assume it's a dead end."

Bones opened his mouth, but Amber beat him to speech. If he wanted to start being conciliatory and taking a back seat, then there was no time like the present to get started.

"Why isn't Mr. Tanaka in the memory ward?" she asked. "Isn't that where the unresponsive patients usually go?"

Giles flicked his ashes into the alley outside the exit. Amber noticed several piles of cigarette butts on the asphalt, giving testament to how often he indulged in his vice of choice.

"He's moving there next week. Open rooms are hard to come by, but I overheard something about an incoming patient falling through." He glanced first at her and then at Bones. "Why the sudden interest in Mr. Tanaka? Don't tell me you think he's the one who erased your security tapes?"

"No, it's not him we suspect," Amber said. She smiled blandly up at the security guard. "*You* are."

As if by unspoken agreement, Bones shifted his position to her flank. Say what she could about her ex, he made one heck of a good bodyguard. Giles could neither attack nor flee without Bones making a very decent show at preventing him.

"Me?" Giles looked first at Amber and then at Bones. He didn't make an attempt to run away, but he did stub his half-finished cigarette under one foot so he could give them his full attention. "Why would I do a thing like that?"

Amber shrugged. "Because you've already proven that you're willing to let people break into podcast studios in the dead of night. Because we have it on good authority that you never miss a shift. Because you're one of the only people here with the skills and access necessary to erase those tapes."

Giles laughed. That sort of response wasn't ideal when questioning a suspect. Either his laugh was genuine, and he was innocent, or it was faked, and he was not. In both cases, he wasn't likely to make it easy to get answers.

"Is that funny to you?" Amber asked.

"A little," Giles admitted. "They were right when they said you were one to worry about."

Bones shifted again, this time in a way that Amber recognized as all his muscles tensing at once. "*They?*" he demanded in a dangerous voice. Instead of intimidating the security guard, Bones's raised hackles only made Giles more amused. It had to be the first time in Bones's life that he faced a man who not only matched him for size, but for indifference.

"I didn't erase those tapes, if that's what you're asking," Giles said. "And no one bribed me to miss that shift. Like I said—my kids had a baseball game. You can ask my husband."

Amber didn't want to believe him, but she had no real reason to suspect Giles of foul play. Granted, she knew very little about the security guard other than that he seemed to genuinely care about his family, but what else did she need? She'd spent enough time with her own relatives to recognize true affection when she saw it.

"Who here *does* have the skills necessary to erase the tapes?" Amber asked. As soon as she voiced the question aloud, she had her answer. "Besides Peggy Lee, I mean?"

"You didn't hear that from me." Giles touched the side of his nose. "But if you ever get a chance to talk to her about her past—and I mean really *talk* to her—see if you can get her to tell you how she met John Draper. Nothing I say or do will get her to spill her secrets."

Bones looked very much as if he'd have enjoyed questioning Giles further—up to and including coercion of the type Amber didn't like to examine too closely—but she reached out and gripped his elbow.

"I think we need to wait and see what happens with Tatiana," she said. "There's no sense in casting accusations until we know exactly what we're accusing people of."

"I'm glad to hear that tortoise is getting on okay," Giles said. He was so wholly unconcerned with the prospect of being charged with accessory to murder that Amber had no choice but to cast her ballot on the side of his innocence. "I saw him a few times on the feed, but he always seemed to move on before I could send someone to fetch him. The Admiral would be pleased to see that he landed in such safe hands. He was anxious to get the poor devil back."

"Of course he was," Amber said.

For once, she had the exact answer as to why. And when Nancy came to find them a few hours later, a hideous twist of gold and diamonds held in the palm of one gloved hand, she was able to confirm it.

Once again, Tatiana was the good luck charm Amber had never known she was missing. The Admiral's family heirloom had been inside him all along.

———————

"I am absolutely not touching that. Someone get me an evidence bag, stat."

Detective Vega, the arresting officer in charge of her grandmother's case, was every bit as hard-assed, by-the-book, and full of wet blankets as Amber had first feared. She was also gorgeous, a statuesque brunette with eyes like black holes and eyebrows slanted like a satyr's—all things that must be a real boon in her line of work. She was *terrifying*.

Or rather, she *would* be, if she wasn't standing with her hands tucked behind her back, her whole body recoiling from a ring that had been polished to the point where any possible remaining evidence had been eradicated on a molecular level.

"It was inside a tortoise's digestive tract, not a barrel of acid," Amber said as Officer Peyton came forward holding a plastic bag. She flashed him a smile as she dropped the ring in. "Hard to believe I was literally carrying it around with me this whole time. Is my grandmother free to go now?"

Detective Vega frowned as she took the bag and dangled it between her forefinger and thumb. That was terrifying too, but for different reasons. The fate of her grandmother's life literally rested in that bag.

"Do you really expect me to believe that this ring just happened to appear from the inside of a tortoise?" the detective asked.

"You're welcome to call Ethan Adler or Nasty N—I mean, Nancy, the nurse who got this ring out of the tortoise. They can both verify that I'm telling the truth. The ring was never stolen—not by my grandmother, and not by anyone else. And you don't have any other motive for George Vincent's murder."

Officer Peyton cleared his throat. "She's not wrong, Detective Vega."

"I can't believe this is happening," the detective muttered. She looked to Bones, her brows in twin arches that only made her look even more like a woodland god. "Is what Ms. Winslow is saying true? You witnessed this event?"

Instead of rushing to Amber's aid, as any good ex-boyfriend PI would, Bones gulped. Actually *gulped*—the sound of his gurgling like a fountain that had been turned on after a decade. From the moment they'd entered the police station and seen Detective Vega round the corner, guttural noises were all he seemed capable of.

His reaction to the woman would have been hilarious if it wasn't so ill-timed. Amber had never seen Bones in such a state. He'd taken one look at the tight knot of Detective Vega's hair and the way her pantsuit looked slept in, and entered a state of catatonic awe.

"Well?" the detective demanded.

Something about the irritated fury of her unlocked Bones's tongue. "I didn't physically *see* the ring come out of Tatiana, no."

Amber came perilously near to stamping her foot. "Bones! You might not have seen the extraction, but you saw the state of the ring after Nancy got it out—and you saw how many strawberry tops Tatiana sucked down as soon as his tummy felt better." She turned toward Vega before Bones could make an even bigger fool of himself. "If you don't have a motive for the murder, then you have no right to keep my grandmother locked up. She's as innocent as the tortoise in all this."

Legally speaking, the police probably had the right to do whatever they wanted—at least, until a judge said otherwise—but Amber wasn't about to back down. Not now that she was actually *getting* somewhere.

"I promise not to let her leave the country in case you have follow-up questions," Amber said. "She's a public figure. A beloved podcaster. She couldn't get very far without someone noticing her fleeing over the border."

Instead of softening, Detective Vega bristled. "I think calling her *beloved* is a stretch. I listened to that podcast of hers. All five seasons. There's not a single piece of factual evidence in any of it."

"Very entertaining though," Officer Katz offered. "Almost like a bed-time story."

"You mean *exactly* like a bedtime story," Vega countered. "How anyone with an ounce of common sense could believe one word of that nonsense is beyond me."

Amber couldn't resist stealing a glance over her shoulder at Bones. Instead of the look of outrage she expected, his head hung slightly, a sheepish reddening about the tips of his ears.

"It's not that bad," he muttered. "You'd be surprised what you can learn when you open your mind to the possibilities."

Amber doubted whether the detective heard this feeble defense of *Death Comes Calling*. With a heavy sigh, Vega nodded at her two subordinates. Amber practically squeaked when they interpreted that nod as a sign to proceed and bustled off to start the paperwork.

"This ring doesn't prove anything except that you bought yourself some time, Ms. Winslow," the detective warned. "It'll get the deceased's children off my back, which is a start, but the fact remains that a man is dead."

Amber nodded gravely. "Understood."

"The number of drugs in his system is highly suspicious," she continued. "That particular combination of nitroglycerin and sildenafil caused an immediate and irrevocable cardiac event—and that doesn't include the vast amount of alcohol used to wash it down. Whoever killed him knew exactly what they were doing."

This time, Amber's nod was more surprised than grave. Nitroglycerin and sildenafil? Why did that sound familiar?

"And of course there's the upheaval of the podcast studio and locked door," Vega finished. "I know you don't think much of my officers, but my department *will* find who's responsible for George Vincent's death, and we *will* prosecute them to the full extent of the law."

Amber felt the hostile undertone to this and would have done no more than swallow the threat, but Bones suddenly found his tongue. She was guessing he'd also found several other of his body parts, but there was no way she was touching any of that with a ten-foot pole.

"In that case, you're going to want to question Nancy Holloway up at Seven Ponds," he said. "She's the nurse who got the ring from the tortoise. We also have reason to believe she's the one who called in your anonymous tip the night of the murder."

"*We?*" Amber demanded, but she may as well not have spoken for all the attention that was paid her.

"We don't consider Nancy a suspect, but she may be able to shed some light on what went down inside the studio that night," Bones continued. "I assume you've also looked into the life insurance policy? The motivation for every criminal activity can be boiled down to one of three things: sex, power, or money. And since money can easily buy the other two, I think we have our answer."

Amber almost snorted to hear Bones plagiarizing the *Death Comes Calling* podcast verbatim, but Detective Vega beat her to it.

"That's the most pedantic thing I've ever heard," she said coolly. "Any other brilliant and patently obvious insights you'd like to share?"

"Uh. Um. Yes. I mean, no. That is—" Bones was so flustered that he started to lean his hip on a chair without noticing it was on wheels. With a stumble and a whoosh, he sent it skittering across the floor…where it was caught in one neat hand by Jade McCallan, looking small but triumphant as she was led across the linoleum floor.

"Grandma!" Amber dashed over to greet her. Despite the fact that her grandmother had been the one to spend the better part of the last week behind bars, she immediately wrapped her arms around Amber and refused to let go.

"Shh, child. It's all right. I've got you. It's going to be okay." The whisper of her grandmother's breath moved over her skin, warming her from the outside in. "From the way you're acting, you'd think I just narrowly escaped the guillotine. It was a county jail, not Alcatraz. I always knew you'd get me out before I was forced to eat the meatloaf."

"Terrible stuff," Officer Katz agreed with a cough. "Not sure it's meat at all."

Amber's laugh was absorbed by her grandmother's tight hold on her. She might have stayed that way for hours, basking in a hug she'd feared never to experience again, if not for the sound of Detective Vega's dry drawl.

"If you're done with this touching scene, perhaps you could tell me exactly how or why that tortoise of the Admiral's ate a piece of jewelry the size of his head?" the detective asked.

At the moment, that seemed the least of Amber's worries. Her grandmother was free, and she'd completed her first official job as a private investigator. This was a moment for celebration, not further questioning.

"Does it matter? He went missing long before the murder, so the two things can't possibly be tied together. That rock has been sitting in his gut for weeks."

"I wonder," Vega said, but she didn't feel the need to elaborate further. "Now get out of here, all of you. The last thing I need is for the press to get wind of this and start demanding my head for letting criminals walk free. That, by the way, is a direct order. If I hear one peep of this investigation on your podcast, so help me…"

"Why, Detective Vega. Are you violating my grandmother's first amendment rights?"

"Out."

"I'm just saying. Unless you get a judge to issue a gag order, we have a constitutional right to—"

"Officers Peyton and Katz, if you don't remove these three from my sight right this instant, you'll be put on probationary leave without pay for as long as it takes my blood pressure to get back to normal. And *that*, I'm happy to report, is well within my ethical and moral obligations to this community."

Officer Peyton flashed Amber a reassuring grin. "You heard the detective. Right this way."

Amber didn't need any further prodding. With her arm wrapped firmly around her grandmother's waist, she followed the two officers out the door. Bones lingered a few steps behind, and she could hear him say something about "keeping an eye on things back at the retirement community," but the response Vega gave him was so scathing that she had no fear he'd be allowed to do anything of the sort.

"Well, that was quite an adventure, wasn't it?" her grandmother asked as soon as she inhaled her first breath of fresh air. The air was hot and dry and not the least bit refreshing, but neither of them seemed to notice.

"No. It was awful, and if you ever do that to me again, I'll—"

"You'll have to call your mother and let her know I'm a free woman again. She'll hate that."

"Grandma, will you be serious for two minutes? I think we should take you to the clinic to get an IV infusion first thing. After that—"

"She might even fly out to berate me for getting you in such a fix. That would be nice. You should tell her that under no circumstances is she needed or wanted here. That'll light a fire to the stick up her ass."

"Grandma!"

Jade laughed and shook her head, the cascade of mahogany and gray tumbling down her back. "What? You don't think she'd come?"

On the contrary, that sounded *exactly* like something her mother would do—and since the last thing Amber wanted was to ruin this moment of triumph, she decided to put the order out of her mind. She'd only just gotten her grandmother back. No way was she sharing her with the one woman on this planet who'd let her go to waste.

"We can talk about this later," Amber said as she started leading her grandmother toward Bones's car. They'd have to wait until he picked up the shattered pieces of his ego from the precinct floor, but for once, Amber didn't mind.

Her grandmother was free. They were safe.

And if a nagging doubt in the back of her mind reminded her that a murderer was still very much at large at the Seven Ponds Retirement Community, she didn't let it bother her. As long as Jade McCallan wasn't the one responsible for his death, Amber had nothing more to worry about.

24

*"Few people kill for love, but
plenty seem to die for it."*

—*DEATH COMES CALLING*, SEASON 4 EPISODE 10

AMBER HAD NO IDEA WHO called an impromptu gathering of the *Death Comes Calling* podcast group, but everyone was waiting for them at her grandmother's condo when they returned.

Including, against all odds, Geerta Blom.

"And thus the prodigal podcaster returns," Geerta said as Amber, Bones, and Jade made their way up the front steps. If Amber had been the one who only just managed to avoid having the book thrown at her, she'd have preferred a chance to shower and get her bearings before facing a woman like Geerta, but her grandmother was nothing if not resilient.

"I hear you kicked my granddaughter out of my home the moment the opportunity afforded itself," Jade responded as they halted on the front porch. "That was rather short-sighted of you, don't you think?"

Geerta acknowledged her words with a frown. "It's company policy, I'm afraid. My hands were tied."

"I believe what you meant to say was, *Thank you, Amber, for solving the mystery of the missing ring*," her grandmother said. "Also, *The check for your services will be waiting for you at the reception desk tomorrow morning.*"

To Amber's surprise, Geerta nodded. "The Vincent children are prepared to be generous for the return of their property. Especially considering the, ah, misunderstanding about your involvement."

If that wasn't enough to floor Amber—she was going to get paid for freeing her grandmother? In a way that was termed *generous?*—Bones followed up with, "The usual finder's fee in situations like this is five percent."

If the ring really was worth three million, Amber's mental math put her share of the recovery at a staggering one hundred and fifty thousand dollars. Geerta's must have done the same because she looked pained for a prolonged moment. "I can probably get the Vincent children to two percent, but it'll take some doing."

"Then do it," Bones said. "If Amber hadn't found that tortoise and taken care of him, he'd have probably died and taken all possibility of recovering that ring with him. Sixty thousand dollars is the least they can do."

"I think I'm going to be sick," Amber said as they watched Geerta walk away, her heels clipping with their usual speed down the sidewalk. She gripped the guard rail so tightly that she felt her fingers starting to cramp. "*Sixty thousand dollars?* For asking Nasty Nancy to give a tortoise an enema?"

"Oh, dear," her grandmother murmured. "I've missed quite a bit of the fun, haven't I?"

Fun was the last word Amber would have used to describe the events of the past week, but as the sound of laughter burst from the inside of the condo, she had to admit that it fit the current situation to a tee. Jade squeezed Amber's free hand before throwing open the door like Norma Desmond making her debut. Amber would have followed her inside, but Bones stopped her with a touch of his hand on her arm.

"You can keep it, by the way," he said before she could issue a protest. "The money, I mean. This was your case, not mine."

A month ago, Amber would have immediately countered his offer with the firm resolution that they were a team and the only fair way to deal with such largesse was to split it. But that was back when she really *had* believed them to be a team—when she was just a few signatures away from realizing her professional and personal dreams, when her future seemed wrapped up in his. In many ways, she still felt that way, especially since Bones had genuinely helped her with this case.

Unfortunately for him, she was no longer willing to accept his scraps.

Judith Webb, a.k.a. Jade McCallan, a.k.a. the brain behind Horace

Horatio, would never split a finder's fee with a man who'd once cast her in the role of secretary. She'd take the money, smile sweetly, and then do exactly what she wanted. Amber might not ever gain her grandmother's level of confidence and brazenness, but there was something to be said for taking what the world offered without apology.

"Thank you," she said. "I accept. And in return, I'm prepared to uphold my end of the bargain. You can have Tatiana."

"Really?" Instead of looking upset at losing out on his share of the money, Bones practically lit up. "Because I was going to ask, but I didn't think you'd be willing to let him go without a fight. I'll take great care of him, I promise. The little guy and I have an understanding."

"Wait. Are you talking about Tatiana the *tortoise*?" Amber reared back as if struck. That animal had basically solved this case. That animal had basically saved them all.

The least she could do was save him in return.

"I was talking about your stupid hula girl—the whole reason you're here helping me, remember? For your good luck charm? You can't seriously think I'd give away my pet that easily."

"Technically he's not your pet. He was the Admiral's."

"Yeah, and I found him. I'm also the one who's been giving him baths and taking him to the vet and—"

He snorted. "Please. You didn't *take him to the vet*. You pulled out the charm and roped that poor guy with the bum hip into doing your bidding."

"Ethan's hip is made of titanium, so it's probably stronger than yours, and he's never once considered me charming. Ask him."

Bones started to swell up in a way that generally preceded his need to air an opinion as loudly as possible, but he managed to get hold of himself before the shouting started. "Fine. I'll sign those papers you keep nattering on about. That's what you really want, isn't it? To be a PI? To start your own shop without me?"

This was said with such an air of injury that Amber was momentarily stunned. She'd always assumed that Bones was holding her back out of self-ishness, but this sounded less about wanting an assistant and more about not wanting to be left behind.

But behind from what? Amber was an agent of chaos. An untrustworthy mess. Even her grandmother's podcast group had assumed she'd come here not to pay a visit to her long-lost relative, but to hunt down a box of jewelry for a man who had no need of it.

"I never said I wanted to leave," she said.

"You didn't have to, Amber. I could always tell." His gaze flicked to an empty spot a few feet above her head. It was the closest he'd ever come to making an emotional confession, and considering how hard he was finding it to look her in the eye, she was guessing it was also the closest he'd ever get. "So it's a deal? I'll sign off on your training, and then I can have Tatiana— *both* Tatianas?"

She thought of the tortoise inside the condo behind her. He was probably whirling around on a Roomba or eating some of Lincoln's kitchen scraps, the last tie the group had to a friend they had yet to mourn. As strange as it seemed, she'd grown attached to her reptilian friend. It was a new and not unpleasant sensation to think that someone actually *needed* her.

"No deal," she said. "Sorry, Bones, but it's too little, too late. I wouldn't even be able to use a Washington PI license down here. I'd have to requalify if I wanted to work in Arizona."

Bones wasn't a man used to hearing the word *no*, but his response had less to do with hearing a negative and more to do with Amber's plans for the future. "You don't seriously mean you plan to stay in this hellscape of armpit sweat and denture cream?"

Amber laughed. The moment she released that light, trilling sound, a similar one sounded from inside the house. Her grandmother was clearly wasting no time getting back on familiar ground.

"I don't know what I want," she said with perfect honesty. "I know I'm too old to say that, and that I'm treading down the same dangerous path my grandmother took, but I have unfinished business here. Including, in case you forgot, a murder that has yet to be solved."

"You don't really think you can do better than Detective Vega," he said, stating it as a fact rather than a question. "She's a professional."

Amber's prickly nature reared itself up to its full, dangerous height. "So am I. I might not have the fancy badge or a college degree, but I'm not ready to call this thing quits. And I'm not giving up Tatiana just because you're lonely without me. You should've thought of that before you treated me like some temp you hired straight out of secretarial school."

Without another word, she turned on her heel and stalked into the house. Bones was the exact sort of man to follow her, so she was careful to slam the door before he could make the attempt.

The moment she stepped through the foyer into the living room–kitchen combo, she was assailed on all sides by the warmth and vibrancy of a set of retirees who were rapidly reaching the point of hilarity. The briny scent of olives and vodka warred with flour and butter as Lincoln stood in the kitchen rolling out pastry. Tatiana wasn't, as she'd expected, riding a Roomba, but was instead munching happily on a plate of arugula that Peggy Lee stood guarding like a sphinx. Raffi and Julio reclined in twin chairs while Camille and a woman Amber had never met stood chatting with her grandmother.

"Bless you, child. It's about time. Did you manage to rid yourself of that overgrown heap of muscles you call a boyfriend?"

"He's my *ex*-boyfriend," Amber said as she accepted the martini glass being held out to her. "And, yes, he's gone for now. But I wouldn't put it past him to stick around until this case is over. Next to me and possibly you, he's the most stubborn person I know."

Her grandmother saw nothing amiss in this statement. She'd changed into one of the flowy, frothy sundresses that showed an indecent amount of leg, her feet bare and her hair streaming down her back. To look at her, you'd think she'd just returned from a vacation in the tropics rather than a six-by-eight-foot cell.

"I'm glad to hear you plan to see the case through to the end," said the woman Amber didn't recognize. Like the rest of the assembled crowd, she was facing her seventh or eighth decade. Her steely loc'd hair was piled loosely on the top of her head, complemented by a pair of gorgeous, chunky earrings that pulled so hard at her earlobes Amber could see right through the holes in them. It took only a glance at the wedding band on her left hand and the way Lincoln's eyes kept sliding over toward her to put the rest together.

"You must be Lincoln's wife," she said as she held out a polite hand. "Veronica, right? It's great to finally meet you. How was the visit to your sister?"

The older woman's deep brown eyes twinkled into hers. "Very restful, thank you. She lives on the beach with her cats, so I pay her a trip every time this group of revelers starts to get to be too much for me."

Camille arched one perfect brow. "Didn't you say the number of her cats has multiplied to an even dozen?"

"Yes."

"And that she had both her kids *and* her grandkids staying with her?"

"It was lovely to see them again, even if baby James was colicky." Veronica heaved a playful sigh. "I haven't slept that soundly in months."

Amber immediately decided that this woman was her new role model. Anyone who found a way to balance life in a place like this and the outside world deserved multiple commendations. "Twelve cats sound downright peaceful compared to the past few weeks I've had," she said.

"So I've been hearing." Veronica winked and placed a hand over her stomach. "The only problem is that I never eat as well when Lincoln's not there to cater to my every whim. I've been dreaming of his croissants for weeks."

"You'll have to dream for about five more hours, love," Lincoln called from the kitchen. He waved his rolling pin like a sword. "Perfection takes time."

"I know," she called back. "I've been waiting forty-six years for you to meet my high standards. A few more, and we might be able to get you there."

Amber was about to release a lovelorn sigh when something about Veronica's words caused her spine to stiffen. Camille noticed, and so did her grandmother, but neither woman was given a chance to mention it.

"It's good to have you back, Jade, but I had you in the clink for a good three more weeks," Julio said, noticing nothing amiss. "Lost an even two hundo. We'll need something new to spice up the pot."

"I expect we'll be busy enough recording the next season of the podcast," Raffi said. Only by a twitch of one eyelid did he expose himself to be interested in anything related to gambling. Whatever else Amber might say about these people, they did seem to have their friend's best interest at heart—*all* their friends' best interests at heart. "A first-person account of your time behind bars will thrill the listeners, Jade. I hope you don't plan to leave anything out."

The discussion that followed this was loud, heated, and accompanied by so much enthusiasm that Amber had to run to the bathroom to compose herself. Once there, however, she lifted a hand to the medicine cabinet and pulled out the now-familiar prescriptions belonging to her grandmother.

"Atorvastatin for cholesterol and lisinopril for blood pressure," she recited as she pulled out each bottle. Her heart leapt to her throat as she closed her fist around the last one. "And sildenafil for reasons I'm not even going to begin to explore."

There was also, she noted, a box of sleep aids that had been opened and placed on the top shelf. Inside, there were two packs of pills missing. She had no way of proving that those pills had been used for anything but to help her grandmother get a good night's sleep, but nothing about Jade's habits hinted that she had a hard time falling asleep.

Amber dropped to the edge of the tub, the box of sleeping pills crushed in her hand. There was no way for her to forget that deep, blissful sleep her first night in the condo, when she'd awoken more refreshed than she'd felt in years. Nor was there a way to deny that Lincoln had been cheerfully sliding a plate of hot croissants in front of her the moment she woke up.

Croissants that take eight hours to make. Croissants that mean both Lincoln and my grandmother were awake at the time of the Admiral's murder.

"Oh, Grandma. No." Amber almost sobbed out loud to think that she'd been such a fool. She'd been so fixated on the pain pills in her grandmother's possession that she hadn't thought to examine anything else in her medicine cabinet. And she'd been too pleased to be welcomed with open arms and fresh baked goods to find anything odd in that first morning.

But both Lincoln and her grandmother had been up the whole night. Other than that first sign of shock, Jade had shown no signs of regret or remorse at her friend's passing. And even though the financial motive was no longer viable, Amber had no doubt that her grandmother's convoluted logic could have easily provided another reason to commit a murder.

For fun? For ratings? Or maybe—just maybe—by accident?

Amber knew it behooved her to step into the next room at once, demanding answers while the memory of jail sat fresh in her grandmother's mind, but she found she couldn't face either Jade or Lincoln in her current state of mind. She'd just freed her grandmother from a lifetime behind bars using nothing but her wits. She was supposed to be the heroine of this story. Not an accessory after the fact. Not a *murderer*.

There was so much noise in the living room that she was able to slip outside without anyone noticing. Without giving herself a chance to second-guess her actions, she dialed the number for home.

"Hello?" Her mom's terse, slightly annoyed voice sounded on the other end of the line. "Amber? Is that you? Where are you calling from?"

"I'm still in Arizona. I'm at Grandma's."

Instead of jumping to the obvious conclusion—that Amber wouldn't have called her unless the situation was desperate—her mother tsked. "I wish you wouldn't call her that."

"Biologically, that's what she is."

"You know what I mean. What's the problem now? Have they set a date for her trial? Am I going to need to come down there?"

That gave Amber pause. "Would you? Come to Arizona, I mean? Because the last time we talked, you said—"

"I'm still not bailing her out. The last thing that woman deserves is either my sympathy or my savings." A sudden silence pulsed next to Amber's ear. Every part of her yearned to fill it, but she forced herself to wait and see what else her mom had to say. "But Dad and I have been talking, and he thinks it might be a good idea if I come get you."

Amber couldn't have been more shocked if she'd discovered that her grandmother and Lincoln were, well, murderers. "Come get me?"

The annoyed *tsk* on the other end of the line did much to restore Amber's sudden imbalance. "You don't need to sound so shocked. I have a few weeks of vacation saved up, and our cruise to Iceland isn't setting sail until next summer." A silence fell again. "I didn't realize that you and that boyfriend of yours had broken up. The guest room is available if you need it."

"Bones, Mom. His name is Bones."

"Which should have been your first clue not to take up with him in the first place. Honestly, Amber. Is he a skeleton? Does he have a passion for paleontology? I see no other cause for saddling a full-grown man with a name like that."

Despite herself, a giggle escaped. "I'll pass your feedback along, thanks. I'm sure he'll appreciate it. But you don't have to drop everything and come to Arizona—not unless you want to, anyway. I'm calling because—well, the thing is—"

Amber stopped, unable to remember why she'd dialed her mom's phone number in the first place. Not for this rare burst of emotional support, which was starting to freak her out, and not to share her growing suspicion that she'd just helped a murderer escape her sentence, because, well, that would be a ridiculous thing to admit in the open.

"She's free," she eventually said. "I helped get Grandma out of jail."

"You did?" The surprise in her mom's voice didn't speak well of her confidence in her only daughter, but there were only so many miracles one could expect in a day. "How did you manage that?"

"Because I'm a private investigator, Mom. It's my literal job."

"Hmm."

Amber let that familiar derisive sound wash over her. "I'm pretty sure Grandma will invite me to stay with her a bit longer, and I'd like to take her up on the offer, only…" She bit her lip as she trailed off. "Mom, she didn't, like, commit any crimes when you were a kid, did she? That's not the thing that drove you away?"

"The thing that drove me away?"

"Yeah. The whole She-Who-Shall-Not-Be-Named situation we've got going on. Growing up, you never told us anything about her except that we were under no circumstances to have any kind of relationship. Before I commit to staying here or helping her or—oh, I don't know—even just letting myself get attached, I'd like to know why. Why do you hate her so much? What did she do to you?"

There. Amber had asked the question. It was out now. Her heart hammered in her chest as she awaited her mother's response—the thing that would help her decide what to do next. Every part of her being longed for reassurance, a promise that her grandmother wasn't the heartless monster she appeared to be, but she had no idea if her mom was even capable of such an emotional response.

She could feel displeasure, yes. True concern for her fellow parishioners, sure. But affection for her daughter? For the one person who'd never been able to break through the shell of her heart?

The jury—and Amber—were still out on that one.

The sigh that heaved on the other end of the phone could have moved mountains. "I don't *hate* her. Must you always be so dramatic?"

"I'm pretty sure I'm not the one who cut an entire human being out of my life."

"Do you know what your problem is, Amber?"

Amber could have recited an entire list of her problems, but she doubted her mother needed the reminder.

"It's the same problem I always had with your grandmother. From the day you were born, it's been as if you can't bear the ordinary things that everyone else has to deal with. You spit up every drop of milk I fed you. Screamed whenever you were swaddled by so much as an inch. And woe to the parent who used a drop of artificial scent in your detergent or bathwater. You've never seen hives like that on a human being before."

"Wait. Are you mad because I was a difficult baby?"

"I'm not *mad* about anything. That's my whole point. From the moment you were put into my arms, I knew that what I had to offer you wouldn't be enough—just like it wasn't enough for your grandmother. Regular life is too small to hold you, so you thrash and kick and invent your own dramas at every turn."

"Mom," Amber said, but her mother kept going.

"Instead of dealing with what's right in front of you, you dream up these wild fantasies instead. For your grandmother, that meant joining cults and marrying a succession of unworthy men, always moving on to the next big adventure without a thought for the child who just wanted to go to the same school for longer than three months at a time."

"Mom," she said again, this time with a plea underscoring everything. What she was pleading for, however, was anyone's guess. For the bitterness she heard in her mother's voice; for the grandmother she, too, recognized as a reckless and beautiful disaster; for the way her whole being longed to throw off the bitterness of the former and adhere to the messy glory of the latter.

"I always knew your brothers would find good jobs and get married, put down roots that the rest of us can depend on. But you…you're exactly like her. You want action and chaos, and if for some reason you can't find it, you go out and make some of your own."

"I'm sorry your childhood was so hard." It was the only thing Amber could think to say, though it sounded inadequate even to her own ears.

"And I'm sorry yours wasn't hard enough," came the short reply. "Look, Amber—I don't know what you want from me. I have no desire to see or talk to your grandmother, but I won't stop you from building a relationship with her if that's what you want. Maybe she's different now. Maybe she's changed."

"She hasn't." Even though Amber knew very little about the family matriarch, she felt that down to her very bones. "But that doesn't make her unworthy of being loved."

"Okay." The word was uttered simply and without rancor—which, for Amber's mom, conceded a whole heck of a lot. "Just remember that I'm a phone call away if you need me. And for the love of everything, don't let her be the director in every scene the two of you share. She will, you know. I've never known anyone else capable of striding into a room and taking it over as easily as she can. Well, except for you."

Amber's mom hung up before she could respond, which was for the best since her words had given Amber considerable food for thought. There was no denying the truth of what her mom had said: that her grandmother was a storyteller, a director. Jade McCallan—even her name was fiction—was a woman for whom the limelight was akin to oxygen. It was why she was the one who wrote the *Death Comes Calling* scripts instead of the group as a whole. It was why her condo was the epicenter of activity—the place where parties were thrown and friends gathered. It was also why everyone had stood back and allowed her to take the fall for a crime that Amber understood the extent of for the very first time.

She picked up one of the pill bottles from the bathroom counter and read the label. Sure enough, it confirmed everything she now knew to be true. All the medications, even the one for the sildenafil, had been prescribed by someone named Dr. Carnegie.

Not Dr. Lopez—the doctor who'd prescribed the Admiral's medication, the doctor who Amber had met that day she'd stumbled accidentally into the memory ward.

"I can't believe it took me this long to figure it out," she breathed. "Or that they let me run around playing investigator this whole time. Oh, how they must have been laughing behind my back."

She slipped back into the living room without making a sound. The party was well underway, the decibel level rapidly reaching that of hilarity. Pausing at the threshold, she let her gaze travel from animated face to animated face. And then she did what she always did when confronted with a case like this: she shifted her focus from the center, Jade McCallan, to the surroundings instead.

Lincoln, busy making his eight-hour croissants.

Raffi, whose dapper exterior made him appear every inch the elite chemistry teacher he once was.

Julio, his breathing ragged as a result of the heart condition he'd never once denied having.

Camille, elegant and broke, but so determined to put a good face on things that nothing ruffled her.

Peggy Lee, whose computer skills and ability to nose her way into anyone's business were legendary.

Tatiana, a tortoise who'd somehow managed to swallow an entire heirloom ring, and who'd been running at large all over the retirement community for weeks.

And, most important of all, the way they rallied together in times of need. As friends. As *family*.

"Everything okay, child?" her grandmother asked as soon as she caught sight of Amber. Amber's response was to stride up to Julio, her hands on her hips.

"Julio, what medication do you take for your heart condition?" she asked. He blinked at her but answered readily enough.

"Beta blockers and nitrates, mostly," he said. "Why?"

Amber's lips compressed tightly but she moved on to the next person without explaining herself. "Camille, you and my grandmother drank a little too much a few months ago and fell on the steps. Is that something that happens often? Intoxication to the point where bodies and furniture start to fly?"

"I wouldn't say it's a *daily* occurrence, but when the gin starts to flow, my love…"

Amber turned on her heel and approached her next victim—only she was rapidly coming to see that the term *victim* applied to no one in this room. "Raffi, if I were to ask you to explain the dangerous interactions between different medications, could you do it?"

Raffi removed his glasses and began elegantly polishing them with the handkerchief from his suit pocket. "I used to do a whole unit on the manufacture of poison using only items in a medicine cabinet. The kids really enjoyed that. The rabid little monsters were never more engaged than when discussing the chemical components of toxins."

By this time, Amber had no need to continue confirming her suspicions, but she was on a roll. "Lincoln, is there a way for you to shortcut your croissants? Like, to speed up the process so they're done faster?"

At Lincoln's gasp of mock outrage, Veronica wrapped her arm around her husband's waist and gave it a squeeze. "This one's a perfectionist through and through," she said. "He'd never do anything so shabby."

Amber nodded, unsure how far to keep pushing. Every single person in this room knew what she was doing…and not a single one of them was making the least effort to stop her.

Because they wanted her to know the truth? Because they *needed* it? Or because Camille had told them that she wasn't the threat they suspected she might be? If Amber hadn't been sent here to investigate for Camille's ex-husband, if she really was just a granddaughter trying to understand her roots, then what more did they have to hide?

She moved to Peggy Lee next. Before she could ask her question, the tiny woman flung up a hand. "I plead the Fifth."

"But I haven't asked you anything yet."

"And if I have my way, you never will. I'm just a poor old woman who only learned to use a computer a few years ago. I refuse to be harassed by a young upstart who doesn't know when to leave well enough alone."

Amber narrowed her eyes but allowed the objection to stand. She had the distinct feeling that getting Peggy Lee to admit anything would require torture at a level not even Bones was prepared to undertake.

"At least tell me this much," Amber said. "Did you know that ConcernedCitizen1443 was Nancy? And that she's been the one harassing my grandma?"

A smile touched the edges of Peggy Lee's thin lips. "There's nothing that goes on around here that I don't know about. If you haven't realized that by now, you never will."

Amber believed her. She also knew that her last stop would be more difficult than all the rest. If her suspicions were correct, then Jade McCallan was the one who'd orchestrated this entire affair.

A death, yes, but not a murder.

Pausing just long enough to tickle Tatiana under the chin, she went to join her grandmother in the far corner of the room behind the bar cart. The look of mockery on the older woman's face did nothing to dissuade her, especially when their eyes met. That warm brown gaze said everything that Amber needed to know—that the death of the Admiral had been a monumental loss, but that this particular group of friends had been granted plenty of time to prepare for it ahead of time.

"You were surprised that first morning," Amber said, her voice pitched low enough that only the two of them could hear. "When the police arrived to inform you of the Admiral's death—you were genuinely upset to see them."

"Well, really. Who wouldn't have been under those conditions?" her grandmother returned.

Amber ignored the question, which had been uttered in a purely rhetorical spirit. "I thought it was because you were upset about the Admiral's death, but that wasn't it, was it? You were only upset that someone had called the police—that *Nancy* had called the police."

"Did she now? Bright of you to have put that together."

Amber felt the familiar well of frustration start to build up at her grandmother's evasiveness, bringing with it a new understanding of her mother. Her mom was a woman who dealt in certainties. God was good. Account figures always added up. Children could be molded to become anything you wanted them to be. The only problem was, Jade McCallan had never done a predictable thing in her life—and neither, Amber knew, had she.

What a trial they both must have been to Moonbeam Effervesence Winslow née Webb. What a disappointment.

"You thought about marrying him, didn't you? Or at least taking over his power of attorney so his care would be in your hands?" Amber continued. She had the doubtful satisfaction of seeing her grandmother wince, but by no other sign did she show she was affected by the words coming out of her mouth. "But what was the point? He was bound for the memory ward one way or the other. His kids, I imagine, were eager to get him behind a locked door so they could get their hands on that three million dollars. That's the only part I can't figure out—if the ring went missing by accident or if you guys fed it to Tatiana on purpose in order to hide it from them. I'm leaning toward the first one. If you'd have known the ring was gone and that his kids would raise such a fuss over it, you might have done a better job covering your tracks."

Her grandmother's only response to this was a blink, but Amber wasn't fooled. That blink hid a gleam of understanding and—did she dare say it?—respect.

"Only you didn't expect to get arrested, did you? You figured the Admiral's death would be ruled a heart attack and no one would think anything of it—a man nearing the end of his life, mercifully taken before his condition advanced too far. But the going-away party you threw—since I assume that's what went down in the podcast studio—got a little out of hand. You trashed the place. Made enough noise to rouse Nancy's interest. Ran off and locked the door behind you, not suspecting that such an action would make it appear as though the Admiral's death was anything but natural."

Amber drew a deep breath. With each passing sentence, she found herself falling deeper and deeper into the narrative. "And then, while Peggy Lee erased the security footage—thanks to Giles, who absented himself from the security booth because I'm pretty sure he's the grandson of the memory ward patient Dr. Lopez told me about—you came home and made croissants with Lincoln. You waited for me to wake up from the sleep you'd drugged me into so you could pull off your farewell without interruption and pretended as though your friend's death meant nothing. When all this time, you've been grieving deeply for a man whose life you helped end. A life *all* of you helped end together."

Amber was ashamed to admit to the feeling of triumph she felt as soon as her monologue was over. Nothing about the tale she'd just unraveled was worth celebrating, unless there was comfort to be found in an ending that the Admiral had been given a say in choosing.

"Well?" she demanded when her grandmother continued to be silent. "Don't you have anything to say for yourself?"

"Oh, my dear sweet child." Her grandmother smiled at her then—a smile that Amber didn't trust for a second, a smile that her mother would have certainly deplored. "We can't possibly put all that in the podcast. Who would believe it? But if that's the kind of solution you're prepared to write for us, I'm sure you'll come up with something just as good. Our next season will be a hit, I'm sure of it."

"Grandma!"

Her grandmother wrapped an arm around her shoulder. From the outside, the gesture was a friendly one, full of comfort and camaraderie, but the way her grandmother's fingers dug into her upper arm told a different story.

"You *can* come up with a different ending, yes?" she asked in a voice that felt as hard as her grip. "One that satisfies just as well? The Admiral would have hated to think that his legacy could be reduced to such a scandalous end. He wasn't that sort of man. He was better than all the rest of us combined."

Amber drew a long, steady breath. Once upon a time, she'd asked Bones why he'd become a private investigator instead of a police officer or detective. With his experience and pedigree, almost any law enforcement door would have been open to him. His response had been typical of him—self-assured and surface deep—but she was starting to wonder if maybe he'd been right.

Laws were never made for men like me, babe. Why follow them when I can bend them to my will instead?

Amber had a strong suspicion that Detective Vega wouldn't agree with this assessment—and that Bones, if confronted with his own words, would deny it to his dying breath—but she was willing to reconsider her stance. If the podcast group *had* killed their friend, and if they'd done it at his request, then there was no murder.

There was a death, yes. A crime, probably. But even though everyone treated her investigative skills with respect, Amber wasn't a licensed private investigator. She was a just a woman paying a long visit to her grandmother. She had no obligations other than the ones Jade McCallan asked of her.

"I want something in return," Amber said suddenly. She stepped aside until the manacle of her grandmother's hand loosened. "I'll write any ending you want, but only if you meet my demands."

Her grandmother's eyes narrowed shrewdly. The sounds of conversation seemed to fade into the background, but neither woman paid them any heed as they squared off behind the bar cart.

"Why, Amber. Are you asking me for a bribe?"

"No, Grandma. It's not bribery I'm after." She grinned, remembering their earlier conversation. "It's extortion."

The ripple of laughter that escaped her grandmother did much to restore the balance between them. Amber had the sensation that as long as that sound still existed in the world, nothing could touch her. People would come and go, friends sent off into their next big adventures. Jobs would disintegrate and boyfriends disappoint. But what did any of that matter when she had a grandmother who would go to jail rather than expose her friend's death as the tragedy it was? Who trusted so much in her granddaughter's ability to free her that she'd carry that laugh all over the county jail?

"Anything, child. If it's in my power to give it to you, I will."

"Good." Amber drove her hand into her pocket and extracted the locket. It dangled from her fingertips, the silver heart bouncing as gravity took hold. Her grandmother sucked in a sharp breath at the sight of it but never wavered. "Then I want to know about this locket, about my mother, and, most important, about how *the devil* you know so much about my life."

25

"It's very rare that the punishment fits the crime."

—*DEATH COMES CALLING*, SEASON 3 EPISODE 6

BY THE TIME JADE FINISHED unfolding her tale, Amber didn't know who she felt the most sorry for: her grandmother, her mother, or herself.

"Your brother Derek has three children—Genevieve, Geronimo, and Muriel, all of which I maintain are the cruelest possible names to saddle on anyone born this side of the century. Mikey has two, though I find it very difficult to tell them apart on his posts. Must they *always* wear flannel and hoodies? Doesn't the sun ever shine up there in Washington?"

"Grandma, don't." Amber took a bite of one of the warm croissants that Lincoln had left heaped on the kitchen counter. The condo felt oddly quiet after all the buzz and activity, but not in an unpleasant way. Like an open field after a rainstorm or the hush that follows a moving speech, there was something cathartic about having the place all to themselves. "Please don't act like they aren't important to you. I know you've been paying close attention to our lives. You even knew Bones's real name—a thing he's taken *very* careful pains to hide."

"Well, really. What else was I supposed to do?" Her grandmother gave a sniff. She had yet to touch her own croissant, but her martini glass remained equally undisturbed, so Amber had no cause for complaint. "The day Mikey was born, your mother told me that under no circumstances was I to reach out, ask for help, offer support, or even send birthday cards in the mail. 'It's better for them to have no grandmother at all than one they won't be able to depend on.' That's what she said to me."

The flaky pastry turned to sawdust in Amber's mouth. "I'm sorry. You didn't deserve that."

"Actually, I did. I missed her wedding—did she ever tell you that? I wanted to go, and I meant to get there with plenty of time to spare, but there was a yacht and the Amalfi Coast and the most delicious millionaire with mommy issues."

"Of course there was."

Her grandmother sighed and leaned back against the couch cushion. For the first time since they'd arrived back at the retirement community, she looked her age. Weary lines settled around her mouth and on her brow, the streaks of gray in her hair overtaking the dark strands underneath. "The truth is, I used Italy as an excuse. I couldn't face your father's family—such good, wholesome, ordinary people. I knew they'd take one look at me and wonder how on earth your mother turned out as well as she did."

"She's not perfect," Amber said. "Take it from someone who used to have to hide her graphic novels inside the Bible. She's got plenty of flaws to choose from."

Her grandmother reached over and patted her knee. "That's sweet of you to say, but we both know it isn't true. She was a good mom to you—still is, in many ways. I was never that for her. Not a safe harbor in any kind of weather, let alone anything with the least sign of wind."

Amber opened her mouth to refute this, but a shadow passed over her grandmother's expression. "I let Effie down in a lot of different ways—more than you could possibly imagine—but that was the one thing I knew I could give her. She asked me to give her space, and I did, but that didn't mean I couldn't keep tabs on you kids. It worked out best for everyone that way."

It was on the tip of Amber's tongue to say that it hadn't worked out best for *her* in the slightest, but something about her grandmother's slumped posture gave her pause. So many times growing up, Amber had heard about the sin of selfishness—of putting her own interests before the family's, of refusing to acknowledge that her actions affected other people—but she'd always brushed it off as her mother being her usual uptight self.

She was rapidly coming to realize that her mother may have been right all along. Grandma Judith was everything Moonbeam Effervescence wasn't: bright and generous and full of a joie de vivre that seemed ingrained into her DNA.

But she *was* selfish. By her own admission, the only thing she'd ever been able to provide her daughter was her absence—a thing that cost her nothing and worried her even less. She'd never reached out, never asked how they were doing, never put herself in a position where she might be made to feel the least emotional discomfort. There was glamour in that kind of lifestyle, and her grandmother had done an exceptional job creating a circle of friends to replace the family that had rejected her, but at what cost?

Us. We're the ones who paid the price. We're the ones who continue to pay it every day of our lives.

"I think, when you're ready, that Derek would like to meet you," Amber said, voicing none of the emotions whirling in her breast. She knew, with a wisdom that hadn't existed a few weeks ago, that there was no point. On the outside, her grandmother was everything she aspired to be, but inside, Amber realized she needed something more. Not security, exactly, not of the type that her mother and brothers idolized, but the sense that she was contributing something to the world.

Something that lasted. Something that *mattered.*

"Derek? You mean your brother?" her grandmother echoed. Her look of fright was quick to pass, but Amber saw it all the same. "Whatever for?"

"Why not? Now that the wall has come down, there's no reason for him to stay away. We might even get Mikey on board, but he's a bit of a hypochondriac, so he might not want to come to a retirement community. He probably thinks old age is contagious."

"I almost reached out half a dozen times, you know," her grandmother said by way of reply. Amber recognized it as the avoidance tactic it was and let it stand. "Not to your brothers, but to you."

"Yeah, you started saying something along those lines my first day here." Amber smiled at the memory. "At the time, I thought maybe you'd been stalking me for nefarious reasons, but that wasn't it, was it?"

Her grandmother reached out and touched Amber's hair. "Of course not, child. It's just that I ached to see you so adrift. You remind me so much of myself at your age."

"Except you had a child and a few husbands under your belt by that time."

Jade waved this off as no more than a casual detail in a life that was allowed to contain nothing but. "They never needed me. Not the way *you* do. You will stay with me, won't you? Finish out the month? I'm sure we can get Geerta to reset the clock—and if not, there's always Camille and the rest of the group to take you in."

Amber flushed, more pleased at this invitation than she cared to admit. At some point, she'd need to settle into a place of her own, find a real job, and get a habitat for Tatiana, but there was no rush. For now, she had a roof over her head and a pair of warm arms to hug her good night—not to mention a grandmother who *wasn't* going to jail for the rest of her life. That was enough.

"Yes, please," Amber said. "I'd like that very much."

"And you can keep that locket," her grandmother said with a nod down at the necklace in Amber's hands. "I don't need it anymore. Not now that I have you."

Amber's fist closed around the locket. She felt a watery sniffle start to overtake her, but nothing more than a prickle of tears escaped before a knock sounded at the door. The fact that her grandmother had guests shouldn't have come as a surprise, since news of her release had gotten around fast, but Amber wished she could have a few more minutes of her grandmother's attention before it was diverted again.

"Oh, Amber. You have a visitor," her grandmother called as she went to answer the door. "A *male* visitor."

She closed her eyes with a groan. "Tell him to go away. He's not getting his hands on my tortoise—I don't care how much history we have or how helpful he's been."

"Well, that's not very nice. Especially after I brought him a going-away present."

"Ethan!" Amber was on her feet in a flash. She rushed to the foyer to find the slight veterinarian standing more or less on his own, a bundle of kale arranged like a bouquet in one hand. "What are you doing here? And what do you mean, 'going-away present'? Tatiana is staying here with me. It's already been decided."

He proffered the bouquet like a knight of old, a slight flush to his cheeks. "Tatiana might be willing to live the rest of his days here, but I hope never to return. Not as a resident, anyway."

Jade took one look at the way Amber stood stock-still, more upset at this news than she had any right to be, and beat a hasty retreat. "I need a long soak to get the scent of all that jail grime off of me," she announced to no one in particular. "If you need me, I'll be in the tub."

"But Tatiana is in there," Amber protested.

Her grandmother winked. "I meant the *hot* tub, child. You wouldn't believe how many people want to talk to me about my time in the clink. I haven't been this famous since that time Emmy Rossum put up an Instagram about the *Death Comes Calling* podcast."

Amber could only watch as her grandmother swept out the front door with another knowing wink. Since Ethan was there too, he saw every deliberate movement of her eyelids.

"I'm glad to see almost going to prison for murder hasn't dimmed her light in the slightest," he said, laughing. "Or yours."

Since Amber couldn't think of a suitable response to the way his eyes glowed a rich, welcoming hazel, she busied herself by taking the kale bouquet.

"The vitamin A will be good for him," Ethan said. "And the fiber, but don't go overboard. One leaf a day mixed with his regular meals should be plenty to—"

Amber interrupted him before he could go any further. "Did you really come here to talk about my tortoise's diet?"

"No." He shifted from one foot to the other, his movements careful in a way that spoke of pain rather than embarrassment. "I meant what I said before. I came to say goodbye. The discharge papers are in my back pocket, and my Uber should be here in fifteen minutes. At the rate I move, that should get me to the front gate with thirty seconds to spare."

"But you're not better," she said. "How can they let you go if you move slower than my tortoise? Does Nancy know? I'm sure she'd have something to say about this."

"Damn, Winslow. You must be really desperate to keep me around."

"I'm not." A flash of heat rushed to her cheeks. It matched the air that was puffing into the condo in huge, yawning gulps. "I just think you should be careful, that's all. What if you end back in the hospital? Or have to come here for another round of rehab?"

"Then I reclaim my reputation from Bruce and the rest of the *Call of Duty* players. Actually—that's a lie. We already made plans to meet up online. I'm going home, but it's going to be a while before I'm back to work full-time. There's plenty more gaming in my immediate future."

"And what about your distant future?" Amber couldn't help asking. She knew she was acting like the blushing schoolgirl she'd never once been, but what else could she do? She was going to miss having the grumpy veterinarian around. He was one of the only rational people in this place. "Are you going to abandon the rest of us to our fates? Just like that?"

His grin grew until it practically split his cheeks. "I'm going across the city, not to the Antipodes. If your fate decides it wants to meet up for coffee sometime, let me know."

"Wait. What?"

He turned and started moving slowly down the stairs, his hand gripping the guardrail as he tested each careful step.

"Ethan, you mean you live here in Draycott? This whole time? Why didn't you say anything?"

He paused just long enough to cast a glance at her over his shoulder. He was laughing again, his every feature so defined that Amber almost felt as though she was taking a picture just by looking at him. "Because you didn't ask."

"And just how am I supposed to call you?" she demanded, feeling nettled. Somewhere in here, there was an analogy between her and her grandmother—a case to be made that they were both so caught up in their own affairs that everyone else in their life either had to get caught up in the dizzying whirlwind or be left behind entirely—but she wasn't about to examine it too closely. Not when Ethan was wearing that particular smirk.

"You're a private investigator now, remember?" he said without another backwards glance. "I'm sure you can figure it out."

EPILOGUE

"I'm Amber Winslow, and you'd better hope
death doesn't come calling for you next."

—*DEATH COMES CALLING, CLOSING CATCHPHRASE*

The following is a transcript from a recording of *Death Comes Calling*,
Season 6, Episode 8

Amber Winslow: Detective Eliana Vega is the sort of woman who goes in swinging. Tall, leggy, and with a scowl that could curdle blood, she—

Horace Horatio: Whoa, there. Slow down. Last episode, you said that the detective in charge of the case would surprise most of our listeners. That sounds *exactly* like a woman I used to work with back in the nineties. Great at back-alley chases but not ideal when informing families of difficult news. I asked her to marry me at least six times. She always said no. Come to think of it, it was probably the right move. I'd have been terrified to fall asleep at night.

Amber Winslow: (Laughing softly) Vega's a surprise because she's like a dog with a bone—and one who won't be satisfied until it's been reduced to shards. Once the Vincent ring was returned to the family, all the motives for murder became circumstantial. The Admiral's life insurance policy barely covered the funeral expenses, so money was off the table, and the anonymous caller who put in the hot tip came forward to say that she might have exaggerated what she overheard that night.

Horace Horatio: Rather convenient, wouldn't you say? Who's to say the caller wasn't threatened or bribed to say that?

Amber Winslow: CUT. Raffi, that isn't in the script. You can't say that.

Horace Horatio: But it's the truth. We *did* bribe Nasty Nancy. We've had to invite her to poker night every single week even though she cheats. Julio caught her marking the cards.

Amber Winslow: Grandma, will you please stop recording this?

Jade McCallan: Keep going, child. I can always cut this part in edits.

Amber Winslow: I am *not* recording a murder confession with the hope that you remember to delete it later. Raffi, you're supposed to segue into the other case Detective Vega is working on, remember? The one about the woman whose body was found on Sunset Lookout?

Horace Horatio: I think our listeners have a right to know what really went down that night.

Amber Winslow: (Incoherent muttering) That's what we're doing. We're trying to create a link between the hiker's body and the Admiral's. They were both poisoned, they were both found in a place they loved, and they both had exotic pets.

Jade McCallan: Well, really, Amber. I don't know that I'd call a guinea pig *exotic*.

Amber Winslow: It weighs ten pounds!

Jade McCallan: I'm still not convinced this serial killer route is the best way to go. Peggy Lee thinks they're overdone.

Peggy Lee: It's true. Did you know that less than one percent of all murders are committed by serial killers? Yet they make up twenty percent of podcast topics. Gives you something to think about it.

Amber Winslow: That's it. I'm taking ten. You guys had better be ready to move forward *as planned* when I get back.

Horace Horatio: Oh, dear. Is she all right?

Jade McCallan: Don't worry about her. She's just upset because Detective Vega told her to stay out of her new murder case or risk being arrested for obstruction. She was really hoping she'd be called in to consult, but that woman won't budge by so much as an inch.

Horace Horatio: Poor dear. We'll have to do something special to liven things up for her. I expect life in her new apartment gets a little lonely. A car theft, perhaps?

Peggy Lee: I've always wanted to try my hand at a heist.

Jade McCallan: Blood, I think. If we want to really distract her, we'll need something with blood.

Amber Winslow: Omigod, you guys. STOP RECORDING. If we're going to commit a crime in the name of podcast glory, I have a better idea. How are you with—

ABOUT THE AUTHOR

Tamara Berry is the Edgar award–winning author of the By the Book Mysteries series and, under the pen name Lucy Gilmore, uplifting romantic fiction. Also a freelance writer and editor, she has a bachelor's degree in English literature and a serious penchant for Nancy Drew novels. She lives in Bigfoot country (a.k.a. Eastern Washington) with her family and their menagerie of pets.

Find her online at tamaraberry.com.
facebook.com/TamaraBerryAuthor
Twitter: @Tamara_Morgan
Instagram: @tamaratamaralucy

Printed in the USA
CPSIA information can be obtained
at www.ICGtesting.com
LVHW090420160924
791024LV00005B/18